HELL AND BACK

By Craig Johnson

The Longmire Series

The Cold Dish

Death Without Company

Kindness Goes Unpunished

Another Man's Moccasins

The Dark Horse

Junkyard Dogs

Hell Is Empty

As the Crow Flies

A Serpent's Tooth

Any Other Name

Dry Bones

An Obvious Fact

The Western Star

Depth of Winter

Land of Wolves

Next to Last Stand

Daughter of the Morning Star

Also by Craig Johnson

Spirit of Steamboat (a novella)

Wait for Signs (short stories)

The Highwayman (a novella)

Stand-alone E-stories
(Also available in *Wait for Signs*)

Christmas in Absaroka County

Divorce Horse

Messenger

CRAIG JOHNSON

HELL AND BACK

VIKING

VIKING

An imprint of Penguin Random House LLC

penguinrandomhouse.com

LIBRARY OF CONGRESS CATALOGING-IN-PUBLICATION DATA

Names: Johnson, Craig, 1961– author.

Title: Hell and back / Craig Johnson.

Description: New York: Viking, [2022] | Series: Longmire

Identifiers: LCCN 2022013666 (print) | LCCN 2022013667 (ebook) |

ISBN 9780593297285 (hardcover) | ISBN 9780593297292 (ebook)

Subjects: LCGFT: Novels.

Classification: LCC PS3610.O325 H44 2022 (print) | LCC PS3610.O325

(ebook) | DDC 813/.6—dc23/eng/20220323

LC record available at https://lccn.loc.gov/2022013666

LC ebook record available at https://lccn.loc.gov/2022013667

Printed in the United States of America

1   3   5   7   9   10   8   6   4   2

For Anthony Red Thunder,
your laughter continues to lighten the way

Hell is oneself, hell is alone, the other figures in it merely projections.
There is nothing to escape from and nothing to escape to.
One is always alone.

—*T.S. Eliot*

ACKNOWLEDGMENTS

All haunting is regret. Whether it's the things we've done or the things we haven't, and in that way, we are all possessed by something—the limbo of unfinished business. *Hell and Back* is a book about the phantoms of regret and loss that hopefully grant the sheriff new life.

Like everybody else, I sometimes dwell on things I shouldn't, such as, What is the scariest thing I can think of? And the answer is pretty simple—not knowing who, or where or why, I am.

Readers who know my books are aware that I like to tread in the margins, the place where different genres can mix and hopefully enhance one another like a fine meal. *Hell and Back* isn't a simple amnesia story, but rather it's about a man fighting to reclaim his very existence against an active and malicious adversary. There are times when the good sheriff doesn't know when to leave well enough alone, and this is one of those times.

I was made aware of the current horrifying problem that involves murdered and missing indigenous women when I came up with the idea for *Daughter of the Morning Star.* I knew there had to be a backstory that would provide an underpinning to the more mystical aspects of the tale and remembered that a few years ago I was talking to venerable Cheyenne Elder Leroy

White Man about the Éveohtsé-heómése, a taker of children, something of a bogeyman to keep the young ones from wandering off too far. I asked him where a being like that could originate, and not so oddly he told me that in his long life he had actually given it some thought.

His theory was that the Wandering Without was a conglomeration of all the lost souls that had been banished from the tribes over the centuries—the murderous and the insane, the ones that had been driven out into the wilderness to die alone. His belief was that there was and always had been something out there waiting to take these souls that no one else wanted, and that they had banded together to satisfy a hunger for companionship.

Where would the perfect feeding ground for a creature like the Éveohtsé-heómése possibly be? A storage place for the tender, young souls it finds so irresistible?

Of the items on the long list of incredible wrongs that have been implemented against the Native Peoples, the boarding schools that separated children from their families, cut their hair, forbade them from speaking their native language, and a million other atrocities must be forefront. With the discovery of unmarked gravesites scattered across the West, the true horror of these places and their genocide is only now becoming known.

These were children.

This book is different, and even though this isn't the first time I've said that a novel goes out there in the topography of loss, where Walt's been for the last seventeen years, it's never been at this depth. Memory is the fuel of haunting, and the complexity of that is that sometimes the unadorned and unvarnished truth becomes camouflaged and sugarcoated by nostalgia in the hostile world I've attempted to create—a Western, gothic-romance with tinges of horror.

The Northern Cheyenne have a saying that you judge a man by the strength of his enemies. I couldn't think of a better statement about Walt Longmire, whose humor and absolute conviction make him truly formidable—but what if the souls he's dispatched are out there, somewhere in a ghost town, waiting for him?

Right off the bat I must thank Leroy White Man, who passed away this past year. His insight into the culture and history of the Cheyenne people will be sorely missed. Another person to thank would be my best buddy, Marcus Red Thunder, the model for Henry. My good friend has had a rough year, but he never lost a step—that's a true man.

Herman Moller, the head archivist for the Absaroka County Sheriff's Department came through for me and David Nickerson, my on-call medico checked me out on that front.

You can't have a haunted house, or haunted boarding school, without occupying it with entities, and *Hell and Back* is no different. First off is that phantom of Time Square, Gail Hochman, and her twenty-sixth floor specter, Marianne Merola. Then the spirit of copyediting, Eric Wechter, and the shadow that goes forth, Francesca Drago. The apparition that haunts Broadway, Brian Tart, and his poltergeist pal, Margaux Weisman. No book tour is possible without the ghost of Route 66, Ben Petrone, and his resident visitant, Bel Banta, and wraith, Mary Stone.

And to my very own ma'heono, Judy, who haunts my dreams.

HELL AND BACK

1

There was the sound of bells and then the silence—the kind of quiet that only comes with snow, capturing the soundwaves of life and smothering them before they can cry out. I couldn't open my eyes, like something was weighing them down, so I brought my hand up to my face and brushed the snow away. My eyes worked now, so I tried to sit up, feeling something strike my chest, something small and metallic, a couple of somethings.

Snow, a lot of it, falling in static sheets. Fat flakes covered everything, silenced everything, as they cascaded from the yellowish-black sky.

I was lying in the middle of the street.

I started to stand but discovered that part of my sheepskin coat was frozen to the ground. Leaning over to one side, I noticed that there were two silver dollars in my lap, so I pulled a glove off with my teeth. I picked up one of the coins that were old ones but looked remarkably unsullied. I glanced around again, couldn't see anybody else on the street, so figured finders keepers. Scooping up the other one, I deposited them both into my pocket and then pulled the glove back on, tugging the tiny red-beaded ends on the straps to snug it. I reached behind me and pulled my coat loose from the ice—I had at least been lying there long enough for it to freeze to the ground.

Raising myself to a kneeling position, I felt something around my neck and pulled the material up to find a red scarf. It didn't particularly look like a man's scarf—silky, with a fringed end— but with current weather conditions I figured I didn't have a lot of options.

Momentarily distracted, I saw a lump of snow beside me and reached over to find it was a pinch-front cowboy hat. I slapped it against my knee to knock it clean. Figuring it was also mine, I lifted it and tugged it over my head. It felt a little tight but that was probably from being as frozen as it was.

I stood the rest of the way and shook off the accumulated snow from my coat like a dog. I was at the top of a hill, which looked down a winding two-lane road that dropped off into a small town about a mile away. Turning, I could see the top of the hill was covered with tiny crosses encircled by a wrought iron fence where, a little farther off, the corner of a stone building still stood, shedding rubble into the snow, a large lump of which was centered on some sort of platform.

Above a gate I saw an arch with the words FORT PRATT IN-DUSTRIAL INDIAN BOARDING SCHOOL. There was some movement at the apogee of the arch, and I watched as a great horned owl slowly swiveled his head from back to front to look at me, golden eyes shining like twin harvest moons.

"Howdy."

He continued to observe me with all the patience of the world.

"Well, at least you didn't ask *who*." Sighing, I turned back toward the town, thinking I might get a little more conversation in that direction. Starting off down the two-lane, I lumbered through the snow for a while eventually passing a few of the buildings on the outskirts—a house or two, a library, and what looked to be an old Catholic church.

There were buildings on either side of the road, the type of single-story storefronts seen in many small towns scattered across the Rocky Mountain West. Plastic wreathes hung from the dozen or so lampposts with a red electric candle in each that flickered yellow and then, one at a time, slowly dimmed.

I couldn't really tell if it was night or day with the skies colored a strange yellowish cast and with the inclement weather, the surrounding distance was darkened to an ocean of obscurity. There were a few lit buildings, a two-story grand vintage structure to my left, the Baker Hotel, and a movie theater down on the corner, with a yellow and green neon marquee that read SUPPORT YOUR LOCAL SHERIFF.

I had a mild headache and could smell something burning, as if there were a forest fire not too far away, and I felt strangely detached for a guy who had been left lying in the street. With a deep sigh, I took a few more steps, trudging toward the side of the road, amazed that I hadn't been scraped up by a snowplow. My back hurt and my limbs and head felt heavy—I must've been lying out there for a while.

There were no cars or trucks parked on the street as far as I could see. I stepped onto the curb and sidewalk. There was a café at the other end of the block, and I decided to walk in that direction even though it appeared to be leading west and out of town. Booths lined the glass front of the place, and the condensation on the inside of the windows promised warmth. A woman with strawberry blond hair was wiping the counter, but no patrons, and I was worried the tiny restaurant might be closed.

I was relieved when I pushed on the wooden bar and the glass door swung open, a bell jingling just above my head.

Appearing to be in her early thirties, the blonde was stunningly beautiful. Dressed in a waitress uniform, she looked up at me, and there was something about her that stuck the words in my throat. I swallowed. "I'm sorry, are you closed?"

She looked up to a clock on the wall that advertised the Red Lodge Soda Company; it was 8:17 p.m. "Not for another forty-three minutes, but I was thinking of closing with the blizzard and all." She looked back at me. "But can I help you?"

I slipped off my hat and stared through the fogged windows back onto the street. "Is it a blizzard?"

She laughed; a silvery, melodic sound that made me turn back to her and smile. "Storm of the century. What, you don't read the papers?"

"Not recently." I walked over, sat on a stool in front of her, and placed my hat on the one next to me. "You know what? I think I need a cup of coffee."

"You got it." She smiled, her hazel eyes sparkling. "The co-op says they aren't going to get the power back on for thirty-one hours." I watched as she plucked a Buffalo China mug from under the counter, walked to the coffee maker, and pulled the pot out by its plastic handle.

I glanced around the well-lit space. "How is it you still have electricity?"

"Municipal generator system on the hill outside of town near the old boarding school. I guess back in the day the power went out all the time." She rested the mug on the counter. "Are you new around here?"

"Yep." I looked back into the street. "At least I think so."

She laughed at the absurdity of my response. "You're not sure?"

I pulled the red scarf from my neck, stuffing it into my hat, and unbuttoned my heavy coat. "Well, to be honest, I just woke up out there in the road a moment ago."

She stared at me. "Are you drunk?"

"I don't think so—drunk feels better than this." I pulled off my gloves, tucking them into my pocket, and sipped my coffee as she studied me.

"You look familiar."

I nodded and smiled. "You know, it's funny, but when I came in here, I was thinking the same thing about you." The coffee tasted hot, rich, and life-affirming. "What's your name?"

"Martha."

I sat there looking at her and thinking that of all the names in the world I could've chosen for her—but that one was perfect. "Just Martha?"

She nodded, stepping back guardedly. "Just Martha, for now."

"That's a great name." I started to stick out my hand to shake hers but then stopped.

She glanced at my hand as I lowered it but then went back to studying my face. "Something wrong?"

"Um . . . I don't want to panic you or anything, but I can't seem to remember my own name."

Her eyes sharpened, and she folded her arms. "Your name is Walt Longmire."

"So, we do know each other."

"No."

"Then how do you know my name?"

"It's on the liner of your hat."

I reached over and picked the thing up, removing the scarf and reading the barely legible gold lettering on the sweatband—THIS HAT BELONGS TO WALT LONGMIRE: A GIFT FROM THE GRATEFUL PEOPLE OF ABSAROKA COUNTY, WYOMING. I looked up at her. "Is this Absaroka County?"

She moved closer, staring at me, pressing the palms of her

hands against the edge of the counter. "Not even Wyoming—welcome to Fort Pratt, Montana, Walt Longmire."

I inspected the hat a bit more. "That is, if it's mine."

"Where did you get it?"

"It was lying on the road there beside me, out at the edge of town, up on the hill to the east."

"Does it fit?"

I placed it on my head, where, after warming up, it fit, if not like a proverbial glove, at least like a custom-made hat. "Yep."

"Honestly?" She looked over my shoulder. "You really were just lying out there in the road?"

"Evidently for a while." I turned and looked outside into the darkness, took my hat off again, and resettled it and the scarf beside me. "Has there been any traffic lately?"

"No, the plow went through about an hour ago, but since then, nothing—I think they gave up." She smiled the warm smile. "You sure you don't want something to eat?"

"Now that you mention it, I am hungry, but I don't want to put you out."

"It's your lucky day, the special is a grilled cheese sandwich and a bowl of tomato soup."

"Is that 'the usual' too?"

She stared at me for a long moment with an unsure expression. "What an odd thing to say . . . Why would you say that?"

"I don't know."

She looked at me a little uncertainly. "One special, coming up." She swung through the doors into the tiny kitchen, where I could watch her busy herself.

Sipping my coffee again, I plucked a menu from the condiment stand to see the name of the place—The Night Owl Café, Fort Pratt.

She called through the opening of the pickup window. "I guess when that gust went through a couple of hours ago it took five poles out." A moment passed. "You want fries?"

"I don't want to be a bother . . ."

"None at all . . . I just need to get them out of the freezer in the back."

Another door opened and closed in the depths of the kitchen. I sat there listening to the ticking of the Red Lodge Soda clock on the wall and tried to remember who I was. What the hell? Had I fallen out of a vehicle, been hit by one? Was she right and I had been drunk and was out there sleeping it off?

With my hands thawed out, I reached up and probed my head. I found a lot of knots and bumps, with one that felt reasonably new but not so recent as to be responsible for how I felt. If I could just find somebody who knew me.

I was about ready to take off my coat when the front door opened behind me and a giant of a man stepped in, strangely dressed, and carrying a long native war staff.

Seven feet tall if he was an inch, his hood was pulled up to cover most of his face. He ducked his head to clear the top of the doorway and stepped into the light where I got a better look at him.

He wasn't just tall, he was big too. He unbuttoned his great fur coat with its grizzly bear hood, which revealed buckskin clothing indicative of the Mountain Crow tribe. What really unnerved me, though, was that staff in his hand, a wooden lance about six feet in length with a large, chipped obsidian spearhead on one end and red-painted coyote skulls on the other, along with horsehair tails, bells, beads, jawbones, and cloven hooves.

He stood there in the doorway and then walked past me with a curt nod, which I returned with a smile, somewhat amused by his seriousness. Sitting at the far end of the counter, he rested the spear against the edge and with little effort straddled a stool, dropping the hood with both hands and staring straight ahead.

He had scars on his face and strong Native features. His dark hair was streaked with more than a touch of gray and flowed down over his shoulders as he sat there motionless.

"How are you doing?"

He said nothing, continuing to look straight ahead.

Figuring he was a regular, I thought it best that I explain. "She went into the freezer to get me some fries, but she'll be right back." There was some noise coming from the kitchen, and I unbuttoned my coat the rest of the way before turning back to him. "You're lucky—she was going to close."

He still sat there, unmoving.

"Excuse me, but are you from around here?"

Nothing.

Shrugging, I turned forward as the woman, Martha, appeared in the opening. "You say something?"

"No, no . . ." I gestured, nodding my head down the counter as she couldn't see the colossus from her perspective.

She smiled and disappeared again, finally resting a plate and bowl in the opening and ringing a small bell in comic effect. "Order up." She then appeared through the swinging doors and picked up my meal, turning and placing it before me. "More coffee?"

"Please."

She pivoted back to the coffee maker and refilled my mug before setting it down. "Anything else?"

"No, no I'm fine." I once again nodded my head toward the strangely dressed man at the end of the counter.

She stared at me. "What?"

I gestured again.

She looked in his direction and then back at me. "Is there something wrong?"

"No, I just thought you might want to—" I turned my head to look at the man and discovered he was now looking directly at me.

My voice caught in my throat as he slowly raised a finger, placing it against his lips. "*Shhhhhhhh . . .*" His breath fogged the front of his face with the freezing air still in his lungs that he must've brought in with him. "Sometimes . . ." He stared at me for a moment more. "It is better to sleep than to awaken."

I turned back to the waitress, who was watching me.

I smiled and shrugged again, then picked up the flatware and unrolled the napkin. I took out the spoon and tasted the soup.

"Oh, my God . . ."

I looked up at the woman, figuring she must've finally noticed the behemoth at the end of the counter. "You're bleeding."

Pulling my coat aside, I could now see that the stomach of my shirt was indeed saturated with blood. "Well, I'll be damned . . ."

Standing, I pulled my coat off and saw that the blood seemed to be heavier toward one side. Martha grabbed a few dish towels from a shelf and started toward the door where the cash register sat and circled round. She knelt beside me. "You're going to have to pull up your shirt so I can have a look, but that's a lot of blood."

"It doesn't hurt or anything." I pulled the shirt loose till we could both see my unmarked flesh, then unbuckled my belt and felt something heavy on it. She examined my side. "You could be in shock, which might be why you don't know your name."

The giant at the end of the counter lumbered off the stool, picked up his lance, and started our way. I watched as he passed without looking at either of us before stopping at the door to fasten the bone closures on his fur coat and pull the hood back up.

Now I could see it was a grizzly hide, the bear features hovering over his own, the jaws separate and on either side of his face along with beads, eagle feathers, abalone-shell disks, and strands of rawhide adorned with tiny cone bells shaped from snuff container lids that made a faint tinkling sound as he looked back and down at me. "You will stand and see the bad—the dead will rise, and the blind shall see."

"Excuse me?"

He said nothing more but slowly turned, pushed open the door, and strode into the strangely colored night, the swirling flakes seeming to swallow him up quicker than the darkness.

"What?"

I looked down at the woman, still kneeling at my side. "What?"

"You said something?"

I gestured toward the now closed door. "I guess he thought he wasn't going to get waited on."

She rose and studied me. "What are you talking about?"

Figuring we weren't going to find the source of the bleeding, I started tucking my shirt back in and fastening my belt as she stepped to the side, looking at me with an odd expression. "What?"

She moved back a few more steps and pointed at my hip. "You're wearing a gun."

After buckling my pants, I reached around to a heaviness I felt there; a weight at my back I hadn't noticed before. It was a sidearm in what felt like a basket-woven leather pancake holster. Adroitly flipping off the safety strap, I plucked the large-frame semiautomatic and swung it around to study it.

"Colt M1911A1."

She stared at me, even going so far as to take another step back. "Is it yours?"

"I guess." I studied it a little closer. "Remington Rand—I don't even know who makes my gun." Lifting the barrel, I sniffed at the deadly looking thing. "It's been fired, not too long ago."

She took another step back. "Look, I think I need to call the police."

I studied the worn stag handles. "Are the phones working?"

She hurried back toward the cash register and a phone without taking her eyes off me.

I hit the magazine catch and counted the rounds.

Six.

She tapped the receiver hook and turned to look at me. "Nothing."

Pulling the slide action, I caught the round from the pipe and examined it. "230-grain jacketed hollow point." I laughed. "It would appear I am a serious individual."

She hung up the phone. "How many bullets are supposed to be in it?"

"Eight, fully loaded—seven in the mag, one in the pipe." I re-inserted the loose round into the mag and reloaded it into the grip. "So, one's missing."

"So, maybe it's not your blood."

I thought about it. "Maybe not."

"Do you mind putting it away?"

"Not at all." I slid the action, and punched the safety before slipping it behind me, holstering the thing and reattaching the safety strap literally behind my back as if I'd done it a million and three times.

"You seem to handle it very easily."

I showed her my hands like a croupier, indicating we were both now safe. "Yep, I guess so."

"And you weren't even aware that it was there?"

"No."

"Then you're very used to carrying it."

"I guess." I smiled, attempting to put her at ease. "Maybe I'm a cop."

"Where's your badge?"

"Good question."

"There's a town ordinance here in Fort Pratt—no guns."

I glanced around. "Look, can I finish my soup and then I'll go and talk to the police? Maybe they know what's going on."

"There isn't any police department here—we just have a highway patrol outpost that's empty most of the time. The guy who mans it is only there two days out of the week, and with it being the holidays I don't know if he's there at all."

I sat and ladled in a spoonful of soup, followed by a few fries and a gulp of coffee. "Where's the outpost?"

"West of town."

Grabbing a few more fries, I stuffed them into my mouth and stood, picking up the mug and gulping down the rest of the coffee. "What do I owe you?"

"Nothing." She looked at me, and there was a sadness that crept into her expression. "I've got a feeling you're in trouble and need help."

I felt around for my wallet, but I didn't have one. "You may be right. I thought I might have a wallet, but as it turns out, I don't."

She waved at me as she backed away. "On the house."

I tucked my hand into the pocket of my coat and pulled out

the two silver dollars, tossing them onto the counter. "At least I can leave a tip."

Pulling on my coat, I watched as she approached from the other side, staring at the coins but making no move to pick them up. "Those are old."

I leaned over as I grabbed my hat. "Yep, but there's something wrong with them. See how her lips look like they're double-stamped or something?"

"Hot lips."

I settled the hat on my head. "Excuse me?"

"That is an 1888-O Hot Lips silver dollar."

Having buttoned up my coat, I took another spoonful of soup and a few more fries. "A what?"

"It was double-stamped; a mistake. See her lips?"

I leaned forward and could see the mismark on both. "Still worth a dollar?"

"A lot more than that. My father used to collect coins."

"Well, it's all I've got on me."

She started to reach for them but stopped. "You keep them. I've got a feeling you're going to need them more than me."

I flipped up the collar of my coat. "No, you . . ."

"No. I'm serious, I don't want them."

I stared at her and then slid them off the counter and deposited them back into my pocket. "Okay." Heading toward the door, I rewrapped the scarf and pulled on my gloves. "I'll come back and pay you when I find out what is going on, okay?"

She folded her arms again. "Sure."

I began to push open the door to leave but then stopped and turned back. "Hey, you mentioned it was the holidays, do you mind telling me which one?"

She looked more than a little puzzled. "It's New Year's Eve, Walt Longmire."

"Right." I gave her one last smile, pushed open the door, and walked out, calling over my shoulder—and it was strange how familiar the words felt as they rolled off my tongue, as if I'd said them my whole life—"Happy New Year, Martha."

The wind had picked up, but like me it didn't seem to know in which direction it wanted to go, diminutive snow devils twirling all around like some subfreezing cotillion.

Trudging along on the sidewalk, I could feel it end as the heels of my boots sank deeper into the snow. I could also see a light above a door on a small, rectangular block of a building, with a car sitting out front entirely covered in a good eight inches of powder.

Walking under the halo of light, I peered through the insignia on the window into the darkened office, only a singular lamp on inside. Backing away, I could see that a Post-it was attached to the inside of the glass with a note reading, "Emergency, be back soon.—Bobby."

Sighing, I started to turn and head back into town when I thought I saw somebody standing out near the road, a very large somebody holding what looked like a war lance.

Taking a few steps out past the car, I watched as a small amount of snow slid from the window, revealing the interior of a late-'70s Ford Crown Vic, with an old Motorola two-way under the dash.

Reaching up, I wiped the snow from the top, revealing the vintage emergency lights with the single cherry. "Huh, they must use it for parades."

"They don't have parades here."

I turned to see the giant from the café, standing at the front of the car. "Oh, hey."

"You are looking for Bobby?"

I glanced back at the office. "The trooper, yep."

"He'll be back later; I called him."

"I thought the phones weren't working?"

He smiled down at me, placing the spear against his shoulder and pulling some kind of candy from his pocket, carefully unwrapping the yellow covering and then breaking it in half and popping a portion into his mouth. "Some calls don't require phones."

"Right." He chewed and then attempted to hand me the other half of the candy cup, which I turned down. "No, thanks."

He shoved it toward me. "You should take it; people don't give things away in this town."

I pulled the half-finished candy from the wrapper, then read the card underneath. "Mallo Cup Play Money."

"See, now you're not broke anymore." He laughed.

"Hey, should you really be out here alone on New Year's Eve?"

He looked unconcerned. "One year is the same as the next; besides, I have business with Bobby, we have a job we need to do."

"Business."

"Yes, that and I'm listening."

I looked around. "Listening for what?"

He turned his big, solid face toward the darkness. "Sometimes when I hear the wolves cry out there in the night, the call of the owl, or the wind that brushes the landscape clean, I hold my breath and listen for a very long time. I travel back to the beginning when I was one with the wolves, the owls, and the wind, when our souls were entwined." He glanced down at me. "Then I am overcome with an incredible sadness."

Not sure of what to say to that, I settled on a question. "Why?"

"For I no longer know how to reply."

Without another word, he turned and walked back toward the road. I stood there watching him disappear again and mumbling to myself. "Wow, this is one weird town."

Starting off toward civilization, I looked down at the card and wrapper in my hand, beginning to throw it aside but then thinking that I shouldn't litter. I looked back up for the strange goliath but couldn't see him. He should've been easily within sight, but he wasn't there. Turning in a circle, I couldn't see him anywhere and worried about him out there on the road somewhere, alone. Holding the card up, I read "Mallo Cup Play Money, 25 Cents." I began walking and stuffed the candy wrapper and card into my pocket. "Every town has got a crazy person." I smiled to myself. "And some have two."

I made my way back to the sidewalk, back to the entrance of the café, and was saddened to find the lights were dimmed and a cardboard sign that read SORRY, WE'RE CLOSED hanging behind the glass door.

I started to move on but then caught sight of her behind the counter. She was dancing. Her moves were lithe and supple, and she was what they call a natural. She turned with her arms in the air, elbows bent and wrists out as she danced to some music that I, try as I might, couldn't hear.

I stood there on the sidewalk, transfixed, my boots having taken root.

She turned toward me, her hair hiding half her face, and I was relieved that her eyes were closed so she didn't see me. I continued up the block and passed a women's clothing shop called LeClerc's, a Culpepper's Hardware, and walked by a Bar 31 before reaching the movie theater. I paused to look at the poster inside the lit alcove beside the ticket booth: James Garner smiling his roguish grin back at me.

"Hi."

I turned and could now see a young woman sitting in the glass-enclosed ticket booth. She was counting money. "Last show was at 8:17."

"Well, I missed that one, didn't I?"

"Yeah."

Close up, I could see she was Native and maybe in her late teens, athletic, and wearing a name tag that read JEANIE. "That's okay, Jeanie. I don't have any money."

She stopped counting and looked up at me through the glass window. "Do I know you?"

"I don't think so, but you do look familiar."

She continued counting and deposited the cash into a metal box. "You probably know my sister, Jaya—she knows everybody."

I watched as she turned with a wave and went out the back door into the lobby of the theater, where I could smell popcorn. I wished I'd gotten here earlier.

Two guys came stumbling out of Bar 31 next door, and I watched as the one in uniform tilted toward the curb and grabbed one of the lampposts before leaning over and throwing up. After another moment, I noticed the second man staring at me— an odd-looking guy made up of random large parts that didn't match and stringy hair. "You got a problem?"

"Excuse me?"

His head kicked sideways and shook in disbelief as he repeated slowly, through his rotted teeth. "I said . . . Do you have a problem?"

"Not that I'm aware of." I glanced at his friend and could now see a patch on his shoulder that read AMERI-TRANS—whatever that was.

He took a step toward me. "That's good because if you do, Calvin *Fingers* Moser can take care of it for you."

"That your name?"

"Yeah, and don't you forget it."

I figured at this rate it would take him another five minutes to navigate the twenty feet between us. "Well, Mister Moser, I'll tell you that what I'm going to do is walk around this town remembering your name."

He looked confused. "What?"

There was a hotel across the street, and the hands of a large clock above the door read 8:17 p.m. I thought about getting a room for the night, which could prove interesting without a wallet or ID.

Leaving *Fingers* standing there on the sidewalk, threatening the air, I looked both ways and crossed the street, ankle-deep in snow. I got to the other side and then saw a man struggling to get a large chair into the stone church on the corner opposite the movie theater.

"Need some help?"

He looked up, and I was surprised to see from his collar that it was the priest himself. Waving me over, he redoubled his efforts in an attempt to get the thing in the door, but it was proving to be too much for him.

I recrossed the street, climbed the church steps, and took the chair by the legs, guiding it in. We sat the chair down in the entryway, and the priest closed the door behind us. I was surprised by how young he was.

Blond, with large, sad, pale-blue eyes behind steel-rimmed glasses, he held out a hand. "Thank you, I didn't expect to see anybody on the streets tonight, especially with this weather."

"I was just on my way over to the hotel when I saw you and thought you might need some help."

"Get stranded in the blizzard?"

"Something like that. I stopped in at the highway patrol sub-station, but I guess he's out at an accident or some kind of emergency."

"There's probably a lot of those tonight."

"Yep." I started to go but then stopped, figuring that if I was going to get any help, this might be the place. "Father, I know this is coming out of nowhere, but I could use a hand. I've been in an accident and lost my wallet. Do you have any setup for ministerial aid in this town?"

He studied me for a moment. With his oversize glasses and Superman curl on his forehead, I could've sworn he was only in his twenties. "Have you been drinking, my son?"

"No."

"Drugs?"

"No, honestly."

He studied me a bit more and then nodded. "So, you need a place to stay?"

"I'm afraid I do."

"We have an understanding with the Baker Hotel on the next block; we sometimes use them when we have people from the diocese in town." He motioned me inside. "C'mon in, I'll telephone them."

"I don't think the phones are working." I gestured down the street. "The woman from the café said the electricity was knocked out too; that you guys were running on municipal generators?"

"The woman at the café?"

"Martha, hazel eyes, strawberry blond . . . Hard to miss, even for a priest."

He laughed and shook his head. "Unless she's Catholic, I probably haven't met her."

"She said the blizzard had taken down five power poles and that it was going to be thirty-one hours before they got everything back on."

He stared at me. "Thirty-one hours?"

"Yep, I thought that was odd too. Your co-op is pretty exact in their estimates, huh?"

"Well, I'll need to get my coat if I'm going to walk you over there."

"You don't have to do that."

"I do, if you want that room."

He pushed the door open to the small church and picked up a dark overcoat from a bench in the vestibule, and I got a look at the masonry and dark woodwork. "Beautiful church."

"Yes, the stone was originally part of the boarding school."

"Somebody else mentioned that—what boarding school?"

"The original Fort Pratt Industrial Indian Boarding School . . . It was here before the town, and it was the reason I came."

"You were part of the school?"

"No, I came here long after it shut down, but I wanted to research it for a book I hope to write." He slipped his coat on and buttoned it up. "You've never heard of the Fort Pratt Industrial Indian Boarding School?"

"No, why? Is it famous?"

He held the vestibule door open for me. "More like infamous."

———

"Are you all right?"

I turned to look at Father Vanderhoven, and it took me a moment to remember who he was and why I was there, and even when I did, I wasn't sure I had. It was like that; I couldn't seem to hold it all there in my mind. "Yep, yep, I'm fine. Just a little disconnected, you know?"

"I do." We were sitting in the tiny corner bar of the Baker Hotel with a parlor stove no more than ten feet away, glowing merrily, as we drank brandy-spiked Tom & Jerrys that Father Vanderhoven had prepared himself.

The owner and operator of the hotel had obviously decided to go celebrate elsewhere but had been kind enough to leave a set of keys to one of the upstairs rooms just in case of emergency.

"Kind of him to accommodate me."

The priest nodded. "He's a good guy. Rebuilt most of this hotel himself."

"When was it originally built?"

He sipped his steaming drink and looked out at the snowy scene just as the lights of the marquee dimmed. "Before the turn of the nineteenth century, so there was some time between the closing of the school and the opening of the hotel; and the opening of the town, for that matter."

I sipped my own drink and spotted the two men still on the sidewalk in front of the bar; maybe they'd wake up in the middle of the street too. "Fort Pratt, was it a military installation before it was a town or school?"

"Named for Richard Henry Pratt."

"Kill the Indian, save the man?"

He sat back in his chair with a look of wonderment in his clear eyes. "You are the first person I've ever met who knows who he is." He leaned back in. "You're not a fallen academic like me?"

"No, I . . ." I laughed. "I honestly don't know who I am." I took another sip of the drink and then kept my hands around the ceramic cup, even though I couldn't feel much warmth left there. "Controversial figure."

"Yes. I think his heart was in the right place, attempting to give the Indians an equal footing in education, but taking them away from their families and denying them their heritage was tantamount to cultural genocide." He glanced up at me. "I seem to have put a pall on the evening."

"Oh, no. You mentioned the school as being somewhat ill-famed. Is there a reason for that?"

"The fire . . . Because of that, Fort Pratt had the highest attrition rate of all of the Indian boarding schools, by far. There's some rubble and a cemetery up near where the gate is that led to the school. In the late forties the Department of the Interior spearheaded an attempt to dig up the bodies of the students who had died, but the number of graves they found held no remains. A lack of documentation made it impossible to discover where the remains of the children might be or how to return them to the proper tribal authorities."

"Funny enough, that's where I woke up; on the hill to the east of town where the ruins are." I sipped my drink. "There appeared to be a lot of graves."

"Far too many, thirty-one in all, and then the staff who were also lost." He gazed out the window. "It was termed a working school, and I'm afraid the administrator, Spellman, took the name literally." He pushed his chair back and stood. "I've kept you up too late, telling old wives' tales. You're probably tired."

"Amazingly enough, I'm not." I smiled. "Must've caught up on my sleep out there on the road."

"That's an amazing story." He held out a hand. "I hope to see you in the morning."

I stood and followed him out of the small bar and into the lobby of the hotel. "I'll make a point of it."

He smiled and started to go, buttoning his coat at the door. "Sleep well, from what I'm to understand the hotel is haunted— but then again, the entire town is."

I stood at the base of the stairs, the red carpeting leading to my upstairs room, number 31. "Haunted by what?"

He smiled, pushing open the door and going out as a cold draft from the street squeezed through the frosted glass, fighting to get in and push me toward the carpeted stairs. "Why, the children, of course."

2

Riley stood on the balcony overlooking Main Street just as one of those fancy new trucks pulled in, all shiny. The kind of truck he wasn't ever going to be able to afford unless he sold the hotel, and as far as he knew, nobody was buying—especially since Dad had died.

"Your clock is broken."

He'd been fixing the upstairs. It wasn't the season for those kinds of repairs, but when the storm had blown through the other evening, it had taken the railing with it. He'd carried it back up the main stairs and fed it out the door after shoveling the balcony and was trying to get it secured before the ever-present wind took hold of it again.

Standing, he looked down at the Native, probably Blackfoot or Assiniboine. "Say what?"

The large man in the black duster pointed to the clock on the exterior of the hotel. It's hands read 8:17. "Your clock . . . it is broken."

"It's right twice a day." Making the old joke, he thought about it. "As far as I know it hasn't ever worked, and I've been remodeling the place for five years now."

The man walked over closer on the sidewalk as a woman let

a large dog out of the truck to nose around. "It is a beautiful building."

"Thanks, it's on the National Register."

Throwing a few screws into the base of the railing, the young man walked across the balcony to a spot just above the large man. "You looking for a building?"

"No, we are looking for a friend who may have been here in the last couple of days?"

"Yeah?"

"Yes, a man in a cowboy hat, with a scar over one eye?"

"I've got a scar." Riley lifted his stained hat to show him the divot in his forehead. "I was racing motocross and went over a berm and into a parked car." His attention was drawn back to the unfinished job. "Let me get a few more screws in and I'll come down."

The Cheyenne Nation smiled up at him. "That would be fine, thank you."

He'd at least done enough to keep the thing from falling off and into the street, so Riley carried his tools and a bucket of supplies inside and down the steps. They were already standing in the lobby, looking around at the place. "It's not finished, but someday we're going to have national conventions and stuff." He shook hands with the man, shrugging in apology for his dirty hands. "Riley."

The man glanced around. "Good bones, as they say."

The man was even bigger than Riley had thought, and one of those guys that looked like, well, like they could do things. "Sure you don't want to buy it, mister . . . ?"

"Standing Bear, Henry Standing Bear." He sighed. "No, I already own a bar, and it is enough to keep me busy."

Riley studied him, noticing the way he talked, really precise. "You guys aren't from around here, huh?"

"No, we are from down near Wyoming." Standing Bear gestured toward the woman, who stuck out her hand.

"Vic Moretti, how you doin'."

Riley thought she was very pretty, but at the same time she looked like she had a mean streak a mile wide. He noticed the tricked-out truck with the stars on the doors. "You guys cops?"

"Absaroka County Sheriff's Department, Wyoming."

He noticed her eyes were a funny gold color, kind of unsettling, and that she talked funny too, like she was from somewhere back east. "I went to Wyoming once; got beat up in a bar and never went back."

Henry Standing Bear walked over toward the windows and looked out onto the empty street and the vacant buildings. "This is Fort Pratt, is it not?"

"What's left of it, yeah."

Henry turned to look at him. "What happened?"

Riley laughed. "The stock market crash of 1929, the dust bowl, they moved the railheads, the interstate highways . . . You name it, whatever bad luck could hit this town did—it's like it was cursed."

Vic Moretti pulled a photo from her Carhartt and held it out to him. "The guy we're looking for, big guy." She gestured toward Henry. "Even bigger than him."

Riley looked at the photo, which was some kind of official thing with an older man in uniform and a light-colored hat—and a gun. "He a cop too?"

"That's right."

He handed her back the photo. "Wow."

"I'll take that as a no?" She studied him. "He wouldn't have been in uniform."

"Yeah."

Leaning back, she read the sign. "Baker Hotel." Lowering her face, she studied him. "Is this the only hotel in town?"

Riley unbuckled his tool belt and laughed. "It's the only anything in town."

The man came back over. "But this is Fort Pratt, yes?"

"Yeah, but we're not even incorporated anymore—that's why there's no sign or anything."

"There are no other places by that name?"

"Well, there's the cemetery and the old archway sign for the boarding school, east of town. There was a fort, then the school, and then the town."

Henry looked down at the young man. "Boarding school?"

"Yeah, some kind of Indian boarding school."

The Cheyenne Nation mulled over the word. "Indian."

"Yeah, I mean, I don't know what the politically correct term is now, but back then it was Indian."

He looked past Riley and toward the stairs. "You Assiniboine, Blackfeet . . . ?"

Henry, heading upstairs, moved past him. "Have you ever heard of a man by the name of Artie Small Song?"

"No, I don't think so."

The Bear continued up the stairs but then stopped and turned to look at Riley. "You do not think so?"

"I mean, no, never heard of him." Riley glanced at the woman, who was also watching him. "He traveling with your guy, what did you say his name was?"

"We did not." Henry studied him some more and noticed the young man was getting a little nervous. "Longmire, his name is Walt Longmire, and we believe that he might be in pursuit of a man by the name of Artie Small Song."

"This Small Song guy, he Assiniboine or Blackfeet?"

"No." The Bear turned and continued up the stairs.

"He do something bad?"

Henry climbed to the landing of the second floor and turned toward the door on the left. "Perhaps."

Riley watched as the large man traced his fingers over the impression on the door where Thayer had removed the old numbers and had sanded it in preparation for paint. "So, you think there might've been trouble?"

"Possibly." Henry reached for the doorknob.

"All the rooms are locked."

Vic stepped into his line of sight. "Why?"

"Vagrants, we get people passing through . . ."

"But not the people we're looking for?"

The large man came back down the steps. "Vagrants, in the winter?"

"All the time, just more in the summer, sure."

"That room at the top of the stairs, it is room 31?"

"Yeah, why?"

"No reason. We will go look at the remains of the boarding school." Henry and Vic surveyed the place one last time before heading for the door.

Moretti looked back at the young man for a long moment. "How about you come with us?"

"Oh, I've got work to do."

"Really." The man holding the door smiled a tight-lipped response to that. "It will not take long, and we would be greatly appreciative." Riley started to speak, but the Bear quickly added. "I think you should."

Walking around and retrieving his coat from behind the counter, Riley rejoined them at the door. "I only have a little time. I mean, I'm the only one working here."

The Cheyenne Nation put a weighty arm around the young man's shoulders, directing him out the door. "Do you have any rooms available?"

"You mean now? Tonight?"

He nodded, the expression on his face unreadable. "Indeed, I do."

"No."

Vic laughed as she followed. "What, you're fucking booked up?"

"Um, the rooms aren't really usable . . . I mean, there's no water or anything."

The undersheriff nodded as they walked into the street. "Yeah, well . . . We can make do."

"No, you don't understand . . ."

The Cheyenne Nation steered him toward the high-powered truck as Vic followed, pulling her keys from her jeans. She smiled. "Oh, I think we do."

It was cold in the room, so I just lay there with my sheepskin coat over me, looking at the ceiling and wishing I could go to sleep. Automatically reaching for something at my side, I pulled out the pocket watch I'd discovered there earlier.

I held it to my ear and listened to it ticking. I turned it toward the light and could see the glass was broken but in place. It showed 8:17—not really that late, so if I wanted to get up and do something, I still could. "Like what, go look for the strawberry blonde?" I shook my head. "She thinks you're some kind of psycho."

I sneaked a glance at the holstered .45 on the nightstand.

"Maybe I am." I stuck my hand out into the semidarkness. "Glad to meet you, Walt Longmire, psycho killer. Walter . . . I wonder what my middle name is?" I rolled over and pulled my coat up over my shoulder when I felt something crinkle in the pocket. I reached in and fished out a brittle plastic sleeve, a booklet of some kind, and what felt like a postcard.

I pulled the chain on the tulip-shaped lamp and sat up so I could look at the collection of items.

There was a regular sheet of paper in some kind of binder envelope, stiff with wear, as was the photo and information printed underneath. Half of the image had faded away, but what was left showed a teenage girl with dark hair and eyes. The words were half missing but they identified her as One Moon and offered a reward as to her whereabouts to the tune of $2,000. There was a phone number, the first set of digits and area code missing.

"Not like you can make a phone call anyway."

Maybe this was why I was here; to look for this girl. Maybe I was some kind of bounty hunter.

Staring at the photo, I couldn't help but feel as if I'd recently seen her.

Next, I picked up the booklet and studied it. It had a brown-leather cover with a strange symbol on it of a hastily drawn circle with a slash through it. Flipping it open, I could see it was only about twelve pages and printed in an old-fashioned text unlike anything I'd ever seen in a language I didn't understand. It must have been printed by a small press, FPIIBS, here in Montana.

FPIIBS . . . Where had I read that before? Looking at the last item, the answer was writ large. It was an old postcard with scalloped edges and a sepia-tone photo on one side. It was the entrance gate I'd seen at the top of the hill east of town, the archway displaying Fort Pratt Industrial Indian Boarding School, or FPIIBS. It was obviously taken a long time ago—in it, there was a looming two-story building, large leafing trees, and what looked to be a couple of dozen boys wearing some kind of uniform. The strange thing was that all of their faces were blurred, as if they had all moved at the moment the shutter opened—all but one, a boy in the front staring at the camera with an intensity that was fearsome.

There was a noise down on the street, and I leaned over, pulling the curtain aside. I could see the girl from the theater box office trying to get away from the two drunks who were still on the street in front of the bar.

Whenever she would try to get around them, they'd step in front of her and shout things I couldn't make out.

Standing, I yanked on my coat and stuffed the postcard, the missing-persons poster, and the booklet back inside. Pulling the heavy sheepskin away so that I could attach my gun and holster, I grabbed my hat and the red scarf before heading out the door and down the steps. Pushing one of the front doors open, I stepped out onto the porch of the hotel and started straight across the street.

The girl was holding a metal cashbox, and the men were accosting her as I approached from behind. "Excuse me?"

The lean one, who had been sick earlier, swung around, and I caught his arm, stepped under it, and planted his face into the lamppost, which shuddered with the impact before he slid to the ground. I stood there in shock at how quickly it had happened, wondering where I'd learned those nifty tricks.

I heard a noise behind me and turned in time to see the guy who called himself *Fingers* swing at me, and once again I went into automatic pilot as I blocked his roundhouse with a forearm and caught him in the gut with my fist, lifting him off the ground. I held on to the guy and sat him on the bar stoop, leaning him in the doorway as he tried to speak, but there was no air in him and not likely to be in the near future.

I turned to the girl, who looked like she was going to run. "Are you okay?"

She stared at me.

"Are you okay?"

"Yes . . . Yes, I'm fine."

I took a quick look at the two desperadoes, who showed no sign of moving, and then stepped toward her. "What are you doing out this late, if you don't mind me asking?"

"I'm supposed to make a deposit."

"How about I walk you?"

She glanced around.

"I'm safe, honest." She swallowed and then looked up at me. "I've never seen anybody do anything like that . . . I mean, not even in the movies."

"Me either." I smiled, and she laughed. "You like the movies?"

"They're okay, but I like basketball the best."

I nodded. "Which way is the bank?"

She pointed behind her. "Right over there."

"Well, c'mon, let's get this done so you can get home."

I studied the side of her face as we crossed the street, and she finally noticed me staring at her as we trudged along in the snow. "What?"

"You remind me of somebody."

She stepped up on the curb and turned to look at me. "Who?"

"I'm not sure . . ." I noticed her staring at me, or staring at my chest to be more precise. "Something?"

She reached out and stroked the fabric of the red scarf. "This is nice."

I'm not sure why, but on an impulse, I pulled the thing off and draped it around her neck. "Here, you have it."

She smiled and stared at me for a moment before her attention drifted up and to the left—she spoke into the sky. *Bring me back, I don't belong here, and I want to go home.*

"Excuse me?"

Her sable eyes came back to mine, and it was as if she'd broken a trance. "Bring me back?"

I stepped onto the curb and turned to look at her, not understanding. "Bring you back where?"

"To the theater, that's where my ride is picking me up."

"Oh, yeah, sure."

"I don't belong here."

I continued to look at her. "Excuse me?"

She glanced around, uncertain. "Really. I want to go home."

"Okay. You mean now?"

She looked at me a moment more as if in a daze and then spoke before starting off again. "I feel like I've seen you before . . ."

Slightly confused, I caught up as we climbed the few steps to the front of the bank. I stepped onto the virgin snow and extended a hand to her as she joined me by the door. "I'm the one that asked about the movie while you were counting the till in the ticket booth."

"Oh." She looked back at the darkened marquee. "It's a really good movie, part of our western film festival. It's really funny."

"I know."

"You've seen it?"

"A couple of times, I think."

She laughed again. "You don't know?"

"To be honest, I'm not so sure I know much of anything these days."

I watched as she opened the door on a night deposit beside the main entrance and removed a manila envelope. She started to drop it in when I stuck out my hand and stopped her, having noticed a strange symbol on the paper. "Can I see that?"

She paused for a moment but handed it to me.

Holding it up in the light, I looked at the envelope and saw what seemed to be a symbol that had been hastily scribbled on there: a circle with a slash run through it. "What's this?"

She peered at it and back to me. "I don't know."

"There's no address or deposit slip . . ."

"It's inside." She stared at me and backed away. "Look, if this was just a way of getting the money, you can have it."

"No, no." I lifted the envelope, slipped it in the opening, and listened to it fall; then I closed the metal door. "There."

She continued to back away. "I need to go."

"Don't you want to go back to the theater?"

"No."

"What about your ride?"

"I'll find another way."

"Well look, I'm not going to leave you out here on the street with guys like that loitering about."

She glanced past me. "They're gone."

I turned to look back at the theater and found that they had disappeared. "Huh, they probably went back in the bar . . ."

When I turned around, she was nowhere to be seen.

I took a step forward, even going so far as to pull on the

handle of the bank door, which did not move. I looked around but for the life of me couldn't see where she could've gotten off to so quickly.

Watching the snow fall in the prismatic glow of the street-lights, I reached into my coat pocket and pulled out the tattered, clear plastic envelope with the missing girl poster, half her face staring up at me—the same face that had just been staring at me only moments ago.

As I crossed the street toward the movie theater, I walked past the alcove and noticed that one of the doors was open. My first thought was that the two thugs had jimmied the door and gone in, but as I approached, I could see a set of keys hanging from the lock.

Pulling them out, I glanced around and then figured maybe I'd find somebody inside that I could give them to.

It was a nice old theater with oriental carpets, walnut wood-work, and brass stands with velvet rope. There was a concession counter ahead and a pale-green and red neon strip that ran around a large mirror, and for the first time I got a look at myself.

I felt my jaw and the scruff of not having shaved in at least a day. Not too bad looking, but then not great either. There was one helluva a scar over my eye and part of one of my ears was missing, showing that there had been a few instances in my life when I'd gotten as good as I'd given.

Sticking my hand out again, I smiled. "Walt Longmire, how you doin'?"

I wasn't sure if I'd trust the guy. He looked a little rough.

There was noise coming from the interior of the theater be-hind the two swinging doors that separated it from the lobby, and I thought about catching a feature even if it was half over. I smelled the butter from the popcorn machine and figured what the hey.

I placed the keys on the back counter and pulled out a cardboard bucket, then opened the door of the popper and used the scooper to fill it. Having gotten that done, I walked over to the drink dispenser and poured myself a root beer. Then I went over to the auditorium doors and peeked through its porthole windows. A movie was playing, but I couldn't see anybody in the seats.

Pushing the green leather-covered door open, I stepped inside. It was relatively dark, but there were chandeliers that faintly glowed, hanging from the pressed-tin ceiling. The oriental carpets ran the aisles, and I walked a few steps before turning and looking at the back row—the place was completely empty.

Onscreen I could see it was the confrontation scene between Walter Brennan and the sheriff.

Figuring I had nothing better to do, I moved into row 31 and sat in the end seat, propping a leg up on the armrest in front of me and munching on popcorn as the two screen veterans duked it out. I'd always thought it funny that Brennan was essentially reprising his role as old man Clanton from *My Darling Clementine*, and for light comedy, nobody had a better touch than Garner.

Brennan had just entered the sheriff's office and pulled his gun, sticking it in Garner's face as the handsome leading man took his index finger and in turn stuck it into the barrel of Brennan's gun.

I laughed, and it was about then that the actor turned and spoke directly to me. "Sometimes, it is better to sleep."

I glanced around, I suppose to see if there was somebody else he was talking to, but I was the only one there. When I looked back at the screen, the actors were playing out the scene. "I don't remember that being in the movie."

Everything seemed normal again when Garner started following Brennan toward the back to a cell where the old man could visit his arrested son. Garner was just about to exit the scene when he turned and looked straight out into the theater. "You will stand and see the bad, the dead will rise, and the blind will see."

The image of the actor stood there still looking at me but then exited the scene.

Standing, I experienced the disconnected quality that I'd felt so distinctly when I'd woken up in the street. Looking around once more, I turned and walked out of the theater before anybody else talked to me.

Pushing the double doors open, I saw a tall, blond woman behind the counter; she was cleaning up. "Howdy."

She turned to look at me and then wiped down the glass counter. "Hello, can I help you?"

"I found the keys to the building hanging in the lock out there and brought them in." I pointed with my chin. "There, on the back counter." I gestured with the cup and bucket. "I actually helped myself."

"That's okay, that popcorn's been in there all day." She flipped a lock back from her face and smiled, and I noticed her sweatshirt emblazoned with VASSAR. "Is the film over?"

I approached and sat the root beer and popcorn on the counter she was cleaning. "No, but I've seen it before. You know there's nobody in there, right?"

"Yeah, but we're contracted to show it a certain number of

times by the distributor. I didn't figure anybody would show up for the festival with the blizzard and all, but I had Jeanie run it anyway."

"Jeanie, that's the young woman out in the ticket booth?"

She looked past me toward the front. "Is she still out there?"

"No, no. I escorted her over to the bank so she could make a deposit and then I assume she went home."

She nodded, placing the cleaning supplies behind the counter. She stood and stuck her hand out—"Vonnie Hayes. Nice to meet you . . . In answer to your question, yes. She's also the projectionist. I trained her myself."

"How long has she been working here?"

She stared at me. "I think that's about all of your questions I'm going to answer."

"Just one more?"

"Look, mister, I'm trying to close this place up and go home . . ."

I pulled the missing-persons poster from my pocket and laid it on the counter. "Does that look like Jeanie?"

She leaned forward and stared at the faded piece of paper.

"Is her last name One Moon?"

She continued studying me for a moment before answering. "Why, exactly, should I be answering your questions?"

"Well . . . You know, I'm not sure." I smiled at her, but she didn't smile back.

"I think you should go."

"Look, how long has she been here?"

She folded her arms. "I've asked you to leave. Now, if you don't, I'm calling the police."

I shook my head. "The phones aren't working, and the HP at the edge of town is out on an emergency."

She stared at me some more and then went over and picked

up a phone that was sitting on the counter. Hitting the button a few times, she listened and then rested it back, her expression changing.

"I'm not dangerous, honest." I cleared my throat. "It's just . . . I found that notice in my pocket and I'm thinking that's Jeanie."

"What if it is?"

"Well, somebody's looking for her."

She slid the missing poster back toward me. "You're not from around here, are you?"

"Actually, no." Picking up the sleeved piece of paper, I folded it and slid it back into my pocket. "Thanks for your help."

"Hey."

I turned to look at her.

She came around the counter and looked up at me. "People in this town, they just want to be left alone. Nobody asks any questions because nobody wants to hear the stories—there aren't any good stories in Fort Pratt, if you catch my drift?"

"That's too bad, because I like stories."

"Really?" She studied me. "What's yours?"

I stood there—silent.

The wind was continuing to orchestrate a ballet for the snow devils as they spun and twirled up and down the lonely street. Looking both ways before crossing, I stopped when I thought I saw something up past the bank—a figure, standing there, swinging something.

Taking a few steps that way, I could see it was the giant who had been in the café and at the HP substation. "Hey!"

He stopped swinging the oversized lance to look at me but then turned and ran in the other direction.

Figuring I didn't have anything else to do, I trotted after him, attempting to not land on my ass in the snow. "Hey, where are you going? C'mere!"

I picked up the pace but could still barely see him up ahead where the town petered out, but where one building past the bank had some lights on. It was one of those old Carnegie libraries, in which the two main columns out front were capped with a reddish stone interspersed with hand-hewn gray ones. The lights were on in the rounded conservatory to the right, below the mansard roof and through the main doors, more lights than should've been on this late at night.

I stopped in the street, looking at the lights and feeling some kind of kinship with the building, like I should know it and know it well—similar to seeing a friend on the street that you haven't seen in years.

I crossed toward the library, thinking that maybe the man had run in there. I got to the steps and walked up with a gloved hand on the iron railing, but paused at the door where the sign said CLOSED. I pushed it anyway and was surprised to find it unlocked, so I swung it open and walked in.

The lights were on everywhere, and the music that was playing sounded familiar although I couldn't place it immediately. Climbing the steps, I realized that it was Faron Young, the "singing sheriff," warbling Willie Nelson's "Hello Walls" to a thrumming rhythm. I was proud of myself for putting two and two together—maybe I was a disc jockey.

Faron Young had committed suicide—maybe I was a psychologist.

I saw that the main counter and a wooden rolling cart were full of books. Stepping forward, I looked toward the back of the building, where I could see someone or something moving among the shelves.

Coming around the counter, I looked to my left and saw that there was an old transistor radio sitting on a different library table. Faron Young segued into another song, one that I didn't know at first but then recognized the signature voice of Hank Williams and "I'll Never Get Out of This World Alive."

I shook my head, walked into the reading room, and glanced around, but the giant didn't seem to be anywhere in the vicinity. Continuing to move forward, I got to the open area beside all the bookshelves where it sounded as though somebody was rolling something across the floor. I walked to my right, but the sound had stopped. Standing there waiting, I heard it again, but this time to my left.

Then I moved back, and the noise stopped again.

Deciding to cut to the chase, I picked a row and walked until I got to the end, where I could see another cart of books. The noise continued, now sounding like leaves skittering faintly across the ground or books being slipped into place on shelves. Taking another step, I could see a pair of very nice legs on a ladder.

"You like books?"

Turning back, I squeezed around another set of shelves and the cart to find Martha, the woman from the café, on the ladder. She was re-shelving. "Howdy."

She tucked a book into the crook of her elbow and looked down at me and I couldn't help but be transfixed. She was wearing a cashmere sweater and pearls and a wool skirt that struck at her knee. She was backlit by the library's old globe light, and I just stood there staring at her. "You're still up?"

"You're still working?"

She shrugged, taking the last book and sliding it into place. "After-hours, part-time job re-shelving books." She climbed down and smiled up at me. "I just turn on the radio and do about four carts a night in an hour. A girl's gotta make a living."

I looked around. "It's a great old building."

"Isn't it, though?" She returned to the cart and picked up a few more books. "There was one like this near where I grew up."

"And where was that?"

"Wyoming." She smiled. "You wouldn't know where."

I stood there, rooted to the spot.

"Something wrong?"

"I'm not sure . . . It's just that there are things I see or hear that resonate, like I should know something about them because they're something about me."

"Wyoming?"

"I think I'm from there as well."

She nodded, a concerned look on her face. "Did you go talk to the police?"

"I tried, but there was no one there, something about an emergency."

"The blizzard, no doubt." Turning, she took the books from the cart and started down the aisle, pulling the rolling wooden ladder with her. "Find any more silver dollars?"

I followed so that I could steady the rolling ladder as she climbed. "No, but there's a man out there on the road that I met."

She looked down at me. "What kind of man?"

I shrugged. "Actually, I first saw him at the café and then just now out on the street."

"Alone?"

"Yep. He's dressed up in what looks like a bear hide and is carrying a spear."

"They tell me that we have apparitions sometimes, here in this town," she said.

"You mean ghosts?" I breathed a laugh. "The priest was telling me about that—from the boarding school?"

"The priest."

"Yep, the one across the street?"

"Well, I wouldn't take his word on everything, he's only been here a short while." She studied me and her look became serious. "It was destroyed."

"The school?"

"Yes."

The music changed on the transistor radio, the wailing sound of Roy Orbison's "Only the Lonely" filling the tiny library. "When?"

She climbed down and stood on the second rung, looking me in the eye as I took in the fragrance of her, which was intoxicating. "Years and years ago."

Breaking the spell, I glanced around. "Are there any books?"

"You mean concerning the Fort Pratt School? No . . ."

"No local history or anything?"

She stepped the rest of the way down and walked past me in order to collect more books. "It wasn't a nice place, and a lot of people would just as soon it never existed." She turned and looked at me as the music sounded louder. "It didn't have a happy ending."

"What happened?"

"It burned."

"Are there any old newspapers or records or something?"

She stared at me.

"Scrapbooks or anything?"

"Oh. Yeah, I guess there are the old ones down in the basement, but I haven't ever been down there." She shuddered. "It looks spooky."

"The basement of this building?"

"Yes, it's to the right as you come up the stairwell at the entrance." She carried the books into the aisle next to me.

"Jo Malone."

She stopped and then leaned back, tilting her head just a bit as she looked up at me. "Excuse me?"

"Jo Malone." I walked toward her, smelling her scent. "The perfume you're wearing, it's Jo Malone, right?"

"I think so."

"I saw you dancing." She studied me questioningly. "At the café. When I was walking back, I saw you through the window."

She grinned provocatively. "Was I any good?"

"Yes." I leaned against the end of the shelf and looked at her. "My wife was . . ."

"Wife?"

"I think I was married, and I think I remember something about that, about her, but it's not really clear." I raised my face to look at her. "I think she's gone."

"She left you?"

Feeling a pain growing in my head, I massaged the bridge of my nose with thumb and forefinger. "I'm . . . I'm not sure."

She placed the books on the shelf as Roy Orbison continued to sing the sad song. "So, do you dance?"

"No." I dropped my hand and shook my head. "I think that's how we met, though. I seem to remember sitting in a stairwell in a school or something, and she came around and asked me if I danced, and I told her no."

She nodded and then twirled toward me. She placed a hand on the lapel of my coat. "Did she dance?"

"She said she didn't." I could feel her fingers slide up my coat and under my collar, her fingernails on the skin at the back of my neck. "I, uh . . . I found out later that she was one of the best dancers in the state."

She pulled my face down to hers, speaking as our lips met. "Maybe she didn't want to dance—maybe she just wanted you."

3

They stood there on a snow-covered bluff overlooking the town, where the road curved away from the remains of the school. Flakes fell from the sky in lazy patterns, so you could see the mountains to the west, the weather hanging on the tops of the peaks as if they were tearing away the sky to break open the storm like a mischievous child would a down pillow.

Vic had kept Dog in the cab and dropped the truck's tailgate. She sat on it, watching as Henry walked toward the spot where the sign still stood, arching over the gate to the old cemetery.

The Bear looked up. "Fort Pratt Industrial Indian Boarding School."

"There was a fire."

He turned to look at Riley. "When?"

"I don't know, a long time ago." The Cheyenne Nation started to trip the latch and walk into the fenced-off area when Riley called out to him. "Don't." Henry turned. "They say it's bad luck, walking through the gate. Ever since I've been here . . . Everybody says so."

The Bear glanced around at the empty hillside. "Everybody?"

"Yeah, including the guy that sold the hotel to my dad." Riley pointed to the missing section of the fence that was to the right of the gate. "Everybody goes through there, even the coyotes."

Henry turned and looked at the collapsed stone walls where the school had once been.

"Anyway, I don't think you're allowed to go in there."

The Bear moved to the opening and looked at the platform and a very large bell. "Why?"

"It's one of those National Register of Historic Places or something."

Henry stepped through it anyway and studied the tiny, snow-covered crosses that were disintegrating and falling apart all over the hill. "There is no sign or plaque."

"No, the state hasn't gotten around to it."

Henry kneeled, brushed the snow away, and examined one of the tiny crosses. "What happened?"

"They say it was a stove that caught fire; the place was an old fort, and it was in pretty rickety bad shape. It was in the winter of . . ."

"1896?"

The young man stared at Henry. "Yeah, I think it was—how did you know?"

"It is on many of the crosses."

"They aren't buried there."

"No?"

"Nah, from what I heard they just dug one big hole and dumped 'em all into it—I mean there wasn't a lot that remained." He pointed to the center of the cemetery. "Under that platform where the bell is."

Standing Bear stood and approached it. "E. W. Vanduzen Bell Foundry, Cincinnati, Ohio," he read. "What is the story of the bell?"

"The only thing that didn't burn." Riley walked to the wrought iron fence, placing his hands on the ornamental spikes. "I mean there were stoves and a printing press, but I think considering the, um . . . incident, they decided to just junk that stuff."

The Bear nodded and turned back to him. "How many?"

"Sorry?"

"How many died?"

"Thirty-one, thirty-one children."

"No adults? There had to be staff."

He thought about it. "You know, that's a really good question, and I honestly don't know. I don't think that includes the adults, but I'm not an expert and really have no idea."

Henry knocked on the bell with a balled fist, his knuckles causing the old metal to release a strange and far-off sound; and then walked back toward Riley. "I am assuming that since the fort and the school were here before the town that that is where it got the name?"

"Huh?"

"Fort Pratt."

"I guess."

"Is there any kind of local library, historical register, or anywhere I could find more information?"

"I've got some old scrapbooks with newspaper clippings in them back at the hotel."

Standing Bear looked down the hill toward what was left of the town. "There was a newspaper?"

Riley nodded. "A weekly, but there's also the historical society over in Helena. They're in charge of the signs and stuff, but they didn't take the materials in the library basement, because I don't think they knew anything was down there."

"But nothing around here?"

"No. Like I said, there used to be a library, but they tore that down years ago—was one of those old Carnegie libraries too."

"Really?"

The young man turned to find the brunette with the funny-colored eyes now standing beside him. "Yeah, which is too bad, it was a beautiful old building."

"When did they tear it down?"

"I don't know that either."

Vic turned and leaned against the fence, the hood of her black Carhartt framing her face as her breath clouded the air between them. "You don't know a fucking lot, do you?"

The Cheyenne Nation tried to not smile as he came around the gate, carefully avoiding the archway. "Do you mind if we look at those scrapbooks of yours?"

"I thought you were looking for your friend?"

"We are, but he is a student of history among other things, and if we are looking for him, we may start with things that would interest him. You understand?"

"Not really."

Henry placed one of his big hands on Riley's shoulder and led him toward the truck. "Then perhaps you will learn along with us, my friend."

I listened to the bells ringing in the distance; at least I thought it was bells but it could've been thunder. There weren't any windows and the basement was dark, so I had switched on an ornate floor lamp that stood near a pile of boxes and set it beside the small library table where I could read the yellowed clippings from the elaborate scrapbooks. I'd waded through several of the books—fortunately they were in chronological order—the difficulty being that all I had to go by was that the fire had taken place in 1896. What I hadn't known was that it had happened so early in the year, New Year's Eve to be exact.

DECEMBER 31, 1896. Thirty-one native boys, ages 9 through 17, burned to death inside a dormitory at the Fort Pratt Industrial Indian Boarding School. The fire mysteriously ignited around 8:17 p.m. on a freezing night following a blizzard that shut down travel in the area.

The incident brought attention to a largely forgotten institution that had been in operation since 1886 when it had been converted from a military installation and was an industrial work farm for wayward boys. The disparities of segregation in philosophy and physical structure between the white and non-white institutions of the state revealed a few documented differences. The annual report to the governor included the vocational training at the white schools as carpentry and joining, cabinet work glazing, bricklaying, welding, plastering, lathe operation, tailoring, and shoe mending whereas the FPIIBS vocations are listed singularly as industrial trades, the details of which are not revealed.

Conditions at the school were said to be horrific with students wearing only rags for clothes, no winter clothing, and it was not uncommon for the youths to go without bathing for months at a time and the potable water was actually only marginally drinkable.

Orville Spellman, superintendent of the school, was unavailable for comment as he is among the missing.

The Montana General Assembly has called for a full investigation of the FPIIBS, but as to date little has been done to discover how, exactly, the fire may have started since the lone survivor has disappeared.

Simon Toga Kte, a previous employee of the school, stated that the amount of corruption and cruelty that he saw while there was far worse than had been reported. Toga Kte said it was not uncommon for the stewards and instructors to use leather straps on the boys when they supposedly misbehaved. After making his statement to the General Assembly, Mr. Toga Kte is believed to have left the country for an unnamed location in Canada.

I made a few notes in the margins, then sat back in the wooden chair and tried to imagine that night, a New Year's Eve not unlike this one. For some reason I felt as if I had to go back to where that school had been and see it once again more closely.

Scooting in, I went through the next scrapbook, but there was nothing more about the fire. I sat it on top of the one I'd just finished and stared at the pile of old, ledger-like scrapbooks, black with red corners.

I thought about Martha, the woman whom I'd kissed . . . Or had she kissed me? I wasn't sure what had happened or what it was I'd said or done, but she'd pulled back and looked at me and then turned, grabbed her coat, and rushed out of the building.

It was something I'd said, something about regret and about how we are all haunted by a measure of melancholy in our lives. I wasn't exactly sure why it was I'd said it, or why I'd chosen that particular moment, but it had frightened her.

Left there in the library and still not remotely tired, I'd decided to explore the basement and look for the scrapbooks she'd mentioned. Now sitting there, staring at the books, I couldn't help but wish that I hadn't.

I stretched my arms and yawned, looking toward the stairwell at the far corner of the room and the shadow there. Leaning forward, I watched—the shadow didn't move.

I stood and slowly slipped my coat from the back of the chair, eased around the desk, and stepped that way, keeping my eyes on the outline cast on the wall by the floor lamp. It was an odd shape, like someone was standing on the stairs but if so, they must've been huge. The head was abnormally wide as near as I could tell.

Carefully creeping across the concrete floor, I'd just gotten to the point where I thought I might be able to see if the shape was an individual when I noticed it was holding some kind of staff or spear.

I moved forward, but it was then that the figure turned and moved back up the steps.

Rushing to the stairs, I took them three at a time, but when I got to the landing, the only thing I saw was a slowly closing door, a skiff of snow blowing in from outside.

Pushing the door open, I ran onto the landing at the top of the stairs; skidding, I grabbed the iron railing to catch my balance.

I could hear somebody—somebody big—quietly thudding up the street as I clomped down the concrete steps, trying to get my coat on. I peered through the snow and up the sidewalk, but there was no one there.

It was hard to tell where the road was with the falling snow, and I could barely make out the edges when I walked, although it seemed that the road curled to the left and led upward.

The priest and Martha had both mentioned that the school was on a knoll to the east, where I'd woken up, so I assumed it was that hill I was climbing. It must've been getting very late in the night, but the temperature and yellowish light seemed to be staying the same and I wasn't cold at all.

As the two-lane road began to turn to the right and the ground became more level, I could see something looming up on my left.

Trudging ahead, I stopped and looked up at the archway spanning above it: FORT PRATT INDUSTRIAL INDIAN BOARDING SCHOOL. The words were faded and peeling. I pulled the post-card from my coat pocket and stared at the boys standing in front of this sign, especially the one in the front whose face was in focus.

Taking a step closer, I watched as the great horned owl turned its head around in order to stare down at me again.

"Have you been here all night?"

He ruffled his feathers, shaking off the accumulated snow, his eyes on me still.

"You haven't seen anybody come by here, have you?"

He blinked.

"I guess not." Dropping my eyes, I stuffed the postcard back into my coat and walked forward to where I could once again see the tiny crosses in tidy rows, stretching across the hillock. Farther away, I could see something large up on a platform of some kind, covered in snow.

"It's an igloo." I turned toward the voice and discovered a highway patrolman standing beside a cruiser without a single light on, having made not a solitary sound. "Just kidding, it's a bell." He walked toward me and then moved past and turned to look up at the guardian. "And that's Spedis, he guards the place when I'm not around."

"And you are . . . ?"

He slipped off a glove and stuck out a hand and when the flat brim of his hat tipped up, I could see the chiseled and fine Native features. "Bobby Womack."

I took the hand. His touch was like ice. "Your hand's cold."

He nodded and slipped the glove back on. "Yeah, well, I've been working." He extended the hand and flapped it at the bird. "C'mon, Spedis, give the cottontails a break tonight." The great horned owl, with a look of disdain, reached out with his six-foot wingspan and lifted himself into the air, drifting silently into the yellowish gloom.

The trooper turned back to me, and I noticed he wasn't a large man, but one of those shortstop types, like a bundle of bailing wire. "And you must be the mystery man in town."

I smiled, spreading my hands in admittance. "A mystery unto myself."

"Walt Longmire."

"That's what my hat says." I glimpsed my own brim. "If it is my hat."

He glanced behind him, where I'd woken up. "Well, at least you got out of the road safely."

I nodded back toward the town. "The citizenry been talking out of school?"

I watched him pull the slicker he wore back so I could see a .357 revolver at his hip. "I also hear you're armed."

"I am."

"Mind if I see it?" I pulled the .45 from the small of my back, aimed into the darkness, and then handed the semiautomatic to him, watching as he examined it. "Condition zero—locked and cocked."

I shrugged.

"Expecting trouble?"

"Not really. I guess it's just something I do naturally."

He glanced down the road toward the town. "You know there are no sidearms allowed in the city limits?"

"What's the story on that?"

"Left over from back when Fort Pratt was a military fort and civilians were required to deposit their weapons with the base commander; it just never got changed." He balanced my weapon in his gloved hand. "We're in agreement that it's a little unnerving having an armed man who doesn't know his own name wandering around town."

"We are."

He studied me a moment. "You don't look like a maniac, but until I get some kind of read on who you are, I think I'll just hang on to this."

"Seems reasonable."

"Got any other weapons?"

"A clip knife."

"We'll let you keep that in case you're attacked by an apple."

"Deal." I watched as he thumbed on the safety. "So, got any missing-persons bulletins lately?"

He started back for his vehicle. "Sure, just none for any big white guys in cowboy hats."

I walked with him toward his cruiser. "How was your emergency?"

He seemed relieved to change the subject. "Oh, a runaway heating-oil truck, a real mess."

"I heard it was going to take thirty-one hours to get the power and phones back on?"

"I heard that too." He opened the driver's side door of the cruiser and beckoned me to get in on the other.

"You don't want me in the back?"

"In case I haven't made it clear, you're *not* under arrest."

"Well, that's a relief." I climbed in and shut the door behind me as he climbed in his side. There was a shotgun mounted on the transmission hump along with a large chrome Motorola two-way radio. "Why don't you call into your district headquarters and see if they've got anything on me?"

"Two and a half hours away?" He snorted a laugh. "Under optimal conditions that thing will go twenty miles at best, and in case you haven't noticed we're currently not having optimal anything except snow." He gave me a funny look. "We'll head down to my office and see if we can raise anybody, but I wouldn't get my hopes up."

We slowly drove through town. I could see the lights were still on in the library, and I felt a twinge of guilt about not having been able to lock it up. "I made a pass at your librarian."

He kept his eyes on the road. "You what?"

"Well, not the librarian exactly, but the one from the café that re-shelves books, Martha?"

He nodded. "Who else have you had contact with since you've been in town?"

"What, you think I'm contagious?"

"I'm just curious as to what a fellow does after finding himself lying out there in the road during a blizzard."

I peeked over the long hood of the car. "You're keeping an eye out for anybody else who might be laying out here?"

He sat up a bit, peering through the falling snow with a smile. "Of course."

We pulled back into the spot where the car had been parked before, when I'd found it covered in snow. "You took another unit to the emergency?"

He shut off the engine and climbed out. "No, this is the only vehicle I've ever had."

I puzzled over that as I got out and followed him to the door, where he unlocked and bid me to enter. I stepped inside and looked around, but my eye was held by the mug on the counter with his name on it—notably, so was the emblem for the Wyoming Highway Patrol. "You worked in Wyoming?"

He had shut the door, taken his note off the inside, and came the rest of the way, slipping off his rainproof long coat and sitting behind the counter. Then he removed the cover from his hat and placed it back over his crow's wing hair. "Excuse me?"

I stared at him and at the brown Eisenhower jacket and tan slacks, but more important was the insignia and badge.

"Something wrong?"

"Why are you wearing a Wyoming Highway Patrol uniform?"

He stared back at me, glancing down at his clothing. "Um, I'm guessing it's because I'm a trooper in the Wyoming Highway Patrol?"

"We're in Montana."

He stared at me, a baffled expression once again creeping onto his otherwise emotionless face. "Who told you that?" Retrieving his mug from the counter, he stepped over to a coffee urn that looked like it might've been brewing since Joe DiMaggio filled it. "You want some coffee?"

I glanced around. "Um, sure . . ."

He slid another mug toward me, a Denver Broncos one with a chip on the brim. "So, you don't know your name, but at least you know what state you're in."

"I guess."

He pulled off his gloves and sipped his coffee, his dark eyes carefully appraising me. "Well, I know one thing."

"What's that?"

"You're a cop, or you *were* one at one time."

"How do you know that?"

"A feeling, and you're just too knowledgeable about the tools of the trade and procedures."

I figured it was maybe time to fess up to a few things, so I pulled the missing poster from my pocket and laid it on the counter between us, spinning it so he could read the portion that remained. "Know her?"

He leaned over, studying the thing. "One Moon . . . That's not Shoshone or Arapaho."

"Cheyenne maybe."

"Maybe." I didn't say anything, but he looked up at my silent face, which was obviously conveying something. "What?"

"Cheyenne, there's something about that."

"They're in Montana."

"Yep, I know."

He smiled. "Try your coffee, I've been drinking the stuff for so long I'm never really sure it's fit for human consumption."

I tasted it. It was terrible. "It's great."

"Good." He moved back to his seat, taking the poster with him, and then, pulling out another chair with the toe of his boot, indicated that I should sit. "So, you woke up with this?"

"Yep." I sat, taking the booklet from my pocket and handing it to him. "Any idea what this is?"

He studied the booklet, turning it over in his hands and then flipping through the pages. "Not Shoshone or Arapaho either." He handed it back to me. "Probably Cheyenne as well. You read Cheyenne?"

"No."

"Me neither." He took the postcard I handed him, and he

breathed a mild surprise. "A postcard of the school; never have seen one of those." Turning it over, he looked at the number on the back. "Thirty-one . . ."

"Mean anything to you?"

"No." He handed it back to me and then looked at the photo of the girl again. "She looks familiar."

"I think she works up at the movie theater."

"Here in Fort Pratt?"

"Yep."

"You speak with her?"

"I did."

"Doesn't sound very missing."

"No, she doesn't, does she?"

He reached behind him and clicked on a larger radio-base unit on the desk, one with a stationary mic and kept hitting the tab at the base repeatedly, but neither of us could hear anything. "You hungry?"

I thought about it as I sipped my coffee. "I had some soup and a few fries—I think I am."

"You like Vietnamese?"

"Huh?"

"There's a great Vietnamese restaurant here in town."

"Some cop, how did I miss that?"

"It's not on the main drag—it's behind the movie theater." Womack stood, reaching for his slicker. "C'mon, my treat."

Ten minutes later we were sitting in a converted garage eating cá kho tộ from tiny ceramic pots, the caramelized fish and vegetables simmered to perfection. As I ate, he did too, but also continued to scrutinize me. "What?"

"I've been eating here for years, and I can't make heads or tails out of the menu, let alone understand what these guys are saying, and you walk in for the first time and it's like old-home week."

I sipped my Tiger beer and shrugged.

"This wasn't even on the menu." He wood-spooned in another bite of the long-braised, sweet-savory stew. "How did you know to order it?"

I jutted a chin toward Bao, the smiling man behind the counter, who nodded at us. "The head guy said he was from Hanoi; every grandmother there knows how to fix cá kho tộ—it's like Vietnamese comfort food."

"Yeah, but half the conversation was in Vietnamese."

I gave it some thought. "Was it?"

"Yeah, it was."

I spooned some more in and thought about it. "I guess I speak Vietnamese, at least a little."

He stared at me. "Look, if you're some kind of CIA spook . . ."

"I don't think so."

"No offense, but you don't know what state you're in."

"Well, you got me there." I studied the sign in the window with the silhouette of a Vietnamese junk and the gold and red national flag in the background. "Funny name too."

He looked at the sign, reading backward. "Tonkin Gulf Yacht Club." He turned back to me. "I don't get it."

I finished my cá kho tộ and moved on to the banh cam. "In '61 when the Seventh Fleet arrived off the coast of Vietnam, it became an ongoing thing with line-crossing ceremonies and plank-owner certificates for the anchor-clankers."

"The what?"

"Sailors."

"Yeah, but what did you just call them? Anchor-clankers?"

I sipped my beer. "Did I?"

"Yeah, you did." He sat back in his chair.

"Huh." I glanced at Bao and what looked to be more than a dozen other guys back in the kitchen constantly checking to see if we were enjoying the food. "Ngon quá!"

They laughed and smiled at me, cheering. "Beaucoup dien cai dau!"

I toasted them with my Tiger beer. "Boocoo dinky dau!"

They all laughed and cheered again as the patrolman leaned in. "Okay, what the hell . . . ? I mean, if you are CIA, you need to level with me."

"Honestly, I don't think I am, but—maybe I'm a soldier." I sat back in my chair and glanced around as I drank my beer. "How did these guys ever get here?"

Finishing his own stew, he shrugged. "Hell if I know. The usual, I guess, one shows up and then a bunch follow—all I know is it's the best Vietnamese food on either side of the Rockies."

Pulling the missing-persons poster back out, I studied half the girl's face. "She's younger in this photo."

He reached over and pulled it to the side so that he could see it. "A little."

"She was scared at the theater."

"Yeah, well, you worry me a little more with everything that comes out of your mouth."

"How long has she been here?"

"I don't know."

"The woman who owns the theater . . . ?"

"Don't know her."

I sat there, looking at him and brushing the strange feeling away. "The woman—she said that the people in Fort Pratt don't have good stories."

He laughed. "I'll go one step further and say they don't have any stories at all." He sat up on one side, pulling out his wallet. "Walt, Walter, whatever your name is, you are literally in the middle of nowhere and you go to nowhere to get away from everything—well, everything but one thing. Now, a lot of people in this town are here because they've run as far as they can, and maybe they just want to be left alone with their regrets."

He stood and walked over to the register to pay as I finished my beer and followed. "Is that a warning?"

"Just some friendly advice."

We walked outside where the snow continued to fall, and the air still smelled like smoke. We climbed into his cruiser. "You got a place to stay?"

"Over at the Baker."

"Let me guess, room thirty-one."

I turned to look at him. "How did you know that?"

He hit the starter, and the Crown Vic leapt to life. "It's the only room in the hotel that's finished."

"If there is a break in the storm and I can daisy-chain out with the other departments or they get the phone lines working, I'll come get you, okay?" He pulled up in front of the hotel. "In the meantime, though, I think it might be best if you stayed in your room until morning—if not for any other reason than you might pass out again and who knows if we'd find you before spring."

"Got it." I extended a hand. "Good to meet you, Officer Womack, and thanks for the help."

"Just Bobby." He smiled at me. "Sometimes you have friends you don't know you have in places you've never been."

I studied his face for a change and noticed he looked tired. "Why don't you head back to your substation and catch a few winks?"

He sighed, pulling off the glove and shaking my hand. "I might just do that."

I climbed out. "And try and warm your hands up."

I watched him drive away and was about to turn when I looked down into the dual-imprint tracks left by his tires and spotted something impacted in the snow. Reaching down, I plucked both silver dollars and held them up.

They were exactly like the other two.

Depositing them in my pocket with the other pair, I turned and headed up the steps into the hotel, which looked exactly as I'd left it, down to the note still propped up on the front desk.

I'd just started up the steps when I saw that there was an individual who was standing behind the bar to my right watching me. I stopped and then walked in that direction, figuring maybe he was the owner and that I should let him know who I was as best I could and assure him that the priest had given me keys to the room and gotten me settled.

As I approached, he set a shot glass of mescal down and turned to look at me, his eyes severe and strange, a washed-out brown.

I extended my hand. "Walt Longmire."

"Yes, I know who you are." His accent was Spanish and possibly Mexican but a shade different. Maybe he was actually from Spain itself. He had a few days' growth on his chin and smiled between the dark strands of hair that covered a portion of his face. He didn't attempt to shake my hand. "Do I look familiar to you?"

"Yep."

"Does the name Thomas Bidarte mean anything?"

"Honestly, no."

His smile faded, and he stared at the surface of the bar between us. Pushing his black cowboy hat back, he reached over and poured himself another from a mescal bottle that had a hand-printed label that read Benesin, and a piece of twine attached to the cork. "You don't know how glad I am to see you, or how long I've been waiting."

I sat on a stool opposite him. "You know who I am?"

He nodded but swiped my words away with a hand and then sat another shot glass in front of me. "Yes, but we don't have time for all that right now."

"We don't have time for who I am?"

He sat forward, looked around, and I was pretty sure he was frightened of something. "Look, I'm not supposed to be here, and if they find out I've been talking to you . . . Well, things could get worse for me."

"I don't understand."

"There've been others, people who've come here before you, but I've been waiting for when you would show up—I knew you would."

Ignoring the drink, I sat forward, resting my arms on the surface of the bar. "Look, Bidarte, something happened to me, and I don't know what it was, but I woke up out there in the street . . ."

Shaking his head, he became more frantic. "That doesn't matter. It doesn't make any difference what happened or how you got here but a lot of people are depending on you."

"To do what?"

He cleared his throat. "Do you ever wonder where you go when you die, Sheriff?"

"Sheriff?"

He shook his head. "Madre de Dios . . . You don't know anything, do you?" He glanced around, and I could tell he was attempting to overcome a brooding silence; fighting to use words, a form he wasn't used to. "I'm not a good man, I admit that—but I don't deserve this."

"Deserve what?"

He leaned forward and became, if possible, more intense. "You need to be careful in this town. When you first get here it seems like you've got all the time in the world, but that's not the case, and the longer you're here the harder it will get to talk about it and then it's too late."

"I don't understand."

"You, your time is running out." There was a sound, like a bell ringing in the distance and he began looking around. "They know I'm here."

"What are you talking about?"

"You're our only hope." The bell sounded again, and he studied me, snatching the shot glass and downing the mescal in one gulp. "You can't believe everything that happens here, you can't trust people, even people you think you know." He stepped back, listening, and I noticed that even with the cold, he was sweating. "Look, I must leave but think about what I've said."

"I have no idea what you've said."

"Think, Sheriff, think . . ." He turned and came out from behind the bar, listening to the bell as it continued to ring. "You've got a gun, right?"

"No."

"What do you mean, no?"

"They took it."

He looked at me, utterly dumbfounded. "Who did?"

"The HP, Bobby Womack."

He continued to look confused. "Who?"

"The guy that just dropped me off, the highway patrolman from the substation west of town."

"There's no cops in this town, that's why we need you."

"We?"

"Everybody here, all of us—well, almost all of us."

"Need me for what?"

"You'll figure it out . . . Look, I've said more than I should, and I can't let them catch me here." He backed away even farther and darted into the lobby. "The thing to remember is that you don't have as much time as you think you do."

I stood, watching him. "What about you?"

"What?"

"How much time have you got?"

"Me . . . ?" He started laughing. "I've got time; I've got all the time in the world." He clutched his sides as if the laughter caused him pain, but he couldn't help himself. "I have nothing but time."

I started after him. "Look, I need to know what you know, or I can't help anybody." I pulled the missing girl poster from my pocket and held it out to him. "I found this in my pocket along with some booklet in Cheyenne and a postcard: Am I some kind of bounty hunter or missing-persons detective?"

"Yes, yes, that's it—she wouldn't be the first one you've rescued." He backed toward the door. "Find the girl in the poster, get out there and find her, and don't let anybody get in your way."

"Right, well first thing in the morning I'll . . ."

"No! No!" He was shouting now. "You have to find her now!" He pointed at the flyer in my hand. "If that's what brought you here, then you need to do it, now!"

He turned, pushed open the door, and ran into the snowy street just as the headlights of a five-ton plow barreled up the road straight toward him. If he'd only kept moving, he could've avoided it, but instead, he simply stopped in the middle of the road and stood there framed in the headlights, the emergency yellows painting the street in streaks. He watched as it approached, showering both sides in a cascade of snow and slush, its great, forked blade coming straight at him, slinging his body into the corner of the building with a deafening shudder.

He lay on the sidewalk, his arms and legs twisting out of the mound of snow at crazy angles, his head turned around almost backward.

I ran toward him, slipping and falling in the snow as I crawled up beside him. One brown eye blinked, and it was more horrific to think that he'd survived.

I reached a hand out.

Blood flowed from his mouth as he whispered, "You've got to remember one thing. . . ." He swallowed. "All haunting is regret." The fingers at the end of a twisted arm flexed, and then he was still.

I stood in time to see the missing-persons poster I must've dropped. The plastic-coated sheet skittered in the smooth path of the plow, and I scrambled off the sidewalk, and slid into the street after it. I'd almost reached the piece of paper when another wind gust blew it just out of reach, and I slipped and fell but was able to pin it to the compacted snow. I sat up and grabbed the paper, quickly looking both ways to make sure I wasn't the snowplow's next victim.

I struggled to a standing position and glanced over to where the crumpled and twisted body had been.

And it was gone.

I scrambled over to where the man had landed and there was simply nothing there, not even an impression indicating where his body could've been. I dug into the snowbank to search, but there were no signs that he'd been moved.

Stuffing the flyer back into my pocket I turned toward the Baker Hotel, where the large clock above the door read 8:17 p.m. Standing there with the wind clawing at me, I ran through the conversation we'd had, trying to remember his name.

Thomas Bidarte.

Find the girl.

Find the girl now.

4

They were hungry, so Riley fixed some cheeseburgers on the grill out back. "The kitchen needs a lot of work, besides, I'm not much of a cook."

Henry smiled and took the paper plate with the burger and some potato chips. "Thank you, I'm sure it will be fine."

Vic was standing by the window looking out at the empty street. "How long has the theater been closed?"

He sat her plate down on the other side of the table. "A long time."

She cocked her head and read the abandoned words that were still on the marquee. "Support Your Local . . ."

"Unless it is actually a public service announcement." The Bear picked up the burger, took a bite, and chewed. "There were two films made back then." Vic joined Riley at the little table, and Henry peered at the moldy scrapbooks the young man had piled up on the stool by the bar. "Those are the books?"

"Yeah."

The Cheyenne Nation nodded and continued eating as Vic glanced around. "How did you come to own this place?"

"My dad got it at a sheriff's auction. Some people out of Arizona bought it off the internet and were gonna fix it up and turn it into a bed-and-breakfast, but then they got here and decided it was too much work—and too much snow." Riley looked around, pushing his Stormy Kromer hunting cap farther up on his head. "They didn't pay the taxes, and after a while it went on the block and Dad had the money."

Vic took the first bite of her burger and chewed. "How old are you, Riley?"

"I'm twenty-four."

"Young."

"Yeah."

"Do you live here in the hotel?"

"No, I've got a camper out back."

She chewed, studying him. "So, what's a handsome guy like you doing buried in a ghost town fixing up a dilapidated hotel when you could be down in Missoula or Bozeman chasing skirt?"

He could feel his face getting red. "Oh, I'm doing this as a favor to my dad."

Henry glanced at him.

"When my parents divorced, they sold the ranch, and Dad bought this place and hired me to fix it up, but then we had to buy tools and materials." He smiled. "Tools are expensive."

"Yes, they are." The Bear finished his burger. "We are sorry to be such a nuisance, but that was a fine meal."

"Thank you, I chop up onions and add onion soup mix with the beef and that makes it better. It's something my mom used to do." The young man took his plate, walked it around the bar, and dumped it and the plastic fork into the trash can there.

When he got back, Henry had pulled one of the scrapbooks from the pile and was turning the pages. "I'm surprised the historical society did not take these."

Riley sat on the bar. "Yeah, they didn't seem too interested in poking around. I think it had to do with the fire and everything."

"There is nothing about the fire in any of these."

The young man glanced at the stack. "One of 'em does. When the library closed, they just boarded it up, but I guess people broke in and took stuff. Finally, it got in such bad shape that the county came in and tore it down as a safety hazard."

Henry reached over and took the entire stack of books, laying them at his feet as he picked up and opened another. "And you are the only one who lives here?"

"Yeah, there was a woman who owned the café, but she finally shut it down and moved away to Billings to be with her kids; I heard she died."

"Then you are here alone?"

"Yeah."

"So, if our friend or the other man had been here you surely would have seen them."

"I guess."

The Cheyenne Nation's eyes came up to look at him. "You guess?"

"Well, I can't be sure, but I think so."

"There is nowhere else that they could have stayed or eaten?"

"No, I mean nowhere."

Henry's eyes finally went back to the pages of another scrapbook, and he began thumbing through it as well.

"Where do you go to get supplies and groceries?"

Moretti was watching Riley again, and he felt his face reddening. "It's almost two hours to the nearest real town, so I drive there, but my truck is getting old and I'm not so sure it'll make it round trip for too much longer."

She glanced at the Bear. "Sounds like your truck."

Henry grunted.

She redirected her eyes. "Was your family ranch near here?"

"No, it was over in Kootenai County."

"Where's that?"

"Idaho."

She looked at Henry.

The Cheyenne Nation spoke as he continued to study the book. "Hayden Lake?"

Riley nodded. "Near there, yeah."

Placing a finger on the page, Henry began reading. "*The deteriorating conditions at the boarding school may have been responsible for the fire that took place on December 31. A board of inquiry formed a commission that found survivor Mr. Toga Kte to be innocent of all charges and is attempting to discover the employee who was supposed to oversee the boys' dormitory that night, namely the school supervisor, Orville Spellman, who disappeared the night of the fire.*"

She interrupted and looked at Henry again. "*Toga Kte,* what does that mean?"

"Assiniboine for enemy killer." The Bear folded back a page and continued to read. "*Attorneys turned over the investigative material to the state attorney general's office and a grand jury was formed but returned no criminal charges. To keep the incident from becoming an embarrassment to the state, surviving family members were given fifty dollars per child, half of which was appropriated by attorneys' fees.*"

He sighed and sat back in his chair.

"There was a guy who used to come back here every year, at least that's what the lady who owned the café told me before she left."

Henry held the book back up, studying it again. "Was it this Simon Toga Kte?"

"No, long after that—I guess they never heard from that guy again."

"Then who?"

"I don't know, some really big guy—he'd just show up and go out to the school in a bear costume and perform some kind of ceremony or ritual. Some of the people even called it an exorcism."

Henry continued to study the scrapbook in his hands. "These books are in rough shape."

"Yeah."

His eyes went over to Vic as he held the book open for her to see, and he pointed something out on the page—she studied it and then flashed a look at Riley as Henry rested the book on the table before bringing his eyes slowly up to the young man. "You say you have not seen our friend here in town?"

"No."

The Cheyenne Nation turned the scrapbook around, sliding it toward him. "Then perhaps you can explain to us why Walt Longmire's handwriting is in the margins of this book?"

The snow continued to fall, and the only lights on were in the bar on the other side of the street. I crossed, figuring that if I was going to launch an investigation, the only open enterprise might be the place to start.

The sign above the door read BAR 31, but there wasn't anything else to identify the place, not even beer signs in the two octagonal windows in the squat facade.

I pushed the door open, keeping an eye out for the two I'd encountered on the sidewalk, but the place appeared to be empty except for the bartender, a tall, bald man with some extravagant facial hair and tattoos. "Closed."

"Really, I uh . . . I just need a beer."

He studied me. "You all right?"

"Um, yep."

He looked disgusted for a moment but then waved me toward the bar as he adjusted the rubber gloves on his hands. "I've got to load the dishwasher, so you've got till I'm finished and then out you go."

I sat on the short side toward the door and the two booths in the front and looked at the tap handles with the fancy names. "Do you have any just regular beers?"

He straightened and gestured toward a glass front cooler. "In cans I got Bud, Coors, PBR, Oly, and Rainier."

"No bottles?"

"No bottles."

"Classy joint." Unsure why, I chose the last. "I'll have a Rainier."

He grabbed a bar towel and wiped off his hands, then opening the cooler he plucked out a can. He popped the top and slid it toward me. "That's a buck fifty."

I reached into my pocket and tossed two of the newfound silver dollars onto the counter, where he looked at them.

"Where'd you get those?"

I threw a thumb over my shoulder and forced out a laugh. "Out on the street, the place is covered with them."

He studied them a moment more and then reached out with surprising dexterity, considering the rubber gloves, and turned one over, revealing the silver Lady Liberty with the pronounced lips. He placed it back down. "You keep 'em."

"Are you sure?"

He placed two rubber-coated, beefy fingers on the coins and pushed them back toward me like a checker, keeping eye contact with me the whole time. "On the house." Then he pulled off the glove and extended his hand toward me. "Deke Delgado, but everybody calls me Big Daddy."

I took the hand, and we shook. His was cold too, like the trooper's. "This your place?"

"No, I just run it."

"Why Bar 31?"

"I don't know, I guess there were thirty other failed ones before it." He plucked a clean glass from the top rack of the washer and polished it with a bar towel. "You're not from around here."

"No, I don't think so."

"You don't think so?"

I took off my hat and rested it on the bar. "No, just no."

"I'm familiar with pretty much everybody in this town."

I picked up the can and sipped the beer in an attempt to settle my nerves. "I'm not even familiar with myself."

"Well, you're a cowboy, I can tell you that much."

I tipped the brim and it spun on the crown just a bit. "Why, because of the hat?"

He ducked his head, looking at the inside of the thing and I was sure, reading. "Nope, Walt Longmire, it's the way you set it down; no self-respecting cowboy would ever think of setting his hat down any other way—keeps the brim from getting bent, but more important, it keeps your luck from spilling out."

I lifted my can. "Here's to luck."

"We can all use a little of that." He continued to examine me. "How'd you get here?"

I laughed, but it sounded hollow. "Oh, I just found myself here."

"The blizzard?"

"Um, yep." I took another sip of my beer, and it tasted good and somehow familiar. "Ever heard of a guy by the name of Thomas Bidarte?"

He reached over and took the can. "Out."

"What?"

He pointed toward the door. "Get out, if you're a friend of that nut, then you go."

"He's not a friend, I just met him over at the hotel and . . . Well, I think he just got hit by a plow and is dead out there, somewhere."

His eyes continued the examination and then he set the Rainier back down. "Nobody dies in this town."

"Excuse me?"

He went back to polishing the glasses. "I can't remember the last time somebody died here."

I nodded and sipped my beer while studying him. "Do you know the young woman who works at the theater next door?"

"Vonnie?"

"No, the one that works the ticket booth."

"Jeanie?"

"Yep."

"Isn't she a little young for you?"

"I'm not looking for a date."

He nodded and carefully lined the beer glasses on the bar. "She hasn't been here long, why?"

I pulled the missing-persons poster from my pocket. "This."

Spinning it around, he took in the half image of the girl and the partial writing.

"Seem familiar?"

He continued to study the faded flyer. "Looks like her, a little younger maybe."

"I thought so too."

"You working for the family?"

"Something like that."

His eyes came up to mine again. "Think she wants to be found?"

"I don't know."

"I used to do work a little like this back when I lived in Vegas."

"What brought you here?"

He laughed and leaned in. "You wouldn't believe me if I told you."

"Try me."

"Maybe someday." He leaned back and placed the last glass in the tidy row. "Drink, your time is up—in more ways than you think."

"Excuse me?"

He gestured toward the washer. "I'm done . . ."

"No, about the time, what's the story about time—you're the third or fourth person to mention that to me."

He smiled an empty grin. "Just sending you on your way, my friend." Without another word, he reached under the bar and brought out a baseball bat. "Closing time."

I downed the rest of my beer and stood, scooping my hat from the bar, and replacing it with the empty can. "Thanks."

He leaned back, having now noticed I was a little bigger than he was, and maybe more practiced.

I placed my hat on my head and turned toward the door when he called out. "East of town."

I turned to look at him as I fastened my coat. "What?"

"I seen her walk east, so I assume she lives that way."

"Past the bank and the library—toward the boarding school?"

He nodded. "Yeah."

"I'll try in that direction then."

Looking a little sheepish, he returned the bat to its resting place. "Good luck."

I gave him one last glance as I headed out the door. "We can all use a little of that, right?"

As I walked under the marquee of the movie theater, cast in the odd, greenish neon light, I checked to see if the doors were locked and was relieved to find that they were. What I was surprised by was a boat of an old Oldsmobile with Colorado plates idling at the curb, the condensation from the leaky exhaust creating a vaporous cloud that blocked half the intersection.

There appeared to be a young couple arguing inside.

It was strange but even with the continual snow throughout the evening, it didn't seem to be getting any deeper than about six inches on the ground. Moving around the rear of the vehicle, I watched as they broke off and the driver, a young kid, lowered the window and called out to me. "Hey buddy, can you help us out?"

Stopping, I turned and walked over to him. "What do you need?"

"You got a few bucks you can loan us?"

I waited a moment before responding. "You mean, give you?"

He smiled a crooked response and glanced at the young

woman with a mop of blond hair who sat in the seat beside him. "Sure, I mean give us."

I stuffed my hands in my coat pockets and looked down at him. "I've got four dollars to my name."

The smile lost a few lumens. "You're kidding."

"I'm afraid not."

"What, you blew the money at the bar?"

"Have you been following me?"

He stared at me a moment and then laughed. "Really, you only got four bucks to your name?"

"Yep."

He pulled his seatbelt out and buckled it. "Well, I'll tell ya, pops, you just hang on to your four bucks . . ." He reached down to pull the thing in gear, but the young woman put her hand on his arm. They spoke for a moment, and I'd turned to go when he called out from the open window again. "Where you headed?"

"Out of town."

"Just out of town?"

"For now."

There was more talk in the car before he shrugged her off and called out to me. "Can we give you a lift?"

I peered into the darkness where the town ended and had to admit that I was tempted. "That's okay, I'm not even sure where I'm going."

She said something to him, and this time he strung a hand out. "C'mon, we'll give you a ride to wherever you want to go."

I walked back over, laying a hand on the shedding vinyl roof. "I don't want to be a bother."

He waved me off, and I pulled the handle on the rear door, opened it, and climbed in.

Settling myself, I looked to the front, where the woman had an arm draped over the seat. I could see a fresh scar at her wrist as she studied me. "Hi, I'm Heather."

"Howdy, I'm Walt Longmire."

The young man stuck out a hand. "Make it Jamie. How come you're leaving town?"

"I'm not. I'm, uh . . . looking for somebody."

He shifted the car into gear and glanced around before doing a U-turn and pulling up to the intersection. "Who?"

Pulling the flyer from my pocket, I held it out to her.

She took it as he turned right and began driving slowly. "She's missing?"

"Yep."

"Somebody hire you to find her?"

"Something like that. She supposedly lives somewhere east of town but I'm not sure where." I studied the blanket, pillow, the food wrappers, and other refuse. "You guys been on the road long?"

He barked a laugh. "Forever."

She glanced at the young man. "Tell him."

He glared at her. "Shut up."

"Maybe he knows . . ."

"Shut up."

We rode along in silence, amplified by the cushion of snow on the road. There were no lights on in any of the tiny houses and I was beginning to give up hope when she spoke again. "We left Denver and we've been driving all night . . ."

He growled at her. "I told you to shut up."

"We got tired . . ."

He turned toward her this time. "Shut the fuck up."

"We go to sleep, and every time we wake up, we're . . ."

He reached out and smacked her, the sound of it echoing in the interior of the sedan.

"Hey."

He turned to look at me. "You got something to say?"

"I've got something to do. If you hit her again, I'm going to drag you out of this car and use you like a piñata."

He said nothing and went back to driving up the hill toward the cemetery and the remains of the school.

She held her hand to her face where she'd been struck, and a few tears lined it.

I reached into my jeans and pulled out a bandanna that I hadn't known I had. "Here you go."

She took it and dabbed the tears. "Thank you." She peeked at the driver again. "Maybe he knows . . ."

Disgusted, he spat out the words. "Do what you want."

She studied him for a moment and then turned back to me. "Do you live here?"

"No, I don't."

"Well . . . Do you mind if I ask how you got here?"

I smiled at her. "I would, but I'm afraid you wouldn't believe me."

She eyed the driver again, and he deigned to glance back at her before her large blue eyes returned to mine. "Tell me."

"I woke up in the middle of the road."

She bounced up and down in the seat. "Out in the street, you just woke up there?"

"Yep."

We had reached the top of the hill, and Jamie pulled the sedan over to the side of the road in front of the arched sign and gate, stopping the car and putting it into park before turning around to look at me. "What, lying in the street?"

"Yep."

They looked at each other again and then he turned back to me, his expression changed. "We drove up from Denver all night, and we got tired and pulled over to sleep and woke up in this town."

I waited for more, but there didn't appear to be any. "And?"

He held my gaze. "It's happening to us over and over again: We leave Denver, drive north and get tired, pull over and sleep and wake up in this shitty town. Then we get the hell out of here, and we're suddenly back to zero, driving north from Denver."

I stared at them, but they didn't appear to be joking. "That doesn't make any sense."

"Yeah, I know."

I choked out a dry laugh. "Why don't you just turn around?"

"You don't think we've tried that?" He shook his head in disbelief. "We pull over at a rest stop, a gas station, convenience store, just the side of the road, and we wake up in that, that damned town down there."

"You mean in the morning?"

She leaned forward, shaking her head. "No, no, it's never morning . . ."

"She's right, it never gets light." He gestured toward the darkness around us. "Have you noticed? It never gets light. There's no day in this town, ever."

I scanned the surrounding gloom and the strange tint of the sky. "Well, I've only been here one night."

He made a sound and wiped away my words. "What time is it?"

"Excuse me . . . ?"

"You got a watch on you?"

"Well, yep." I started to pull the pocket watch out from my jeans.

"It's 8:17 p.m."

I stared at him and then held the timepiece up in the available light, to see that it was 8:17. "How did you . . . ?"

"It's always 8:17 here." He switched off the engine and turned completely around. "We can all sit here for eight hours discussing this and then turn around and look at a clock and it won't have moved." He gestured toward the analog at the center of his dash. "Think about it: since you've been here have you seen a single clock that has shown any time other than 8:17?"

I thought about it. "You're right."

"You're damn right, I'm right." He turned and started the car again.

"What are you doing?"

He slipped the Olds into reverse and threw his arm over the seat. Then he looked past me and backed onto the road. "Getting the hell out of here."

"Wait, wait . . . What good is that going to do? You're just going to drive until you get tired and then wake up here in Fort Pratt again."

He looked uncertain.

"Stay here and help me work all this out."

They looked at each other and then Heather turned back to me. "We've done that too. We've stayed here and run around asking questions and it varies: There are people here who are the same as the three of us, not knowing who they are or how long they've been here. Then there are others who claim to have been here forever, and I think that's what happens to you in this place."

"What do you mean?"

"I think people are here long enough, and they forget that they don't belong here—and then they do."

I looked out at the pristine snow that sloped away from the knoll and all the tiny crosses that populated the high ground.

Heather turned back to me. "He thinks it's hell, but I don't."

I took a deep breath and shuddered as I forced it out. "What do you think it is?"

"Someplace between, someplace we're not supposed to be, someplace where we can't stay."

"You got that right." He pulled the selector into gear and started to hit the gas.

"Stop." I reached over and pulled the handle, opening the door and climbing out as they watched. "What are you doing?"

I closed the door behind me. "I'm staying here."

He lowered his window. "Haven't you been listening? It doesn't do any good, it just happens all over again, and again."

I pulled on my gloves and cranked down my hat. "Then I'm going to have to find some way of breaking the chain, won't I?"

He shook his head. "You won't."

"I've got to try." I shrugged. "Anyway, the roads are closed."

"Yeah? Well, I'll open 'em back up."

He studied me for a moment and then reached into his jacket, pulled out a cheap pistol, and tried to hand it to me. "Here."

I stared at the glinting revolver. "What's this?"

"Protection."

"From what?"

He glanced back at her and then back at me, extending the thing out farther. "In the time that we've been here, we've seen some pretty strange shit."

I took a step closer. "Like what?"

"Hard to explain . . ."

"Like dead people disappearing?"

He stared at me. "And other stuff." He opened the door and got out, pushing the revolver at me and laughing a nervous laugh. "Take it. We're just gonna drive all night and then wake up back in this fucking ghost town and I'll have this gun again."

"You've given it to others?"

He nodded his head. "Yeah, brother. I feel like I have."

"Ever see any of them again?"

"Who knows?"

I stared at his hand. "You keep it." Turning and walking away, I tapped the rear quarter panel of his Oldsmobile. "By the way, you've got a taillight out."

I listened as he climbed back in and spun the tires in an attempt to spray me, which only resulted in him sliding sideways and slithering onto the road.

Standing there I watched as the sedan disappeared into the falling snow and darkness with just a bit more speed than conditions would allow. The last thing I saw was the pale face of the young woman, Heather, as she stared out the rear window.

I shook my head and turned to look at the cemetery and the sign with its solitary occupant. I walked over and stopped a few yards away from the arch as once again the great horned owl stared down at me, unmoving. "So, we meet again."

He continued to stare at me with the amber, deadpan eyes.

I pulled the flyer from my pocket and held it up for his inspection. "You haven't seen this young woman, have you, Spedis?"

He didn't answer, not even a hoot.

"I didn't think so." Stuffing the poster back into my pocket, I looked around. "Pretty slim pickings up here tonight."

I took a few more steps, resting my hand on the gate under

the archway, wrapping my fingers around the ornamental arrowheads at the top. The shape of the bell was more pronounced, now that I'd been informed of what it actually was, but it was different somehow, and it looked as if the snow had actually piled up much deeper in the cemetery itself.

It was as if whatever it was that controlled the town held no dominion here.

There was a heavy latch with a loose logging chain hanging from the gate, a vintage padlock tapping against the metal. Evidently it had at one time been deemed fit to lock the place, but that time had passed. Not only had the lock fallen apart but also there were entire sections of the wrought iron fence lying on the ground buried in the muffling blanket of snow.

I reached down and pushed the latch as a bell sounded in the distance.

Staring at the mound of snow that held such a bell, I half expected the thing to rise up and swing, but it just sat there, inscrutable and silent.

I pushed the gate open and it swung wide with an agonizing squeal.

There was an explosion above my head as the great horned owl reached out and flapped the frigid air, driving himself up into the darkness with a powerful flux of his six-foot wingspan. He didn't go far this time, though. Instead, he pivoted on his wing tips and swung around over the massive bell, landing at the top, where the brush of his feathers swept away the snow there. He stretched his neck to one side and then settled, folding his great wings around him. He stared at me, and before long the only thing I could see of Spedis was his unblinking eyes. I became aware of something telling me that I shouldn't be here, that I mustn't disturb hallowed ground, that there would be repercussions for what I was about to do.

I reached over to the gate and started to swing it back closed, but something made me stop. Looking up at the great horned owl, I read the words on the archway to myself. "Fort Pratt Industrial Indian Boarding School." Reaching inside my coat, I pulled out the booklet, opening it to the title page and the publisher's imprint, reading again where I'd used the candy play money and the postcard as bookmarks. "Fort Pratt Industrial Indian Boarding School . . . FPIIBS."

Closing it and returning it to my pocket, I stared up into that owl's eyes again, more words formulating in my head like whispering smoke, words that I'd heard—words from a dead man's mouth.

Feeling them form like an incantation, I spoke, my voice sounding distant and hollow. "All haunting is regret."

Tugging the front of my hat down by the brim—I lifted a boot and stepped through the gate.

5

Riley studied the page. "That writing has always been there, at least since I've looked through them."

Henry took the book back from him and turned it around. "And how long has it been since you have looked through these books?"

The young man thought about it, his Adam's apple bobbing. "Well, awhile."

The Cheyenne Nation stood, looking down at him. "Riley?"

"My head is starting to hurt." He took a step back and turned, walking toward the lobby of the building. "I have these spells, and I'm not feeling very well."

Vic picked up the scrapbook, carrying it around the bar to where he stood. "That's Walt's fucking handwriting." She continued toward the young man, holding the book up for him to see. "Listen, if there's something you're not telling us, I'm going to drag you out into that street and . . ."

The Bear approached and raised a hand. "Riley, you say this writing has always been here?"

His eyes wide, he finally broke off from Vic. "Yeah, I mean, as well as I can remember."

"Is that all you remember?"

"My head hurts."

Henry studied him, finally reaching out and placing a hand on the young man's shoulder. "Maybe you should go take a rest in your trailer, you have been doing an awful lot today taking care of us."

He clutched his head. "Yeah, but I want to straighten up your room and get it ready for you . . ."

"You can do that later. Go out to your trailer and take a nap and we will take care of the room ourselves." He added. "Do you mind if we bring the dog in? He is very well behaved."

Riley waved a hand. "No, that's fine."

Vic followed him as he disappeared through the swinging door leading to the kitchen and then out the back. She stood there for a moment and then turned to Henry. "What. The. Fuck."

Closing the book and tucking it under his arm, he held out a hand. "If you give me your keys, I will go get Dog."

She brushed past him toward the front door. "I'll get the dog, but when I'm back, I want some explanations."

He watched her go and then looked to the stairs, turning in a slow circle and examining the interior of the hotel as if looking for something. But failing in that, he pulled the book from under his arm and opened the page to where there was writing. He played his fingers along the cursive words as if reading braille, looked up again, and sighed.

The front door blew open and the beast charged inward, dragging Victoria Moretti with him. Pulling her toward the middle of the room, he paused to sniff the Bear's leg and then sniffed the carpet, working his way around the room before stopping at the base of the stairwell and looking up.

An instant later, the 150 pound mongrel pulled the leash from Vic's hand and bounded up the steps. He began sniffing the carpet at the landing before moving over to the door to the left and then scratching at it. After a moment, he backed away and looked down the stairs at Henry and Vic and barked a single bark.

The Cheyenne Nation moved toward the stairs and then turned to look at Vic.

After watching the dog, her eyes came back to his. "What the hell?"

Reaching over the front desk, Henry plucked the key and fob from the cubby marked 31. Vic followed, and Henry stepped past Dog. The Bear placed the key in the lock and turned it.

The door opened and Dog was the first one in the darkened room, held back only by Henry, who had grasped his collar. Henry hit the old-fashioned button switch and the overhead chandelier came on.

There was no one there, but someone had been.

There was a large impression in the made bed, and the curtain to the window that looked out onto Main Street was pulled aside, revealing the empty road below.

Kneeling, the Cheyenne Nation could see impressions in the carpeting where someone had walked after it had been vacuumed. Releasing Dog, he watched the beast sniff the floor toward the bed, where he rested his head and sniffed the cover.

Henry stepped in, followed by Vic as they perused the room, Moretti the first to speak. "You see anything?"

"Someone has walked in and out of the room, they moved the curtain and they laid on the bed—a large someone."

The Bear stood there and placed the scrapbook on the blanket that covered the foot. Flipping the book open, he studied the page with the handwriting in the margins. "This is very odd."

Vic came around, looking from the corner of the bed. "What, that's Walt's handwriting."

"Agreed, but it is the instrument that was used which is interesting." He held an elbow and cupped his chin in a powerful hand as he examined the book. "When I was very young, my grandfather had a box of surplus pens he did not use, leftovers from when the Department of the Interior sometimes dumped the strangest items on the Rez."

Vic looked up at him. "You're going somewhere with this, right?"

The Bear placed his fingertips near the writing. "Like the Vulcan Ink Pencil of J. M. Ullrich & Company, Twenty-seven Thames Street, New York. The only perfect, nonleakable ink pencils at moderate prices. Agents wanted. Big profits." He smiled the thin smile. "I still remember every aspect of those pens and the writing on the box they came in; by the time he gave them to me as a child, they must have been almost fifty years old . . ."

Vic leaned in to look at him. "What the fuck, Henry?"

He looked up at her and then walked around her to the nightstand, where he reached down and picked up a hard, rubberlike writing instrument. "I would wager anything that the writing in that book was done by this Vulcan Ink Pencil, a pen that has not been available for over a hundred years."

The town was missing, and I fought the notion that my mind was too.

It was snowing, but it was a different kind of snow and a different kind of sky and a very different time. I looked behind me to make sure that I was somewhat in the same place. The geography was the same, overcast but the foothills of the mountains to the west were now visible and the smell of smoke was gone.

I pivoted in a circle, thinking that maybe I'd gotten turned around, but there was nothingness in every direction. The ground sloped away, and the S-shaped curves of the thoroughfare were still there, even if the road was a snowy, muddy, two-track now.

There was a horse-drawn wagon plodding up from the flats where the town of Fort Pratt should've been. There were two people riding on the buckboard, one large and the other small and wrapped in a quilt.

As near as I could tell, it would take them another couple of minutes to get where I stood, so I turned back to the only architectural feature on the central Montana plain.

The facade of the Fort Pratt Industrial Indian Boarding School was a battered-looking two-story building with stone walls joining it to another building in back, which formed a square in the middle. There was a gate at the center, leading into the square, overshadowed by a bell tower at the center of the rear of the building on the other side of the open space.

I pulled out the postcard from the booklet and held it up—the match was exact.

It had been some kind of prison, the imposing walls decidedly giving the impression that they could keep anything out or anything in. There had been additions, portions of the school that had been added on with barred windows in an attempt to make the place less forbidding, an effort that as near as I could tell had failed miserably.

There was no cemetery, but there was a platform where the bell had been swallowed by the imposing structure. The wind struck at the building as flakes scooted through the air, trying to escape the wind that carried them along. There was a shutter that banged against the facade of the building, which kept time with the wind and with the consistent, muffled *clomp* of the single draft that pulled the wagon to the top of the hill.

I turned to look and could see that it was a man driving the buggy, which was actually a sleigh, easing it toward me with the reins in his chapped and calloused hands.

He was a severe-looking individual with an old-fashioned fur hat and a cigar clamped tightly in the left corner of his handlebar-mustachioed mouth, a heavy, mottled, hide coat wrapped around him.

There was a bundle in the seat beside him. I might've taken it for a simple bundle except for the two scuffed shoes that stuck out of the bottom like worn buttons.

I was standing there in the middle of the road, and wasn't sure if he meant to stop, so I moved to the side and raised a hand. "Howdy."

He kept his eyes level and straight, acknowledging me in no way.

Raising my eyebrows, I shrugged and followed along after the sled—the horse kicking up snow like half-moon divots that fell in front of me as I trudged along after them.

They came to an abrupt stop at the gate, and I was surprised to see the man reach up and pull a chain that was suspended there. Impatient, he pulled it again and then stood in the sled, looking about within the square but seeing nothing.

He had just started to get out of the sled and open the gate himself when a teenage boy, who looked to be about fifteen years old, ran across the square and scrambled to open it. After a moment of fussing, the boy unlocked the latch and swung both sections wide open, allowing the sled to enter.

I doubled my time to get to the gate before the boy in the jacket and service cap closed it, but he swung it shut in my face. "Hey!"

Ignoring me, he ran after the sled as it circled the square, finally pulling up to the double doors below the bell tower.

Reaching down, I tripped the latch and stepped inside, looking up at the stone archway toward the gray skies where the snowflakes continued to dodge and weave in the wind, also trapped inside the square.

"Damn it to hell!"

I looked over to see the bundle in the sled had dropped over the side; and now that bundle was clumsily moving toward me in a kind of side-hitched and disjointed way as the blanket fell. I could see that it was a boy of eight or nine with a wild mane of hair. His hands and feet were manacled, allowing only a hobbled stride as he swung his way to the gate, his shoulders swinging forward and back.

The driver had leapt from the sled and was in stumbling pursuit, even though he was impaired by his heavy coat. "Close the gate, close the damned gate!"

Foolishly touching my hand to my chest to inquire whether or not he was speaking to me, I then saw the uniformed boy from before racing to reach the gate before the smaller boy did.

Figuring it wasn't any of my business, I stood still and watched as the chained bandit hopped by, only to have a foot tangle in the manacles, sending him sprawling in the snow and slush and into the stationary portion of the gate, where he crumpled against the wrought iron bars.

The teenager pounced on the smaller boy, who was at something of a disadvantage.

I was about to reach out and disentangle the two when the man brushed by me and grabbed them both, swinging the manacled boy against the fence and slinging the other to the side, where he stood with his head hanging down. "I told you to close that gate, Ty."

"I did, sir."

I raised a hand. "It was me, I'm the one that . . ."

He continued to look at the older boy, who now was suffering a bloody nose. "When I tell you to close a gate, you do it and that, double-quick."

The teenager wiped the blood from his nostrils and then took off his hat and rung it in his hands. "Yes, sir."

I stood there glancing from one to the other, but neither of them would look at me.

The chained boy stomped his feet, but the man held him tightly, like he would a wild animal. A voice called from across the square. "Mr. Crawley, are you delivering the boy or assisting him in his exodus?"

The man known as Crawley turned as a tall, very thin bald man approached wearing a heavy, dark-colored wool suit. "Sorry, Superintendent, but this is a wild one and if yon boy there hadn't left the gate open . . ."

"I didn't, Mr. Spellman. I swear I closed it."

Crawley turned and barked at the boy. "Then how did it get open, eh?"

I raised a hand again, figuring it was past the time to introduce myself. "It was me . . ."

"Well, let's get him over to the office and put together his paperwork and assign him a bed before it gets dark, and you can't see your hand in front of your face." Spellman turned and walked away without another word as I stood there with the rest of the unfinished sentence in my mouth.

I watched Crawley drag the boy along behind Spellman as the child struggled to escape. The older boy fastened the gate, and I noticed that his clothes were too small for him; the legs of his trousers and the arms of his jacket probably four inches too short. Crawley continued to pay me no mind even though I was no more than a step away from him.

"Hey?"

The larger boy strung a chain back through the bars, attached the old brass lock and then stepped back in order to watch the trio crossing the square, studiously ignoring me and wiping more blood from his nose.

"Hey." He still acted as if I weren't there. "Hey, I'm talking to you."

He turned and ran away without even looking at me.

The three others moved across the square toward the horse, which stamped the ground with his large hoof.

The three were almost across the square when I raised a hand to my mouth and bellowed. "Hey, over here!"

Nothing.

Again, they didn't give any indication that they had heard me or knew that I was there.

I was a little unsteady, so I gripped the bars to get my bearings. I'd stepped through the gate and the world appeared to have changed again. The place where I'd come from wasn't the place I belonged, but I didn't belong here either. At least in the other world I could be seen and heard.

I tripped the latch with my fingers, feeling the cold metal and watching the mechanism open, so at least some aspect of me was here and having an effect. But am I dead? I felt like I needed to sit down. I could turn around instead and walk back through the gate, but if I did, what kind of world would I find, the same one or something different?

I started across the square and moved behind the wagon toward the glass-paned doors. I reached down, thumbed the latch, and stepped into a hallway with a polished wood floor. The walls were whitewashed, and there was nothing on them, giving the place a kind of antiseptic feel.

There was a small sign hanging over the doorway to my right, so I took a step in that direction just as a red-haired young woman in a prairie skirt and felt jacket turned the corner with a stack of clothing in her arms.

I stepped forward and leaned in and could see an office where the superintendent, Spellman, sat at his desk conversing with Crawley, the boy standing behind him.

The red-haired woman came out again and walked past me toward the doors. As she walked by me, very closely, I blew a breath of air in her direction and then watched as she shivered, touching her hand to her neck on the spot where I'd blown on her.

I stood in the doorway behind Spellman as he listened to Crawley explain why it was that he had been so late in arriving with the boy.

"The agents said he was there, but when I arrived, they'd hidden him out in a shed more than a mile away from the house."

Spellman studied some papers in his hands, raising his hawk-like nose to look over them at the man, his eyes a pale, washed-out green, like algae that had died. "Near?"

Crawley adjusted the cigar. "Pryor."

"Why didn't you take him to Saint Xavier?"

"They didn't want him, besides, they're full up."

"So are we."

Crawley shrugged. "I'll take him back to Helena, if you want, but they're the ones who sent me here."

"We have no other Crow children." Spellman's eyes went back to the papers, studying them with a Talmudic intensity. "White Buffalo, doesn't that last name mean something auspicious to the Natives, Mr. Crawley?"

The man removed the cigar, gesturing with it, the embers at the end glowing orange. "A sign of hope and abundance, an indication of good times ahead."

Spellman looked at the boy, still standing there in chains, his head hanging down, the dark hair hiding his face. "Eight years old; big for his age."

"So is the rest of the family; if I hadn't had those two troopers with me, I might've feared for my life." He chuckled. "His mother is as big as me."

"We carry the burdens the Lord gives us, something I learned with the Seventh Cavalry." The superintendent placed the papers on the desk in front of him and addressed the boy. "Young man."

There was no response.

"Young man, I am speaking to you."

Crawley used his foot to poke at the boy. "Answer the superintendent."

White Buffalo remained silent.

Spellman stood, walked around the great desk, and sat on the corner next to the pile of clothes, shoes, and personal items that the woman had brought in. Looking down at the boy, he cleared his throat. "What is your given name, boy?"

Silence.

Spellman turned to Crawley. "Does he speak English?"

"Damned if I know, not a peep for over two hundred and fifty miles, so I couldn't rightly say." He sat forward in his chair. "I recollect they referred to him as Marcus."

The superintendent, a glimmer of light in his eyes, looked at the boy again. "Ah, the emperor and believer of stoicism, a dedicated student of fate, reason, and self-restraint—all philosophies that will assist you in the coming days." He clasped his hands between his knees and leaned back, quoting to the ceiling, his eyes slowly dropping to the boy. "'And, to say all in a word, everything that belongs to the body is a stream, and what belongs to the soul is a dream and vapor, and life is a warfare and a stranger's sojourn, and after fame is oblivion.'"

More silence.

"Very well then." Turning his head, he called through the door that was beside me. "Simon!"

I heard someone approaching in the hallway. After a moment, a young man in his twenties appeared, wearing the same uniform as the boy in the square who had unlocked the gate, his hair shorn close to the scalp and his cap in his hands. He placed his weight on his left foot in order to avoid the right, which I now saw was clubbed. "Yes, sir?"

"We have a new student. If you would, please take him down and have him prepared for his new life."

The young man placed his cap on his head and kneeled in front of the child looking up into his hidden face. "Háu . . ."

The child didn't really respond, but his head lifted just a bit.

Simon looked at Crawley, who removed the cigar again. "Crow."

Spellman straightened the turkey wattle by stretching his neck. "We don't speak those devil languages in this school."

The young man reached out a hand, but the boy pulled back. "It's okay, it's okay . . . I don't speak any Crow anyway." He looked at Crawley again. "Does he . . . ?"

"Don't know."

The young man nodded, looking back at the boy but still talking to Crawley. "Do you have keys to the manacles?"

"As far as I know, he doesn't bite—so there's a blessing in that." Crawley struggled, getting them from his vest pocket and tossing them to Simon. "But I'd be careful if I was you; you give him half a chance and he'll be out the door and gone like a scalded dog."

Simon held the keys out for the child to see, holding his own hands out in hopes that the tiny prisoner would mimic him, and to everyone's surprise, he did. Carefully unlocking the chains, he then reached down and released the boy's legs. He then leaned in very close to the boy and spoke again in a voice so low that none of us could hear the actual words.

Handing the chains back to Crawley, he stood and gently placed a hand on the boy's shoulder.

Crawley took them, roping them over one knee and puffing on the cigar. "Well, I warned you—he's going to run."

Simon picked up the stack of clothes and steered the boy between the two men, and we watched as they went out the door and to the right.

"What kind of horse trader are you, Spellman? That bay I've got out there, he isn't much for the distance anymore and I'd just as soon leave the whole kit and caboodle with you if you'll give me a good saddle horse for the whole conveyance."

The superintendent stood and returned to his chair behind the desk. "Well, that's a handsome offer, Mr. Crawley, but I'm afraid we're fresh out of horses, having eaten the . . ."

I turned just in time to see the boy flash by the door, followed by Simon, the young man running after his charge as best he could. I stuck my head into the hallway in time to see the boy fighting with the door mechanism as if he'd never seen such a thing.

Once Simon laid a hand on him, however, the boy became submissive and did as much as he could understand of the sign language directed at him by the young man's hand. I stepped into the hallway and watched as the boy allowed Simon to turn and usher him back down the hallway and past the doorway.

Spellman and Crawley exited the office to watch them as well.

They washed the boy with the help of the young woman. The redhead used large sponges that had been soaking in a pail of water, which had been heated on the wood-burning stove.

There was also a fire in a cooking hearth in the kitchen, where Simon stood at the door, effectively dissuading the boy from attempting another of his escapes—five since I'd been watching.

I stood by the fire, not to feel any warmth from it but to try to stay out of the way until I figured out what would actually happen if I were to touch somebody.

They sat the boy on a stool and began cutting his hair off with large shears, finally finishing the job with a pair of hand clippers as he sat there wrapped in a large, stained towel.

His back was to me as they had him stand, and I watched as the woman held the clothes up to him to see if they would fit. They appeared to be close enough, or as close as they were going to be, and she started dressing him before he began taking the clothes from her and doing the chore himself.

She wasn't beautiful in a predictable way. Her face was marked by what I surmised had been smallpox, but her hair was very red, almost a burnished brass, and her features were strong. When the light struck her face just right, she was breathtaking.

Simon moved from the door, but not too far, before kneeling again and looking at the boy, placing a hand at his chest. *"Simon Toga Kte."* He then took the same hand and reached out, touching the boy on his own chest. "You?"

Silence.

The woman picked up the ragged clothes she'd taken off the child with thumb and forefinger and tossed them into the fire. She'd started to reach for his hair that was scattered on the floor, but the boy threw himself down, covering it up.

She and Toga Kte shared a look, and then she went to the cabinets behind her and pulled out a small flour sack with a red ribbon drawstring and handed it to him.

Looking over his shoulder, the boy reached out a hand and took it, gathering up the loose locks and placing them inside.

"No lice, nits, or fleas?"

The woman smiled and responded in a Scottish brogue. "Nothing, which is surprising in that he's been traveling with Creepy Crawley."

They both smiled, and Toga Kte reached out to get the boy's attention, then he pointed to the woman. "Madie."

The woman curtseyed in jest. "Pleased to meet you."

The boy had no reaction. The irises of his eyes were as dark as a seasoned skillet, so dark that you might not notice the frantic movement there, like a cornered animal.

I stared at him, and for a moment he seemed to look my way, but his eyes were on the door beside me, always looking for a way out.

Simon collected the few items that were left on the mantle of the cooking hearth and hobbled back over to stand beside the boy. "Come on, time to throw you to the wolves."

I followed them from the main building in back to one of the connecting wings that turned out to be the boys' dormitory. There were beds strung along both walls, more like cots, really, and there were small brackets that divided them with sheer curtains that might provide a limited amount of privacy as well. Small cabinets between the beds were for clothing and personal effects.

The wing had a hard, used look about it from its years of military duty. There were tall, shuttered, and mullioned windows set in the thick-walled embrasures, giving the impression of many realities attempting to get in and held in check, just.

There were two glowing potbelly stoves, one on each end of the room, standing in the center of the hallways like burning afterthoughts, small wooden boxes of found firewood set beside each.

The floors were green and white tiles worn to shades of institutional neglect, many of them broken with pieces swept to the painted baseboards like parts of jigsaw puzzles never to be joined.

There were boys standing in a group like a school of fish, ready to dart away if the need should arise, and they watched warily as Simon brought the boy in through the French doors.

They were dressed alike, and the fit of their uniforms told the story of how long they'd been at the institution, rising pant hems and foreshortened sleeves that had lost the ability to protect bodies that persisted in growing.

The teenager who had opened the gate where we'd earlier come through stood at the front, his nostrils still bloody from the battle there before. The others clung nearby as he looked warily at the newcomer.

Simon stopped in the center of the room, his hand still on the boy's shoulder. "Men, we have a new member joining our ranks." He glanced down at the boy. "Until we receive some other notice, his name is Marcus, and I want you to make sure and welcome him, making him feel at home here at the school."

The teen stepped forward, extending a hand. "My name is Ty."

Marcus didn't respond, only stood there clutching the small cloth sack.

Simon cleared his throat. "We'll give him time and let him get used to things." He looked around. "Is there a free bed?"

"Tiny's bed is the only one left." Ty dropped his hand and stepped back, pointing toward a cot at the far end of the room. "Nobody wants it."

Simon studied the bare bed. "Well, that's certainly not the fault of the cot, now, is it?" He reached out and placed a hand on the tall boy's head. "Ty here is the leader of the pack and will teach you the ropes—think of him as something of a platoon leader."

Simon stepped away, leaving the two standing face-to-face.

Then he noticed a clock hanging on the nearby wall, the pendulum swinging in the case. "Eight-seventeen and far past your bedtime, gentlemen. I would advise you to prepare yourselves for bed before Mr. Spellman makes his evening rounds."

He turned and started to leave as I moved to the side and watched him hobble his way out, finally turning back around to watch the two boys, standing there in a face-off.

"You don't talk, eh?" Ty leaned in over Marcus. "That's okay, we've had mutes here before—deaf, dumb, crippled, and feeble-minded, but it doesn't matter. Whoever you are, you've got to make it to your bed."

He stepped back and began unbuckling his belt, stripping it from his pant loops. "And you gotta run the beltline to get to that bed."

I watched while the others began taking off their belts with varying degrees of enthusiasm, gripping the leather straps in their hands and lining themselves up along the foot of the cots.

I knew I couldn't allow this to happen, but what could I do, grab a sheet off one of the beds and prance around the room? Looking up and down the elongated space, I made a decision and took a deep breath.

Walking over to the nearest barred window, I reached up and slammed both towering shutters closed with a loud slap. As the boys all looked at that window in amazement, I walked across and did the same on the other side, careful to step between them as I crossed back and forth, I worked my way down the walls slamming each set of shutters closed.

The screams and cries from the boys grew as they retreated to the far side of the room, clustering behind the stove as I approached.

When I finished, I turned to see that the only two who hadn't moved were Ty and Marcus, both of whom still stood at the center, Ty looking around at the closed shutters, his eyes wide.

After a moment, Marcus quietly walked around the taller boy and made his way to his assigned cot.

I stood at the last window beside his bed as he walked past me, sat on the cot, and stared at the floor.

After a moment, the others crept past him toward their own

beds, pulling their curtains and removing their clothes and quietly climbing in, the murmur of their voices the only sound.

Ty, looking unsure as to what to do next, went about the room blowing out the oil lamps and then finally walking past the bed where Marcus sat. He raised a finger and started to say something, but then his eyes wandered to the shutters, and he grew silent, the finger dropping like a flag without wind. Standing there for a moment more, he finally blew out the last lamp. He stood there in the darkness looking at the shutters, one after the other, then retreated to his bed and began removing his clothes. After a final glance at Marcus, he covered his head with his blanket.

I moved along the wall, sat on a side chair, and watched the young boy, the steady breathing of his sleeping roommates softening the air.

I'd never felt so brokenhearted for anyone.

Maybe that was the true hell of things: to be an unwilling witness to events but to be unable to stop them—apart from opening and closing shutters.

When my eyes came back to the boy, he'd raised his head and was looking straight at me, but I'd grown used to people looking my way when they really weren't looking at me at all.

The words were whispered so quietly I wasn't sure I'd heard them at all, but when I leaned forward to examine his face in the darkness, he was still looking at me, and I watched his lips slowly move as if speaking to someone on some other, faraway plain.

"Thank you."

6

"I'm taking my gun out for a walk." Vic hung in the doorway, one hand on her holster, and Henry lay fully dressed on the bed with Dog lying beside him. He was still studying the Vulcan Ink Pencil and the scrapbook. "Do you have to do that a lot?"

She nodded, threading fingers through her thick blue-black hair. "Twice a day, or it has an accident."

"Does it ever have accidents on the walks?"

"Occasionally."

The Bear lowered both the pen and the scrapbook. "You are going out nosing around."

"I'm not."

He shook his head, placing the pen behind an ear and raising the book back up again. "You are bound and determined to find something?"

"He's out there somewhere, Henry."

"And you think we will find him in the dark?"

"Fuck you, sometimes dark is all you get." She walked back into the adjacent room to retrieve her jacket. She pulled it on, Dog raising his big head to look at her as she pointed a finger at him. "Fuck you too. You're not going, because I'm not going to be responsible if you run off chasing a deer."

He grunted, letting his head fall back onto the bed.

Henry reached down and petted the dog's broad back. "He wants to go."

"Fuck the both of you—I'm just walking my gun."

The Cheyenne Nation shook his head and sighed. "Do not let the gun off the leash."

"Cross my heart." And she did, before opening the door. "Leave the door unlocked."

"Cross my heart." He didn't but went back to studying the book, finally reaching down and giving the animal's fur a tug. "Personally, I think we are now safer."

There was a lamp on at the front desk when she came down the stairs, but Riley was nowhere to be found. She zipped up her jacket, popped the collar, and even went so far as to pull on her tactical gloves.

Her truck—the Banshee—was the only vehicle on Main Street. She missed Walt, not in some corny valentine way but she missed his company, like a part of her was missing when he wasn't around. She wasn't used to him not being around and over the years it had become more imperative to be in his company; a soothing effect unlike anyone else she'd ever met.

Vic was annoyed.

Where the fuck was he and wasn't this just like him to disappear and leave everybody tearing their hair out trying to find him?

Asshole.

She thought about taking the Banshee, but the town was only a few blocks long and if there was anybody out there, she'd wake them up with the sound of her exhaust. Besides, when she hunted, she liked hunting on the q.t.

She'd just crossed the street when she saw a light glowing behind the hotel, but then she saw it was the camper the guy had mentioned.

She shook her head and continued quickly before the dopey guy showed up. She'd made the curb when she looked back at the old movie theater and noticed the building had collapsed in the back, the ragged edge of the bricks looking like teeth. There were other foundations around and even what looked like the remnants of an old church that had been torn down and hauled off—not like the Catholic church to give anything away. There was an archway that still stood. It reminded her of the archway up at the school where the guy—what's his name, Riley?—had told them not to walk through because it was bad luck.

The edge of the town was ahead, and the only thing in that direction was the road that snaked up the hill toward the cemetery and that old sign for the school.

She shuddered.

As she stood there, she looked to the north where there seemed to be another road, but not really a road, more like a snowplow had suddenly gone rogue and wandered off to die alone and away from the herd.

There were piles of snow in that direction, large piles, so she assumed that was where the plows must dump their excess. She was about to turn when she caught a quick flash of something off in the far distance, something reflected in the partial moonlight.

She pulled out her mini flashlight and shone it in that direction, reaching to the small of her back and pulling out the Glock semiautomatic that felt so natural in her hand. Pointing in the direction of the beam, she kept walking and estimated the distance to be about two hundred yards, an easy shot out here in buffalo land—to shoot a shot like that back in Philadelphia you'd have to go out on the Delaware River or maybe the end zone at Lincoln Financial Field. Of course, the way the Eagles were playing lately you wouldn't hit a soul.

The piles of snow looked like a miniature mountain range, and she wondered why in the world the plow driver had pushed the snow all the way out here?

As she got closer, she could see she'd entered a broad area where the plows must've turned around. There was some junk to one side along with some rolled-up wads of barbed wire. The piles of snow were maybe thirty or forty feet high in spots and a quarter of a mile long.

She heard a noise to the right and swung around, the front sight trained on a shadow that stopped and looked at her, a light-colored coyote out for a nightly hunt. Pulling the barrel up, she smiled. "You can get killed out here, Wile E."

The undersheriff watched as it worked its way along the snow foothills, sniffing for holes the western cottontails might've made there.

Turning back, she shone the flashlight up—something that looked like a two-way whip antenna was sticking out of the powdery surface. With a sigh, she began slugging her way up the steep slope, her boots sinking to her knees with each step.

Finally, she stretched her fingers and pulled at it, and it easily came out of the snow. "Well, hell."

Steadying herself, she studied it, trying to figure out what kind of vehicle the thing might've come from, but then finally flipped it over her shoulder.

She'd just started to turn around and climb down when her boot struck something solid, providing more support than she'd felt in the snow up until then. She stomped her boot in the snow and could hear a metallic, hollow sound.

Holstering the Glock and pocketing the flashlight, she began digging, moving the freshly plowed mounds away in great heaps, stopping to rest for a moment and then digging again, tearing away at the slope until her gloved hands finally struck something. Scooping a few more handfuls away, she threw the snow to the side and then wiped the metal surface. Pulling out her flashlight and clicking it on, she could see the gold and black lettering—Absaroka County Sheriff's Department.

Fuck me.

"You can see me?"

He nodded.

"Why didn't you say something?"

His voice was very soft. "It gets me into trouble."

I looked up and glanced around the dark dormitory of the boarding school. "Like speaking English?"

He smiled—the first time I'd seen him do it.

Moving from the bench, I sat on the bed beside him. "Why can't they see me?"

"I don't know."

"But you've seen others? Other people that they can't see?"

"Yes."

I couldn't help but glance about the dark room. "Are any other than me around right now?"

He smiled again. "No."

There was a light reflecting off the walls past the double doors leading into the other room at the far end of the hall and the sound of a familiar step. Picking up the stack of clothes and belongings, I placed them on the bench and then motioned for him to stand, which he did as I pulled the covers down on his bed.

Plucking off his shoes I settled him in and then pulled the bedding up and under his chin. "Act like you're asleep." He did as I said, and I stepped back against the wall as Toga Kte loped into the room with an oil lamp. He set it down to pick up a poker and tossed in a few pieces of wood from the crate at the side before adjusting the flue damper.

The fire caught, and the young man peered at the closed shutters and then walked between, toward the window, to partially open them.

He got the nearest potbelly stove glowing in the same manner as its mate. It occurred to me that I hadn't felt any heat or cold since arriving at the school and wondered if I ever would feel either again.

He stood at the foot of Marcus's bed and spoke softly. "I know you're probably not asleep, but I figure you don't want to talk. When they first brought me here, I didn't talk either, but I was only about two months old . . ." He paused, the soft glow of his lamp lighting only one side of his face. "Somebody left me out on the stoop where anything could've carried me off, I guess because of my foot and all. The only reason they knew I was Assiniboine was the blanket I was wrapped up in." He took a breath and chuckled. "There was a woman who worked here, Mrs. Peal— she had Madie's job, and she pretty much raised me—I'm what they call institutionalized."

I took one step toward him, just to see if he had any idea I was there, but he didn't seem to notice me.

"I learned English. When you got here, whenever anybody

gets here, I hope they might be Assiniboine so they could teach me. I wanted to tell you something, but it can wait till tomorrow, so if you're sleeping, sleep well. If not, then go to sleep, okay, hawkshaw?"

He smiled to himself and then started to go, but spotted the shutter beside me, which still remained closed. As he walked around the corner of the bed, I stepped back, giving him plenty of room. He reached up and pulled the shutters open, and then turned in order to glance around the dormitory, pretty sure he was getting played.

He finally started off again, back in the direction he'd come. "Happy New Year's, guys."

I watched him go and then kneeled down again and looked at the sharp, dark eyes that studied me from under the folds of the blanket. "Howdy."

"Kahée."

"So, your name is Marcus?"

"Yes."

"Marcus what?"

"White Buffalo."

I kneeled there, looking at him and thinking about it.

"Is there something wrong?"

"I feel like I've heard that name before."

He sat up a bit. "Have you ever been on the Crow Nation? They call it a reservation now."

"I'm not sure."

"It's a long way from here."

"That's okay, I think I'm a long way from home too." I smiled at him. "So, what other people have you seen that nobody else can?" I watched as his eyes diverted. "Don't worry, you can tell me."

"There's the Big Man."

"The Big Man?"

"Yes, he is Crow and looks out for me, do you know him?"

"I honestly don't know."

"He is a great warrior. You would know him if you saw him—he's very big, even bigger than you, and he carries a large staff."

I thought of the man I'd seen back in Fort Pratt at the café and then again on the road—the one carrying a war lance. I wasn't sure how to bring up the subject of seeing him, or someone who looked remarkably like him, more than a hundred years in the future. "Does it have coyote skulls on it and hooves and horsehair?"

He sat up. "You have seen him too?"

"Virgil."

"Are you a friend of his?"

"I'm not sure, but I think so." I was about to say more, when I noticed the boy in the next bed had sat up and was looking at us. Carefully, I raised a forefinger to my lips and then pointed to the next bed.

The boy was small but had enormous eyes. "Are you talking to yourself?"

Marcus turned to look at me, and I almost laughed out loud, for all the effect it would have, I should've. He then turned back to the boy. "Yes."

"You can talk to me, I'm not sleepy. It's New Year's, and I'm going to stay up till midnight."

Marcus stared at him. "Why?"

"Because it's been a year."

"So? It was a year ago yesterday and the year before that."

"That's not how it works." The tiny boy climbed from his

bed and walked over in bare feet, wearing threadbare cotton pajamas. "What's your name?"

"Marcus, what's yours?"

"Thirty."

Marcus sat up a bit more, whispering. "That's not a name, that's a number."

The boy sidled up onto Marcus's bed and sat. "We've all got numbers; don't you have a number?"

"No, I don't think so."

"Tiny was number thirty-one, so you can have his number."

"Who's Tiny?"

"He's the one that had this bed before you. He was my friend."

"What happened to him?"

"We don't know, one day he just disappeared."

Marcus turned to look at me and then turned back to the boy. "Maybe he went home."

"Nobody goes home from here."

Marcus seemed surprised by the idea. "I'm going home."

The boy said nothing.

Marcus reached out and touched his hand.

"What's your real name?"

"It's Cheyenne, and too hard to pronounce; that's why they call me Thirty, but my real name is Ma'heo Háahketa-Noo'ōtse.

"What does it mean?"

"Medicine Something Something."

"Something Something?"

The boy looked down, ashamed. "I don't know what the last part means."

"That's a great name, better than Thirty." Marcus repeated the name with great solemnity. "Ma'heo, I'll call you Ma'heo."

The boy's face came up, smiling. "You want to have an adventure?"

There are few enough universals in any world, but the one that I would count on is that children will play—whether they're in the middle of a war, starving to death, or trapped on an island. Children will play, and that's how I found myself walking along behind two small boys through the dark hallways of a boarding school. It was approaching midnight as they scurried along next to the walls like mice, while I strolled down the middle without a care in the world, pretty sure that with the exception of one of the boys, I was invisible to all.

"Where are we going?"

Ma'heo turned and held a finger to his lips to silence Marcus as they both crowded into a corner beside a doorway. "To the bell tower, that way we can see the new year coming."

"You can't see a year coming."

Now clothed with his uniform and a cloth jacket, hat, and shoes, the boy shook his head. "How do you know, have you ever looked for one?"

"No."

"So, there." He peeked around the corner and then gestured for Marcus to follow as they entered the kitchen where, in the afternoon, they had scrubbed the Crow boy clean. The place was dark, but it had a welcoming feel to it. The smoldering fire was still popping and crackling in the hearth as a pot of water heated on the swing-away arm.

"What are we doing in here?"

"If we're going on an adventure, we need supplies." He continued toward a large table at the center of the room next to a large chopping block, reached up, and uncovered a cast-iron skillet that emitted a wonderful smell. Carefully taking it from the table, he sat it on the ground and began digging cornbread from it with his fingers, filling his pockets.

Marcus approached. "Won't we get caught?"

"Not if you help."

Marcus kneeled and began filling his pockets. "What will they do when they find it gone?"

"Madie always bakes extra, but just in case, we'll leave it on the floor by the back door and she'll think a raccoon came in and got it."

"Why would she think that?"

Ma'heo reached into his pocket and pulled out a raccoon paw, showing it to his accomplice. "I got this off a dead one behind the stables."

Marcus watched as the boy reached up and took some flour from a sack and scattered some on the table and then a little by the back door where he'd left the skillet and then carefully dabbed the raccoon paw in it a few times, leaving prints. "Won't she notice it's only one paw?"

"She ain't James P. Beckwourth for goodness' sake. She's Scottish, and they don't know things." He pointed to something hanging on a peg by the door. "Get that blanket canteen, it's always got water in it for when Simon goes out."

Taking the canteen, Marcus returned. "Out where?"

"I don't know, just out." Ma'heo hung the canteen over Marcus's head and shoulder. "I just hope Madie cleans up before he sees it, because he'll notice."

"I like Simon."

"Me too. He wouldn't turn us in, but he might give us a stern word." He turned and started out just as lamplight cast across the hallway outside the kitchen. Ma'heo whispered fiercely. "C'mon."

Marcus followed as they huddled in a small space by the hutch near the fire, which was far enough to be out of sight. The light continued to approach, but the footsteps were different this time, softer and steadier.

I stood in the middle of the room and watched as Madie entered, carrying a bundle and placing it on the table along with the oil lamp. She made a sound when she saw the skillet was gone and that there were prints in the flour, and so quickly wiped them away with a cloth, having followed them to the back door, where she picked up the pan and shut the door smartly before returning the skillet and setting it back on the center counter.

Looking exhausted, she sighed and placed her hands on the edge of the butcher block.

One of the boys moved, making a noise, and her eyes went in that direction. I decided to become even more complicit by reaching over and tipping a knife from the counter near the door, allowing it to clatter onto the floor.

Distracted, she walked over to where I stood, retrieved the wood-handled knife, and carried it back to the butcher block. She stood there for a moment, casting her eyes around the room. She looked at the knife in her hands and then placed it back on the counter, then looked around the room until her gaze landed on me.

I didn't move.

It was about then that the light of another lamp cascaded down the uneven surface of the hallway walls and reflected in the square panels above the transom.

The young woman picked up the knife again, placing it at her side as the man, Crawley, appeared in the doorway.

She stiffened. "Go away."

"I just came by to make a greeting, we didn't get much of a chance in old Spellman's office this afternoon."

"You've said it, now go."

Instead, he shouldered into the doorway and then adjusted the fur hat on his head before placing one hand in his pocket, still holding the lamp in the other. "Now, is that any way to speak to an old friend?"

"You're no friend of mine, and I don't want you here."

He didn't move. "That saucy line hardly concerns me. I was hoping that we could spend a bit of time together, like we did before."

Her face hardened in the amber light. "I'll never do that again."

"We have a history, young woman." He moved into the room as she stepped back. "I'm here tonight, but I'll be gone tomorrow."

Raising the knife to where he could see it, she shook her head.

He didn't move but smiled at her, and I couldn't help but take a few steps forward, placing myself between them. I could open and close latches and shutters; what was to keep me from knocking the shit out of this character?

I glanced at the hearth where the water in the pot steamed.

He changed directions, sauntering to the other side of the center island. "I like a well-provisioned and orderly workplace—it denotes a well-ordered and provisioned mind." Reaching into his pocket, he pulled out the remains of the cigar he'd been smoking that afternoon and tucked it into the corner of his mouth. He struck a match against the counter to light it. "But here we are, a fair than middling piece from Massachusetts—surrounded by savages."

"Truly." The both of them started as Simon stood in the doorway and looked at the floor. "Having trouble sleeping, Mr. Crawley?"

He cleared his throat, removing the cigar from his mouth, his eyes darting back and forth between them. "It's the altitude, makes me restless."

Simon continued into the room. "Madie, I thought you might need some help with the baking?"

"That would be very kind of you, Mr. Toga Kte."

Crawley stood there on the other side of the center counter, still looking between the two of them as he picked some cornbread that had been left in the skillet. "You two do your baking at night, do you?"

Simon crossed past him to where Madie stood, carefully taking the knife from her hand. "It's the only time there is. We stay very busy here at the school, Mr. Crawley."

Removing the cigar, he munched on the cornbread leavings, his mouth moving mechanically without pleasure. "Perhaps not for much longer."

Simon slipped the knife into the sleeve of his jacket, his hand cupped where the man couldn't see it. "And what, pray tell, do you mean by that?"

He licked his fingers. "Did I not mention that during my stop in Helena I was charged with an appointment?"

"Congratulations."

"My thanks." The man pulled a piece of folded paper from his vest pocket. In the process he removed a Colt M1892 revolver from a shoulder holster under his coat and rested it on the counter between them. "I have been engaged by the state to examine the conditions in the boarding schools and decide which ones are in need of being closed, the charges therein moved to other facilities." He flattened the paper and slid it toward them. "It is not a task I relish, but it is a piece of work, and I need not tell you that times are indeed hard."

Madie reached out and stared at the paper, my guess being that she could not read it.

"My report to the administrative committee will bear heavily on whether or not this institution continues to operate."

Simon didn't bother looking at the paper. "Does Mr. Spellman know this?"

"Not at this time."

"Do you not think he should be informed?"

Crawley picked up the paper and refolded it, replacing it in his pocket. "I will notify the superintendent in the morning, upon my departure."

"And yet you brought us a new boy."

"Exceedingly unfortunate, but there was nowhere else to take him."

"And yet they are going to close our school?"

The heavyset man plucked the double-action revolver from the counter and held it. "Without funding, these mission schools will be realized into the federal programs."

Simon studied the man and then glanced at Madie. "You're not here because you simply wished to see us?"

Crawley smiled, slipping the Colt back into the shoulder holster. "Well, that is always the case, but there is also the issue of the missing boys. This institution is responsible for the loss of seven students, more missing pupils than any other such establishment in Montana."

"We don't treat the students as prisoners; consequently, there have been escapes."

"Yes, but none of these children were found, Simon. What are we to make of that? Even with your extraordinary tracking skills not a single child has ever been found."

Simon remained silent, looking at him.

"Well, I may have a solution for the interim—another reason for my visit." He turned and started for the door, but then stopped when he noticed that the young man wasn't following. "I will need your assistance, please."

Reluctantly, the young man followed after Crawley with one last glance at Madie. "Please—go to your room and lock the door."

She watched him go and then stood there for a long while before continuing to clean up the skillet. She'd finished the job and took the remainder of the cornbread and wrapped it in brown paper before turning toward the hearth and cocking her head. "You can come out now."

I turned to look at the boys, now sure that we hadn't put anything by her.

She turned and sighed, leaning back on the butcher block and shaking her head. "I know it's you, Thirty."

Ma'heo answered from the darkness. "How come?"

"You're the only one-legged raccoon in the place." She turned and went toward a sink where she began cleaning the skillet the rest of the way. "I hope you haven't eaten all that cornbread yourself, or you're going to be sick."

Ma'heo stood, stepping out into the light. "I got an accomplice."

"The new boy?"

Marcus stood, stepping into the light with his friend.

Wiping off the skillet, she hung it on a rack above her head before turning to look at the two of them, hands on hips. "So, you're off to the clock tower?"

He moved in a little closer. "How did you know?"

"It's where you always go, you little urchin." She stepped forward and then kneeled to look him in the eye, taking his chin in her slender fingers. "You have enough supplies to last the night?" He nodded and then she looked at Marcus, with the canteen over his shoulder. "Make sure you return Simon's canteen before you go back to your beds."

"Yes, ma'am."

She studied the other boy. "Are you easily led, Master Marcus?"

He stared at the ground. "I . . . I don't think so."

She nodded. "Just as well . . ." She stood. "Make sure you're in bed by midnight this Hogmanay or firstfoot may well trip you up."

"What's that?"

She smiled down at the two. "What?"

He seemed stunned. "Everything you just said?"

She held out two fingers, counting off. "Hogmanay is the Scottish name for your New Year's Eve and firstfoot is the first guest of the New Year, and you'd do well to make sure it's not ghosts that visit you for they are restless tonight." She turned her profile to look directly at me, then to my left and then my right. "The wallydraigles are out, and they've been known to make away with delectable young boys . . ."

Ma'heo nodded. "Éveohtsé-heómése." The other two turned to look at him as did I, overwhelmed by a strange feeling that the word had evoked. He stared back at them. "The Wandering Without, the Taker of Souls that waits in the wilderness. If you stray too far from the people for too long, it comes and takes you away."

We were all staring at him.

"It is older than the véhoe, the people with the white eyes, older than the known nations." He turned back to them, and I stood there feeling like a ghost that had just had his grave stepped on.

Éveohtsé-heómése. Where had I heard that before?

They continued to talk, but I couldn't hear them anymore, almost as if I were drifting away from this place—a place to which I didn't belong. I could feel my breath growing short and my eyesight becoming fuzzy.

"Off with you but do be careful." Brought back with her words, I watched as the boys scurried toward the door. "Not that way, if Crawley discovers you, it'll be the death of us." She pointed toward the back door. "That way and through the stables; there's a back door to the printing press room and then you can reach the spiral staircase." She shook her head at Ma'heo. "How have you not gotten caught, you little ninny?"

She brushed a hand through his hair as the two of them shot toward the back door. They opened it and allowed a stiff breeze to cool off the inside air and a skiff of snow to dust the stone floor of the kitchen. After they had gone, she went to the door to shut it, but then thought better and held it open. She turned and looked about the room. "I don't know what you are but look after them and be sure that no harm comes to their young souls."

I caught up with them in the stables, where they had climbed up on the stall divider and were petting the bay that had delivered

Marcus to the school. There were at least a dozen stalls, all of them empty except the one.

"I'm going to have a horse of my own someday."

Ma'heo shook his head. "They won't allow that."

"Why?"

"They're afraid we'll run away on them, that's why they lock the stables, so no one can steal a horse."

"How come you never run away?"

"I got nowhere to run to."

"What about your family, your tribe?"

He continued petting the bay as he whiffled and turned to look at me. "I don't know where they are, or even if they're still alive."

"I have heard tell of the Cheyenne, so they still exist." He paused before adding, "The Crow and the Cheyenne are sworn, blood enemies."

Ma'heo continued petting the horse. "Don't you think we have enough enemies?"

"Probably."

They laughed and climbed down, continuing through the stables and out a door on the other side, where there was another door leading back into the main building. I watched as they trudged through the snow and then reached up to struggle with the knob.

"It's locked."

Marcus looked around. "What are we going to do?"

Ma'heo looked up. "The window up on the top is open."

"We can't get up there."

"I can climb on your shoulders."

"We still won't reach."

The smaller boy looked around. "We've got to try; I don't

know any other way than back through the stables and the kitchen."

Marcus sat the canteen down and hunkered over, inviting Ma'heo to climb on his back. "C'mon, then."

I watched as Ma'heo wrestled his way up, finally standing on Marcus's shoulders. He reached for the partially open transom but was still a good foot short. The smaller boy stretched, but there wasn't any way he was going to make it. "Stand on tiptoe?"

Marcus turned his head to look at me.

I figured what the heck, I was eventually going to have to find out what happened if I touched somebody. Stepping forward, I grabbed the one named Ma'heo by the waist and lifted him up, sticking him halfway through the window, where he scrambled through.

Marcus looked at me, then at the transom, and then back to me again. "Are you really a ghost?"

I smiled. "I hope not."

There were noises from the other side as the door was unlocked and swung open, the Cheyenne boy sticking his head out and looking up to where he'd climbed through and then back at Marcus.

White Buffalo shrugged. "I'm much stronger than I look."

7

After scraping the snow away, Vic saw the print of a bloodied hand, his hand, stamped on the interior of the side window, with a sliding trail of blood below it. Dropping to her knees, she moved the light around, searching every aspect of the interior, but still not seeing him. There were piles of snow inside where the windshield had been blown out, some of it stained with blood.

Continuing to shine a penlight beam into the interior of the three-quarter ton, she could see it had been in a monumental wreck, the whole other half of the cab partially pushed into the driver's side.

She stood, but try as she might, she couldn't pry the door open, even while standing on the side of the cab. Evidently, the frame was twisted.

Vic looked at the polymer gun in her hand—the thought of using it as a hammer running across her mind. Boy, would he have had a laugh at that. She glanced around, playing the beam over the mountains of snow, and finally seeing the piles of crap where they'd been pushed by the plow, her eyes focused on a bent metal fence post with a spade end that is used to pound it into the ground.

Holstering her weapon, she hurried down the slope, only stopping to put on her gloves before picking up the frozen metal. Climbing back, she positioned herself over the window and raised her arms, aiming for the bloody handprint at the center of the glass.

She had a moment's pause, thinking she might impale him with the damn thing, but then figured he deserved it.

Bringing the spade end down, she watched as it cracked the glass, shattering the area around impact but not completely breaking through. She struggled as she twisted it out from the damaged glass, but then raised it again, slamming it into another spot close to the first one, and again the glass shattered and some broke away.

With her gloved hands, she sat the fence post to the side in the snow and then pried the safety glass up, pulling the still-attached broken pieces back and then tossing them down the snowy hillside.

Finally, she had thrown the majority away and so pulled the flashlight from her pocket and shone it inside the cab. Carefully easing her legs into the opening she'd made, she braced her boots on the side of the center console and lowered herself into the truck's interior.

The airbags had deployed, and there was more blood on the misshapen steering wheel, along with one of his boots on the floorboard. Setting the boot outside she began digging in the snow, frantic to find him. First, she searched the passenger side, thinking he must've fallen there, but after a while she saw that she would've reached some part of him already, unless he was underneath the heavy truck, a thought she refused to entertain, so she dug in the back with the flashlight still locked in her teeth.

More snow, more blood.

What the fuck?

She dug harder, until she conceded to herself that he wasn't here.

Maybe that was good. Maybe he'd survived somehow, but how? And what could've done this kind of damage to his truck? He would've had to have been hit by a train.

Crawling back into the front of the cab, she saw a shadow move across the window above her. She paused for a second. Could it be that coyote, returning to see if there was an opportunity after all?

She pulled the Glock from its holster again—what she knew about coyotes would fit on the head of a pin, so she figured it was better to be ready. Finally getting under the opening she'd broken into the window, she looked up, but there was nothing there. She positioned her legs and had just started to stand when the fence pole she'd used to break the window shot into the cab with enough force to stab the seat by her booted foot.

Raising the 9mm, she aimed at the center of the shadow that was above her—large, male. "Henry?"

The pole jerked free and caused her to slip and fall against the headliner. As it did, she lurched to the side in the limited space but then quickly wrapped her arm around the pole. She fired just as he let go, and he threw himself back, falling from view off the pile of snow.

Lodging a boot in the steering wheel, she pushed up and out, lunged after him, but slipped and hit her chin on the sill as he fell. Reaching up and wiping the chunks of glass from her skin, she pulled herself out and climbed onto the door.

Moretti stood and looked at the fields of snow, highlighted by the moonlight directly overhead and trained the semiautomatic in every direction.

Nothing.

The snow was higher behind her, and it didn't look as if he'd climbed over in the immediate vicinity, but it was the only direction he could've gone. Struggling out of the hole in the snow she'd made when uncovering the door, she stood on the piles to one side and investigated the darkness, where she finally saw a figure running in the distance.

Yanking the flashlight from her pocket she shone it in that direction, but the beam wasn't strong enough to reach. Raising a hand to the side of her mouth she screamed after him. "Halt, police!"

It had no effect, and she thought about throwing a few rounds out there for good measure, but figured it was at least a hundred yards and she might need the ammo if she was going to run him down.

Grabbing Walt's boot, she flashed a look back at the hotel and the remains of the town. The smart move was to go and get both Henry and Dog as backup . . . Fuck it.

She started off, feeling a slight twinge in her left ankle; she must've tweaked it climbing in and out of the totaled truck.

She moved northeast, shining the flashlight down to where a single set of prints led onto the hill at the edge of town. Kneeling, she looked at one of the tactical-boot prints that appeared to be about a man's size eleven. She moved again and was a little concerned that there was no blood.

"I know I hit you, fucker."

Tucking Walt's boot under her arm, she quickly made the distance to where the prints changed direction and turned to the right and then toward the hill where the cemetery and the old boarding school had been.

Following the tracks, she shook her head, slowly becoming

aware of an acute pain in her ankle but ignoring it. "Run fucker—you just get to die tired."

Reaching the top of the hill, she looked at the backside of the cemetery, where the tiny crosses were barely visible in the drifts that the predominant wind had carved into extended ice shelves.

She scanned around with the flashlight, but the prints had stopped and, turning in a circle, she saw that they ended right beside her. Shifting the light forward, she took a step and discovered why—the scouring of the wind had made a perfectly shaped ice field where her weight and obviously the weight of her attacker couldn't push through.

When she shone the flashlight about, she could see the archway gate, more crosses, the platform for the massive bell, and some piles of rubble, half-standing monuments to the doomed school.

She thought she heard a noise in the direction of the damaged wall and brought her other foot up on the icy shelf, immediately sliding about a yard. Catching her balance, she extended an arm to steady herself and crept forward.

The snow had built a drift in front of the remains, but she saw the imprint of a boot at the far side, near the wall.

She played the light across the facade of the structure until she reached what was left of a window and through it could see someone, a man, looking in the other direction and sitting on a large stone.

Moving along in the rubble, she came to a corner where she raised her pistol and approached closer, finally pressing the muzzle against the back of his head.

His voice wheezed in his chest like busted bellows. "It took you long enough to get here."

The other wing of the boarding school was the work area, housing a hand-set press, cutters, stitchers, and binders—all strange-looking devices that neither Marcus nor I had ever seen before.

Ma'heo hung an elbow over the frame of one of the complex machines. "I'm a print monkey."

Looking around at the exotic contraptions, Marcus turned back to the smaller boy as I moved forward, studying the strange apparatus. "What's a print monkey?"

"The one that retrieves the letters from the rack on the wall and sets them in the press."

"You must know your spelling pretty good."

"Not really, but I can memorize, and I've got small hands, which means I can set the type faster than anybody else."

"What do they make?"

Ma'heo moved down the aisle looking at the machine with something akin to an affection. "Books, pamphlets, legal documents, and stuff for the state."

"About what?"

He turned and shrugged, standing only about two feet from me as I examined the machines. "I don't know; I can't read."

Marcus stared at him. "At this school, they haven't taught you to read?"

"No."

"What do they teach you here?"

"I can set a page in less than ten minutes." He paused for a moment and then reached into the bag he carried. "And I have something I'm wanting to print."

"What?" Marcus watched as he pulled out a sheaf of handwritten pages. "Something for yourself?"

"This was entrusted to me." He stared at the sheets of paper. "It was given to me by another boy."

He looked over Ma'heo's shoulder at the strange language. "What does it say?"

"I don't know, it's in Cheyenne."

"You don't read that either?"

"No."

"You think it's important?"

"I don't know." He stared at the words. "Tiny, the boy who used to have your bed, spoke Cheyenne and said it was important. He was working on translating it when he disappeared." He looked at the other boy, clutching the papers. "I think these had something to do with that."

"With his disappearing?"

"Yes. He said there was something that was coming for him, and this would be a way of stopping it."

"What is it? The thing you were talking about in the kitchen?"

The boy nodded. "Yes, the Éveohtsé-heómése. Tiny said that if we were to battle it, that this would be a powerful weapon, we just didn't get it done before he went missing."

Marcus stared at him. "That's why you brought me."

Ma'heo looked ashamed. "Can't run the press or the binder by myself."

I walked to the barred window and looked out over the snow-covered hillside. The words echoed back at me as I stood there. *Éveohtsé-heómése, Éveohtsé-heómése, Éveohtsé-heómése* . . . Maybe that was why I was here. Was it something about these pages? I pulled the booklet from my inside pocket and stared at it, at the brown-leather cover with the strange insignia.

I was once again tempted to just walk back to the arch and return to the tiny town where I'd been before, but was that really where I belonged? Where did I belong, and how could I get back there if I figured it out?

When I turned back from the window, Marcus was looking at me but speaking to Ma'heo. "I have something to tell you."

"What?"

"There's somebody else here."

The boy looked around. "Where?"

"No, not somebody who's really here, like a ghost, but I don't think he's a ghost."

"What are you talking about?"

Marcus glanced at me again, and I figured I might as well play along. Stuffing the booklet back into my pocket, I crossed from the window, now standing before them as Ma'heo surveyed the room. "Is he here now?"

With a last look at Marcus, I reached over and took Ma'heo's hat and then held it out to him to take.

The boy's eyes grew wide, and he stepped back.

Marcus reassured him. "It's okay, he's friendly."

Ma'heo didn't move. "Is he the one that slammed the shutters?"

"Yes, he's véhoe, but he is kind and helpful."

Carefully, the boy reached out and took his hat. "Is he from the school?"

"I don't think so—I think he is from someplace else and maybe a different time."

The smaller boy reached out in an attempt to touch me, but I was standing too far away. "Is he the one who pushed me through the window?"

"Yes."

"Does he talk?"

"Yes, but I think I'm the only one who can hear him."

"Have him say something."

Marcus glanced at me, and I responded. "Howdy."

He turned back to the other boy. "Did you hear that?"

"No."

"Then you can't hear him." He reached over and took the pages from Ma'heo. "We need to get busy on this, before they discover that we're missing."

The first three copies sat on the laminating table with simple brown-leather covers stitched into them, looking exactly like the one hidden in my pocket, with the exception of the strange marking on the cover. At only a dozen or so pages I couldn't say it was a great achievement, but I took a certain amount of pleasure in providing assistance when I tried not to laugh as the boy's eyes had widened every time a lever was turned, or pages levitated from one place to another.

I watched as he scooped up the copies and the loose pages that he'd used to create the booklet, having returned the equipment to its original state.

Marcus studied him. "Why three copies?"

Ma'heo handed him one. "One for each of us."

He held one of the other copies out in my direction, but I glanced at Marcus. "You take mine, if you don't mind?"

"He says I can carry his." Marcus took the two booklets and looked around. "Shouldn't we be heading back?"

"Don't you want to see the bell tower?"

"Isn't it getting late?"

Ma'heo pointed to the clock over the doorway leading to the back of the building. "It's only eight-seventeen." He started toward that door. "They don't check the beds until midnight, c'mon."

Watching as he started to open the door, I walked over and reached down, picking the boy up by the collar and setting him back with his friend before opening the door myself.

I figured if I was invisible, I might as well take full advantage.

It was lucky that I had. I could see both Crawley and Simon carrying something at the far end of the hall. Simon looked back in my direction but kept going as I held a finger to my lips, which Marcus transmitted to Ma'heo.

I waited until the men went through a set of doors and then motioned to Marcus to follow me. Then I moved down the hall in order to look in the entryway where we'd first come in.

There was a light on in the superintendent's office, and I motioned for them to stop, Ma'heo doing whatever Marcus motioned for him to do.

Walking toward the main doors, I stopped, leaned forward, and saw Spellman seated at his desk, where he was poring over a ledger. I watched him for a moment and then noticed it was two ledgers he was studying. I worked my way along the wall so that I could peer over his shoulder.

On the one side was a set of government documents and a ledger from which he was copying the numbers into another, the figures, however, being different.

"You see the problem, Mr. Spellman?"

I turned to see that Crawley had returned, the cigar pinched into the corner of his mouth.

Looking past him, I wondered what had happened to the boys.

"How did you know?" Spellman pushed back from the desk, an elbow on the arm of the chair and a hand covering his mouth.

Crawley placed his coat on a chair and sat. "It wasn't particularly difficult to figure. There was money coming in, but every time I visited, there didn't seem to be a great deal of improvements around the school—so, where could the money be going?"

Spellman sat there, looking at him.

"And since you are not only the superintendent, but the keeper of the books . . ."

Spellman cleared his throat. "My wife, she was ill."

"Your wife has been dead for three years, Mr. Spellman." He sat there looking at him and then pulling the cigar from his mouth to examine it. "I really don't care; I simply want to know how much of the money you have squirreled away now."

The superintendent said nothing.

"I've gone through the ledger and can come up with a close approximation, if you would excuse the English, but I'd rather hear it from you."

Spellman stood, folding his arms behind his dark suit and looking like a bird of prey. "What is it you want?"

"If it's as much as I suspect, half should do fine."

The superintendent stared at the wooden floor. "Half."

"This school is going to be closed imminently, and there are going to be a lot of questions asked. Now, I am the only state official that's actually laid eyes on this place for how many years? I can vouchsafe that the school has been in fine condition and that the students have been treated with the utmost of care."

Spellman sighed. "And what of the children?"

"What of them?"

"They're likely to have another tale."

"I have a contingency for that also."

"What about Simon and Madie?"

"I'm sure that with the proper financial inducement, they can be depended on to see the light—the same way many of your fellow cavalrymen turned a blind eye at Wounded Knee."

Crawley shrugged. "Now, shall we open that safe of yours and see just how much money we're looking at?"

I watched as Spellman moved toward the safe in his office, and then I slipped out the doorway and into the hall. I would've liked to have stayed to hear more of this very interesting conversation but the hallway was empty; the boys no longer there. I needed to find them but had no idea where they might've gone. Ma'heo had mentioned the bell tower, but I didn't know how to get up there. As a ghost, I was turning out to be something of a bust. I finally found a narrow doorway to the left of the double doors leading to the stables out back and turned the latch, pulling it open and peering inside.

There was a circular stairwell that led up into the darkness, where I couldn't see, but figured it had to be the bell tower. Glancing to my right, I could see a set of hemp ropes with leather sleeves, which reaffirmed my suspicions.

Pulling my shoulders in, I began lumbering up the steps in an endless circle, finally reaching a trapdoor that was blocked open with a piece of firewood.

I lifted it up, turned, and sat, still holding it as I looked around.

The bell tower was only about twelve feet by twelve feet with half walls all the way around. I could see the massive bell hanging from a bell yoke by what I thought was referred to as canons, or the braces that provided a place to attach it. I had to lean far to one side to see past the lower lip and the clapper, which was as big as my arm.

The two boys were sitting in one of the far corners wrapped in a weather-beaten horse blanket, eating cornbread, and taking sips from the canteen they passed back and forth.

Marcus held out a piece of cornbread to me as Ma'heo's eyes grew wide. "Want some?"

"No, thanks." Pushing the trap the rest of the way open, I climbed from the stairs, onto the platform, and ducked under the bell.

I'd just started to close the hatch when Marcus called out to me. "Leave it partially open, the warmth from below comes up through there. We only closed it because we thought those men might follow us."

Using the piece of wood, I did as they said.

The view, in the brightness of the full moon was nothing short of stunning. Walking around the bell, I could feel the slightest of breezes on my face. A feeling of isolation swelled in me as I further explored the tower, taking in the mountains in the distance to the west, where a cloud bank was brewing, and the endless plains to the east.

If you were to run away from this place, where would you go and how could you survive?

I looked down at the boys still sitting there covered in the blanket and munching cornbread while they talked to each other.

You'd find a way, that's how—you'd find a way.

Other than the murmuring of the boys, there was no sound, not even from my boots as I took another turn, drawn by the view.

It was like being in the crow's nest of a ship and looking out onto an endless sea. The moon was very high and gave the sculpted drifts a glow that enhanced the impression of waves. The mountains to the west looked like the ragged edge of a torn page, the stars the tiny punctuations that had been thrown into the heavens.

I started to turn and take in the other side when I thought I saw something move.

Taking out the gloves from my coat, I pulled them on and

then placed my hands on the railing, keeping in sight a fold in the faraway snow. Unfocusing my eyes, I could definitely see something moving in the sage, again looking like a brushstroke that had suddenly come to life.

It was something big, but not human. Its head was large and the thing in its entirety was massive as it lumbered toward us. I was pretty sure it was a bear, which appeared to be walking on its hind legs and dragging something behind it.

"Holy Moses!" I looked down to see that both boys had joined me at the railing, Marcus lifting a finger toward the figure. "Is that a bear?"

"Too big to be human."

Ma'heo, who was the shortest, was having trouble seeing over the rail. "I can't see it, what's it doing?"

"Coming straight toward us." Marcus looked up at me as he helped lift Ma'heo. "What are we going to do?"

I shrugged, holding the jacket of the smaller boy to ensure that he would not fall. "Stay up here."

He stared at me. "You're not very brave for a ghost."

"What, do you want me to go fight a bear?"

He went back to watching the big grizzly. "It's going toward the stable."

The thing was indeed headed that way.

"He probably smells the horse." Marcus looked up at me again. "You've got to do something." He looked back at the bear, which had grown bigger as it came closer. "He can't see you; I don't think."

"Even invisible, I don't think it's a good idea to fight grizzlies."

"What's he going to do—you're already dead."

"We don't know that for sure."

"We've got to save the horse, he's part of my escape plan."

I looked down at him. "Your what?"

"My escape plan." He held up two fingers. "The Crow and Cheyenne Reservations are side by side, so Ma'heo and I are going to escape on the horse and go back there."

"That's over two hundred miles away."

"We will make it." He looked back down at the bear, which had stopped at a rock outcropping at the edge of the hill, probably trying to figure out what the boarding school was and how it had gotten there. "But we have to save the horse, he's our only hope."

I looked back at the bear.

What did I have to lose?

Why not fight a bear?

I figured I'd go down there and just throw snowballs at the thing until it ran off. Hell, it might even be fun. "All right, but you two stay up here no matter what happens, you got me?"

They both nodded, and I crouched under the hanging metal, bumping into the clapper but catching it before it could strike the bell.

Opening the trap, I slid the piece of wood back and started down the circular staircase, easing the lid shut behind me, but then remembering to reinsert the piece of firewood so that the two adventurers wouldn't get locked in the tower.

What was the boy thinking? There was no way they could survive a trip like that, in the dead of winter, on the high plains.

I sighed, figuring I'd take it all one at a time; first, I had to fight a bear.

When I got to the door leading to the hallway, I turned the latch, pushing it open gently, disguising myself as a draft, just in case there was somebody in the hallway.

And there was.

Across the way, the man Crawley stared at the door. Startled for a moment, I took a step out and continued pushing the door all the way open.

He moved his cigar to the other side of his mouth and then looked up into the staircase and the tower. Fortunately, the two boys weren't making any noise.

I watched him draw his head back in and then reach over and close the door. Then he glanced around, made a face, turned, and walked down the hallway toward the boys' dormitory, a canvas bag slung over one shoulder.

Moving to the main rear door that would lead to the stables in the back, I did the same thing with the heavy door, once again trying to give the impression that it was the wind pushing the thing. I ducked through the opening, closed the door behind me, and walked down to an entryway with doors on either side and then into the tack shed and eventually the stables.

The bay was munching away and raised his head when I entered. I figured he was just responding to the opening and closing of the door, but then his eyes followed me as I crossed the breezeway toward the large doors that led to a holding corral out back.

I stopped and then changed directions, his eyes staying on me the whole time.

"Well, hell . . . This does not bode well for that damned bear not seeing me."

I reached over and gave the horse a pet, which he graciously accepted. Then I walked over to the heavy doors, removed the timber that secured them, and hoped to God that there wasn't a grizzly bear waiting on the other side.

I slid some snow back and looked into the sculpted landscape, the moon still shining as I stepped out, but I was not particularly reassured in that I couldn't see the bear. Then I saw it at the rock outcropping where I'd seen it before with its head stuck up past the wind-scoured portion of the rocks. He seemed to be looking the other way.

I closed the door and started walking in that direction and trying to not make any noise, but when I looked back, it appeared that I wasn't even leaving any footprints in the snow.

Strange.

There was a noise from above, as if somebody was whistling to get my attention.

I looked up and could see Marcus hanging over the railing and pointing toward the outcropping.

Gesturing for them to hush up, I turned back and could now see that the bear had lowered onto all fours. He still wasn't looking at me, which was a good thing, but he could at any moment, which would be most certainly bad.

I moved in the opposite direction toward the ridge behind him and marveled at the size of his head as he turned back, looking east.

From about a hundred feet away, I stooped, scooped up a handful of snow, and cupped it in my gloved hands, compressing it into a ball. At least partially knowledgeable of my limitations, I kept moving in its direction until I was directly behind it and maybe forty feet away.

Rearing back, I let loose with the snowball and watched as it missed the bear's head by a good four feet and continued down the hill, where it skimmed along the surface and became bigger.

I stood there for a moment, not moving, then bent down to scoop another handful in order to begin compacting again.

It was then that the grizzly stood up on its two hind legs.

The thing looked like it was at least ten feet tall and the thought that this was a monumentally bad idea rushed over me. The bear didn't move, but just stood there.

I considered moving closer, but then I thought about quietly retreating to the stables and securing the door.

The bear made a noise but still didn't move, probably confused.

I stared down at the snowball in my hand and figured what the hell, I could run, or I could throw the snowball and run.

Launching the thing, I watched as it homed in with a curve and slapped the back of the bear's head.

The giant began turning and all I could think was, even as a ghost or soon to be, I'd neglected to bring any other kind of weapon with me.

A cloud crept across the moon from the bank to the west, but I could still see the glistening of the piggish dark eyes reflecting in the mass of fur as what looked to be about a thousand pounds of bear turned and looked directly at me.

There was no doubt in my mind that he could see me, and even less as he dropped down onto all fours and began lurching over the outcropping and ambling my way.

I turned and figured the chances of me outrunning him were relatively slim, but it was then that I saw two individuals about halfway between me and the stable door—two small figures.

The two boys stood there making snowballs.

I ran toward them, waving my hands and shouting, "Get back in the stable, get back!" Marcus froze, but then the two of them began running in that direction as I turned and saw that the grizzly was once again up on his hind legs so as to look me over, and I was certain at them as well. "Run!"

The bear dropped back onto all fours and began loping in

our direction as I started to race behind the boys, still a good thirty yards away.

They were about to reach the stable doors when Ma'heo slipped and fell, sliding in the snow. Without a thought, Marcus scrambled back and grabbed his arm, pulling him toward the door.

I turned and could see the bear was only ten yards behind me and gaining.

I doubled my efforts, turned, and watched as the boys slipped through the opening, the great bear huffing and snorting just behind me. "Put the timber back in the door!"

There was no way I was going to make it but still wasn't sure what the monster was going to be able to do. That was answered quickly enough as I felt something swipe at me and carry me off my feet and into the door, which slammed shut with my impact.

I hit the solid wood, collapsed at the base, and rolled over to face whatever the bear had in store.

The grizzly towered over me, breathing heavily, chuffing air from its massive lungs; backlit, I could now see that the thing hanging from its one paw was a highly decorated war lance. I watched in wonder as the great beast leaned the lance into the crook of one hairy arm and then seemed to peel back it's great head, replacing it with a human one, a little less backlit in the now uncovered moonlight.

He looked down at me with the broad face smiling, and extended a giant hand to help me up. "Sho'daache, Lawman."

8

"You shot me."

"You're damn right I did, and I'm about to do it again." She moved around in front of him, the Glock still aimed at his head.

There was blood saturating the left side of his abdomen and when he breathed, there was a rasping sound and a burbling as he ended his statement. "Got me pretty good; part of a lung at least."

She tossed the boot down in front of him. "Where's Walt?"

He smiled, blood in his teeth. "Walt who?"

"Walt." She extended her arm, wishing she could cock the thing or jack the action to let him know she meant business. "Try again."

He continued to smile. "I don't know what you're talking about."

She lowered her aim. "Maybe if I give you another 115 grains of lead in your left big toe it'll improve your memory?"

"You know, I do remember something . . ." He nodded, then dropped his head and looked at the targeted foot. "I want a lawyer."

She cast about the snowy hillside. "We appear to be fresh

out." She retrained the 9mm in his face. "We appear to be fresh out of everything except bullets and you—and your name is?"

"Artie." They both turned to see a large shadow leaning against the remains of the stone wall. "Artie Small Song."

"It's about time you showed up—this fucker tried to skewer me with a fence post."

The Cheyenne Nation limped over, kneeling in front of the wounded man, draping a hand over the spot in his leg where a bullet had pierced it no more than a few weeks before. "Is that true?"

"I don't know what she's talking about."

"Really." The Bear nodded and then stared at him. "We have met, náheševéhe Henry Standing Bear."

The wounded man's face remained motionless. "Got any ID?"

The Bear threw a thumb Vic's way. "She does, but she seems to have her hands full." Crouched there, he wrapped his arms around himself. "Nétonétomóhtahe?"

Artie laughed softly. "Násáapévomóhtáhéhe . . ."

The Cheyenne Nation smiled a sad smile. "Working on the assumption that Vic's round did not hit your heart or any major blood vessels, I think we can surmise that from the froth in your mouth and around the wound that one of your lungs is collapsing." He leaned in close, his nose only a few inches from that of the wounded man. "You see, when you breathe, the outside air pulls through your windpipe and into your lungs, but when there is a hole in your chest wall the air comes through there, gathering around the lung and collapsing it. If it is air causing the collapse it is called a pneumothorax, but if it is blood causing the collapse, then it is called a hemothorax and a combination of the two, which I believe is what you are dealing with now, then it is called a pneumohemothorax."

"Thanks for the lesson."

"In layman terms, your lung is going to deflate like a flat tire unless we do something, otherwise you are going to slowly bleed to death from the inside, Artie."

"How slow?"

"Slower than you are going to want, Artie, trust me." He continued to study him. "This officer here, she wants to shoot you until you tell us what we want to know, but there are far better ways to achieve our goals. You see, she is civilized and restrained by the rule of law, and that puts her at a disadvantage. I, on the other hand, am not civilized nor restrained by any laws and from experience have cultivated a number of techniques that will persuade you to tell me what I want to know."

"Do these techniques work on everyone?"

"Everyone." The Bear reached out, pushed the wounded man's jacket aside, and looked at the blood soaking his clothes. "The best scenario is that you cooperate, we compress the wound, sealing it and saving the lung, and then transport you to the nearest regional hospital, which is a good two hours away." He glanced at the Banshee, parked by the side of the road. "Even in the race truck."

"And if I don't?"

"I will torture you and get the information I need, and then you will die from trauma."

Artie raised his face and looked up into the star-laden sky. "There is a fault in your reasoning, Standing Bear."

"What is that?"

"What if I don't care if I live or die?"

"Then you will care about pain. You have far too much imagination to play this game, Artie." Slowly, he pulled his stag-handled bowie knife from a sheath at the middle of his back, the foot-long blade gleaming in the moonlight. "Fear is the perfect tool of inducement. What do you fear most—what do you take the most pride in, your physical self, your sight, your manhood? Whatever it is, trust me, I will find it."

The wounded man took a deep breath and then spat in Henry's face.

Henry slowly wiped the blood froth away and picked up the boot that lay between them. "With your silence, you are holding a very dear friend of mine hostage and I do not think you understand how far I will go to find him."

"We need to know where Walt is—now." Vic stepped forward. "I found his truck—what happened?"

He glanced at her and then rested his eyes on the Bear.

There was no expression on the Cheyenne Nation's face as he said the next words. "If you do not begin talking, Artie, I will insert my finger in the hole in your lung and pull the words out like a beer tab."

The wounded man stiffened, just a bit. A long moment passed before he finally spoke. "There . . . There was an accident."

"What kind of accident?"

He coughed, saliva and blood dripping from his lips in long strings. "A wreck."

Vic leaned in. "Where, asshole?"

He gestured with a nod toward the road. "Right over there, and then the truck was moved to where you found it."

Vic stepped forward again, raising the barrel of the Glock. "If you don't tell us exactly where he is right now, I am most certainly going to kill you."

"Then you lose him forever."

She placed the barrel of the 9mm against his head, again. "That's it, I'm shooting him."

Henry raised a hand to stop her. "I am not so sure how long I can keep her from shooting you—again."

Concentrating on breathing, he didn't move for a moment. "I don't know where he is, exactly."

"What are you saying?"

"There was a crash, and I was knocked unconscious. When I woke up, I looked for him, but he was gone."

"You hit him?" Vic continued to hold the muzzle against his head. "He's not in that truck, Artie."

He nodded. "I know, I looked for him everywhere."

"What are you saying?"

"Listen . . ." The man coughed, holding a hand to his chest. "He's gone somewhere else."

"It took a long time to find you, Lawman." He offered me one of the enormous hands, pulling me from the ground with little or no effort.

Dusting myself off I stood and got a closer look at him and was sure it was the same man from the café and the highway patrol substation back in Fort Pratt. "Thanks."

"The Big Man!" Marcus ran around me and gripped the giant by the legs. "Where have you been?"

He reached down and petted the boy's head. "Kahée, little one, how have you been?"

The boy raised his face. "They kidnapped me and sent me to this place."

"So I see." The large man looked up at the building. "What are you going to do?"

"Escape."

He lip-pointed toward me. "Is the lawman helping you?"

"Not really."

I gave Marcus a look. "Thanks a lot."

Glancing back, I could see the other boy, Ma'heo, moving up to the side to study his friend. "Are there more than one of them here?" Ma'heo interrupted, taking a step forward and tugging on Marcus's shoulder. "Now?"

Marcus pulled away from the giant and gestured in his general direction. "This is the Big Man I told you about."

"Is he going to help us?"

Marcus looked up at him. "Are you going to help us escape?"

The giant chuckled again, and it was impossible not to like him. "Certainly."

I turned to Ma'heo. "So, you can't see him either?"

Marcus stepped toward me with a look of dissatisfaction. "He still can't hear you."

"Right, but he can't hear the . . ." I glanced at the shaman. "Can you tell me your name?"

He looked at me as if it were something I should know. "Virgil, my name is Virgil."

Marcus smiled up at me and then back at the large man. "White Buffalo; he's a White Buffalo like me."

"You two are related?"

Virgil continued smiling, reaching down and palming Marcus's head. "He is my great-great-grandfather."

I sighed, trying to gather it all in and then finally giving up. "I'm having a hard time remembering who can see and hear who right now. Is there anyone else around here I need to know about?"

Marcus surveyed the landscape. "No, not that I can see, but that doesn't mean they aren't here."

I turned back to the large individual. "Virgil, if you don't mind my asking, why are you here?"

He shifted the war lance to his other hand. "I am here to assist in any way I can."

"Assist who?"

"Those who need assistance."

I didn't particularly care for the vagueness of his answers. "Are we in some kind of danger?"

"Some more than others." He then said nothing but just stood there looking at me.

Ma'heo hugged himself, the clouds of his breath almost hiding his face. "I'm cold, can we go in now?"

Marcus led the way toward the stable door. "C'mon."

Virgil looked down at me as I gestured. "After you."

I watched as he lumbered forth, ducking his head as I pulled open the door, peeling back the snow that lay against it where I'd fallen. Inside the stables, he immediately went to the big bay and reached out a hand, stroking its withers as the horse turned to look at him. "Does the escape plan include you, old boy?"

I leaned in so Marcus could see my face. "Just for the record, animals can see us."

He looked momentarily confused. "So?"

"So, if it had been a real bear, it could've eaten me." I glanced up at the shaman, lowering my voice so that the boys couldn't hear, or at least the one who could hear me. "This is not a particularly good place."

He studied me as the two climbed onto the sides of the stall to pet the horse along with him. "I know that and especially tonight."

I sighed. "It seems like a long one."

"Be careful, Lawman." His face tightened. "This night can

last a lifetime if we allow it. There are things that want us to stay here so that they can feed from us—from our fears, desires, loves, and regrets. They have lost the ability to generate that warmth in themselves, so they rely on those that they abduct for that comfort."

"Abduct?"

"Exactly, those they waylay in their rightful journeys."

"I wish I had some idea of what you're talking about."

He turned and looked at me. "The thing you need to remember is that all the heavens and hells reside within you, as you look out into this world particularly, there is always only the reflection of ourselves."

"What the heck is that supposed to mean?"

The smile faded. "There are laws, even here, Lawman."

"So, if my hat is from the people of this place called Absaroka County, I must be a sheriff's deputy or sheriff or something."

He nodded, just barely. "You see, you are working things out already."

"But then why am I here, or why was I in Fort Pratt where I saw you the first time?"

He placed a large paw on my shoulder. "I have faith in you, Lawman. You will work all of this out on your own and do what needs to be done, but you must remember that just as in life, our time here is not endless."

"That sounded like a warning."

His eyes met mine and it was as if there were no light within them. "Yes, it did." He handed me the lance he carried and turned to lean against the stall and talk with at least one of the boys. "So, what have you young gentlemen been doing in your time here?"

While he and Marcus talked, I studied the spear. The head

looked as if it had been hand-knapped from black obsidian and was as long as my hand and exceedingly sharp. It was attached with sinew along with what looked to be two coyote skulls and jawbones. There were deer hooves attached like rattles with horsehair tails and buffalo teeth. The shaft was covered in red felt and there was an ermine pelt attached to the upper end with brass beads and red paint making strange markings on the skulls.

I gave the thing a shake and listened with satisfaction to the sounds emanating from it. It felt good in my hand. I spun it in a circle, ending with the point behind me, my feet braced, then snapped backward with it as if I'd done this before.

Frozen in a moment of sensory memory, I felt as if this was something important.

When I turned, both Virgil and Marcus were looking at me, although Ma'heo still continued petting the horse.

More than a little embarrassed, I straightened and casually lifted the lance onto my shoulder. "Hey."

Virgil held up one of the small books we'd printed. "You have been busy?"

Shrugging, I walked toward them. "I helped, if that's what you mean."

He nodded, leafing through the pages. "Do you know what this is?"

"Not specifically." I gestured toward the boys. "But maybe they do."

Marcus reached over and tapped Ma'heo on the shoulder. "Hey, they want to know about the book."

The smaller boy looked around, unable to see us. "How do we know we can trust them?"

Marcus made a face as he climbed up on the stall divider. "I've known the Big Man my whole life—he's family."

"That doesn't mean you can trust him."

"He's saved my life, numerous times."

Ma'heo thought about it. "What about the véhoe? How do we know he isn't who has taken Tiny or the other missing ones?"

"He never heard of Tiny, until you told him." Marcus looked at me. "I think we can trust him; he helped us make the book. If it was something that could be used against him, he could've just not helped."

The smaller boy looked around the stable, and I felt for him. "Where am I talking to?"

There was an uncomfortable silence as I moved over to stand next to Virgil in an attempt to make it a little easier on the boy. "Tell him this is the first time I've ever been here, and that I'm sorry about what happened to Tiny."

Marcus repeated my statement to the boy and then gestured to where we stood. "They're right here."

Ma'heo lowered his head but continued to pet the horse before speaking. "The boy, Tiny, came here when he was young and because he was small, he got treated badly. He would escape sometimes, and they would find him. He didn't go far, and they would just find him out there a mile or two from the school. One time when they brought him back, I asked him why he kept doing it and he said that there was a sorrow here that drew the Éveohtsé-heómëse and used it as a feeding ground, and he was afraid that at some point it would take him. He said that if he was to be taken, he would prefer to be taken alone so that he could fight it with the words he had brought from his people."

Pulling the folded sheets of paper from his jacket, he held them up.

"These are the sheets he gave me the night he disappeared." He unfolded the pages and looked at them. "I was afraid that night and he gave them to me, but something must have happened. There is no way he would've ventured out to do battle with the Éveohtsé-heómése without these words. I do not know what happened to Tiny. He was just . . . gone."

He wiped away a tear and then folded the pages back up and tucked them away.

"I thought that maybe if I made a book of the words, I could give them to all my friends and then we would be safe." He smiled and laughed. "But if you are ghosts, then you are beyond my protection."

Virgil studied Ma'heo. "How many copies of the book did you make?"

Marcus answered for him. "Three."

Ma'heo pulled his copy from his jacket. "Since there were three of us, we made three, but I have the original so if he would like he may have mine."

Virgil shook his head. "No, but may I see it?"

Marcus translated and Ma'heo handed it toward Virgil, who pulled it up close to his broad face and perused a few pages before asking. "He was Cheyenne, this Tiny?"

Marcus nodded, not bothering to translate.

Virgil looked at Ma'heo. "This one, does he read Cheyenne?"

Marcus shook his head. "He doesn't even know his Cheyenne name."

"What is it?"

Marcus translated and the small boy drew himself up and spoke. "Ma'heo Háahketa-Noo'ōtse."

"Medicine Small Song, his name is Small Song." Virgil thumbed through a few more pages and then turned back to the beginning. "I know this book, but it is powerless unless the words are spoken."

Marcus's face took on a look of concern. "But none of us speak the language."

"None of us?" Virgil grunted as I leaned forward, looking over his shoulder, a few of the words recognizable. "You know the language of the Tsis tsis'tas, the 'beautiful people,' Lawman?"

"Heck if I know."

He breathed a laugh and closed the book, reaching over and plucking the strange pen from my pocket and then biting off the top before turning it and drawing a symbol on the cover.

I stood there, immobile. "What's that?"

"A symbol." He extended it toward Ma'heo. "It would appear that I am the only Cheyenne speaker here."

Marcus watched as the giant kept moving the book back and forth until Ma'heo burst out in laughter. "But you're Crow."

The medicine man tossed the book to the small boy and then turned to Marcus. "Words are important, no matter what the language—they are perhaps one of the most powerful things we have. Words can preserve life or invoke death and should be handled with the same care as any deadly weapon." He reached out and tapped the cover in Ma'heo's hands. "These words particularly are very strong and should not be misused."

"Are you saying we shouldn't have them?"

"Not at all, even being in possession of them might be enough . . ." He stopped speaking abruptly.

"Enough to what?"

"Pray you never know, Lawman." He turned to look at me, stuffing the vintage pen back into my pocket. "I need your help."

"Certainly, anything I can do."

He reached into his pocket and brought out a wad of what looked to be twine made of sinew. "Put this in your mouth and chew it."

The yellowish and greasy string looked like it had just been pulled off a cadaver. "You're kidding."

He pulled out another and stuck it in his own mouth. "You said you would help." He gestured with a hand that I should eat up. "So, help."

Reluctantly stuffing the thing in my mouth, I was surprised by the fact that it tasted even worse than I'd ever possibly imagined. Between bites, I croaked. "This is horrible."

"Is it?" He chewed some more. "I suppose I have gotten used to it; do not swallow."

"Now you tell me." I fought the urge to throw up and kept chewing as he walked toward a wall where a few dried-up saddles hung on braces. He selected one and pulling it off with one hand, gauged its size with the spread of his massive hand. He returned, having plucked a blanket from one of the stall dividers, then folded it and placed it on the big bay's back before lowering the saddle.

The horse twitched, unused to the tack, having evidently been recycled mostly as a sled and buggy puller.

The boys watched with the utmost interest, Marcus the first to speak. "What are you doing?"

Virgil tucked the wad in his mouth to one side and spoke out of the other. "Preparing for your escape, yes?"

Marcus climbed off the stall divider and looked uncertain. "When?"

Virgil returned to the wall, retrieving a bridle with braided reins. "Why, tonight."

"Tonight?"

Hanging the gear on the pole there, he turned back to me, having retrieved his lance. "Yes, you must leave tonight." Reaching at his side, I watched as he pulled a stag-handled hunting knife from his belt and began cutting the bindings that held the obsidian blade on the decorated shaft. "You have other plans?"

Marcus watched him. "No."

Ma'heo joined Marcus. "What are they saying?"

"He says we have to leave tonight."

"Why?"

Marcus turned back to the giant but remained silent.

"It is foretold." The shaman turned away from them, pulling the sinew from his mouth and spitting as he spoke under his breath. "Whenever anyone argues with you about something, just tell them it is foretold—usually works."

I happily pulled the sinew from my mouth and spat a couple of times. "It probably helps that you look the way you do."

"Perhaps." He wandered past me, finding some head loops lying on the ground. Picking through the barrel staves, he held up one piece of metal and examined it. It was about ten inches long and triangular, ragged on one edge.

I watched as he moved back to the farrier's stall and pulled out a hammer, gently tapping the thing straight on the anvil that sat there on a sawed-off stump. "Do you mind if I ask what you're doing?"

"For different enemies, we need different weapons." After straightening the metal, I watched as he took it to a sharpening wheel that was mounted to an abbreviated worktable, scattered with other hand tools. Grabbing a pair of tongs, he began spinning the wheel and honing a blade on both sides of the thing, the sparks arcing through the air, with some of them landing in the straw at our feet.

Using the toe of my boot, I stamped out a few glowing embers. "I have something to show you." He cocked his head but said nothing as I pulled the booklet from my inside pocket, the one with the exact emblem he'd applied to the version we'd printed.

I handed it to him, and he studied it. "Where did you get this?"

"I don't know—I just had it when I woke up in the street back in Fort Pratt." I pointed at the insignia, the circle with the strike through it. "What does that mean?"

"Many things . . . The end of the world—or something else." He took the pen from my pocket again and took the Mallo Cup Play Money card that I'd used as a bookmark and wrote something on the back of it before returning it to the folds of the booklet and then handed it back to me. "I have left you something in this book, Lawman. Something that you may read when you feel the need but only then." He then pulled the metal shard back up and looked at it and began attaching the blade to the lance with the sinew we'd been chewing. "There may be a point when we need to leave these boys, and it would be good if they had a map to lead them back to their home."

"Why would we have to leave them?"

"We may be needed elsewhere." When I didn't move, he eyed me. "How did you get here, Lawman?"

"What do you mean?"

"This is not your time or place, so how did you come to be here?"

"I'm not sure what you mean."

"Where were you before this?"

I held the booklet in my hands and thought about it and was a little worried. "You know, the longer I'm here the harder it gets to remember."

"Unless something from your past jolts you into remembrance." He nodded. "That is the way of things."

"It is foretold?"

"You're getting the hang of it." He smiled. "But be specific, where were you before here?"

"Fort Pratt, Montana, but a different Fort Pratt, Montana—a different time, I think."

"And how did you get here from there? Be exact."

"I walked through the gate of the boarding school . . . There was a cemetery, and a bell on a platform, but the school was gone."

"Do you wish to go back there?"

"I . . . I think so. I think I have unfinished business there; besides, it's closer to where I'm really supposed to be."

"And where is that?"

"I'm not so sure anymore."

"You need to be." He folded his huge arms on the grinding wheel, which had slowed to a stop. "Listen carefully because this is important. When you travel as we have in this land of dreams and shadows, it is easy to lose yourself and your place, but there is a way to be reminded."

"And what's that?"

He reached out and tapped the booklet with a finger like a truncheon. "Bring to mind your loved ones, they are the compass points in your existence, no matter where or when you are—they will guide you home, even if it is only their names."

I laughed a hollow, lost guffaw. "That's just the problem, though. I can't remember anything or anyone, only bits and pieces."

"You will when things become desperate, and they are about to become very desperate."

I studied him. "What does that mean?"

He went back to turning the wheel and honing the blade. "Go find us a map."

I stood there for a moment more in an attempt to digest every-thing he'd said, but it seemed impossible without any point of ref-erence. "We'll talk more when I get back?"

"Sure." The sparks flew, and he grunted. "Put that booklet back in your pocket and do not lose it or the bookmark under any circumstance."

I glanced at the embers in the straw as I did what he said. "What good does it do me if I can't read Cheyenne?"

He continued grinding. "Perhaps you will find someone other than me who does."

The boys wanted to go with me, but I was able to convince them that if I was invisible, it bore certain advantages in this type of situation.

I moved down the hall, thinking about what the shaman had said and about how he seemed so familiar. I thought about the woman, Martha, back at the café in Fort Pratt. I thought about her face, but it had melded into something else—a face like hers mixed with my own and a child with a trace of the same fea-tures.

Family?

Children?

Grandchildren?

Why couldn't I bring anything into focus when I tried to re-member these things?

I leaned back on the door and pinched the bridge of my nose, trying to concentrate, but it was like there was a wall; some-thing holding me at a distance from myself. The disembodied feelings that the Medicine Man referred to were almost palpable, along with the warning that I didn't have all the time in the world.

Crossing the hallway, I turned the knob to what looked like a classroom, but the room was relatively bare. There was a pull-down map above the chalkboard, but it was of the entire United States and the lack of detail in our portion made it relatively useless.

There was a desk, but all the drawers were locked, and evidently my powers didn't extend to unlocking drawers either.

Running a finger across the top, I looked at the stripe in the dust and got the feeling that the classroom wasn't being used all that much.

Figuring that maybe there was a usable map in the administrative offices, I started toward the center of the hallway. Taking the right toward the front door, I was surprised to find the light still on in the superintendent's office.

Slowing, I looked around but there wasn't anyone else in any of the other offices as well.

Glancing inside, I could see that what should have been a neatly ordered desk was now a mess with the blotter and stationery and pens and pencils scattered on the floor. The oil lamp was burning on the windowsill, and from that light I could see that the safe I'd noticed the first time I'd been in the room now hung open, papers and a few bank bags also lying on the floor.

Taking a step in, I could see that the young woman, Madie, was crumpled against the wall in an awkward position, her face turned away from me.

There was a smell, a smell that most people don't know but one with which I seemed to be familiar. It was a stillness in the air where the most heinous of smells refuse to invade, an action that was but is no more, a stillness that occupies the space of things that have been.

It was strange in that I didn't hesitate and stepped across the room to kneel and touch a hand to her throat only to pull away and find my fingers covered in blood. Placing a hand on her shoulder, I pulled her back and could now see that the blood on the other side had run to the baseboard and leaked beneath.

Her clothes were soaked, and now I could see that someone had practically cut her head off.

The blade, a large one would be my guess, had sliced deeply from left to right, strong enough to do the deed with only one pull. The look of shock in the woman's eyes was crippling. You couldn't help but feel the pain, the confusion, and the absolute terror that was there in those still and lifeless pupils.

It was strange as the blood also seemed to be flowing from her mouth; maybe that was simply drainage from where her throat had been cut. I turned her head carefully so as to not disconnect it from the body, when I noticed her mouth was hanging open in moderate rigor mortis.

Dead for an hour or more.

How did I know that?

I was unconcerned that her foot kicked out because my hand still held her jaw. Cadaveric spasm or postmortem spasm, instantaneous spasm, instantaneous rigor cataleptic rigidity, or instantaneous rigidity—a rare form of muscular stiffening that sometimes occurs at the time of death and persists into the three periods of rigor, livor, and algor mortis.

I caught my breath, again considered the thoughts that had just effortlessly flowed through my mind and how nonplussed I'd been in responding to the words that had been conjured up in my mind.

Mumbling to myself, I continued examining her. Maybe I was a doctor.

The body stilled, and I was about to lower her head back to the wooden floor when I thought to loosen the jaw with thumb and forefinger. I cocked her head back, then took the lamp from the window and held it near the face so that the reluctant shadows were chased away. I peered into the cavity.

Someone had pulled out all of her teeth.

9

"What do you mean, gone?"

Artie coughed again, a splatter of blood hitting the snow between his tactical boots. He wiped his mouth with the back of his hand. "If one of you would be kind enough to give me a blanket or something, I might be more inclined to discuss this with you."

Vic nudged the side of his head with the barrel of her Glock. "Why did you attack me, Artie?"

"I thought you were someone else."

"Who did you think I was?"

"One of the ones hunting me."

"Who?"

"Someone else."

She nudged his head once again. "If it'll help your memory we've got a boot we can stick up your ass if you don't tell us exactly where Walt is, right now."

Henry dropped Walt's boot and then stood and slipped off his coat. He swirled it and allowed it to settle around the man before kneeling in front of him again. "Talk. Now."

Clutching the leather coat a little at the collar, Small Song closed it at his neck. "Why did he follow me?"

"They found the girl, Jeanie One Moon."

He nodded, the last nod dropping his face. "Of course, they did."

"Did you have something to do with that?"

"No."

"No?" Henry leaned in, his nose almost touching the crown of the man's head. "Tell me what happened when he got here in pursuit of you."

Artie's words fell from his mouth. "It was not me he was after."

"Then who?"

"He has many enemies on this side and the other."

"For now, I am concerned with this side."

His voice became more conversational. "You know, I have found it is always easier to be the pursued than the pursuer, to act rather than react—it is that small increment of time that is an advantage. When he arrived here, he thought he held the advantage, but it proved otherwise."

"Yes?"

Artie smiled. "He did not die in the fight between us or in the vehicle."

"He has not died at all."

After a moment, the man continued to talk to the ground. "How do you know, Standing Bear?"

"Because I would feel it."

"You're sure?" Artie's face rose again, smiling.

The Bear reached forward, driving a finger into the bullet hole as the wounded man jerked back only to be held in place as the Cheyenne Nation clamped the other hand on the nape of his neck, effectively holding him in place. "Answer my questions or I will pull your lung out from the inside."

The man shuddered but remained silent as his face rose in a grimace, blood edging his teeth.

"Walt followed you here because there was something about Jeanie One Moon that did not end with her death. She called out to him. I know he is alive and near, and I will find him before he dies because I will not allow him to pass into a realm where the Wandering Without will have dominion over him."

"Kill me and you have no say." A stream of blood and saliva dripped from Artie's mouth. "I am . . . its advocate."

"Explain."

Artie shuddered again. "To . . . to talk to it, you must talk through me."

"Tell it to return my friend or face the consequences."

"The sheriff, I thought he would have to die to do the task I have prepared for him, but he does not. He must, though, first pay a price."

"What price?"

"There are many who call out to him from the other side, many he must answer for who would take him with them if given the chance—he is now fighting a battle for others. If you interrupt before he finishes you will be doing more harm than good." He raised a hand and then dropped it. "Would you please remove your finger from my lung?"

"No."

He uneasily took a breath and wheezed out the question. "Why?"

"Because it is the only thing keeping your lung from collapsing and I do not want that to happen until you are through telling me what I wish to know." The Bear stared at him a good long while before turning his head to look at Vic. "You have emergency supplies in your truck?"

She glanced at him, keeping the 9mm on Artie. "Yeah."

"You have a medical bag?"

"Sure."

"Would you get it, please?"

She shook her head. "Not till he tells us where Walt is."

"I honestly do not think he knows, and it is to our benefit to keep him alive."

"Fuck him, where's Walt?"

The Cheyenne Nation sighed. "I know you are very upset right now . . ."

"Fuck upset, Walt is out there, and he needs our help."

"And we are helping him by helping this man. Now would you mind getting those medical supplies so that I might remove my finger from Artie?"

With an exasperated gasp, she lowered her weapon, stuffed it into her holster, and walked toward the truck.

"I think she would rather shoot me." Artie grunted.

"I can guarantee it." Henry nodded and then studied him some more. "How do I know what you are telling us is the truth?"

"I have proof."

"Let me see it."

He stretched his neck, attempting to be at least partially comfortable. "After you patch me up and take me back to the hotel."

"You are pushing your luck."

Artie shrugged. "I thought we should at least be comfortable while we wait for your friend."

Vic arrived with the medical supplies and a roll of duct tape. "Here, but that medical tape doesn't work worth a shit when there's that much blood."

Henry glanced up at Artie's sallow face. "I am going to take my finger out now. I suggest that you should compress the wound yourself?"

"That might be best, yes." He prepared himself, placing his hand beside Henry's in preparation as the Bear pulled his finger out from the man's body. "Mmmmph . . ." Covering the wound quickly, Artie froze and then nodded, looking up at Vic. "Mind if I ask what round you're carrying?"

"Federal Premium, 115 grain. They have one of the best large-wound cavities."

He smiled. "I can attest to that."

Opening the kit, the Bear drew out gauze pads and began assembling them and then tore a few strips from the roll of duct tape. "I am to assume from this conversation that there is no exit wound?"

Artie nodded. "Agreed."

"Are you ready to move your hand?"

"I am."

He did so and the Bear pasted the makeshift bandage onto his abdomen as they both froze for a moment. "Are you all right?"

"I think so."

"Can you be moved?" The man nodded and Henry reached forward, scooping him up as he stood. Carrying him toward the truck, he motioned for Vic to open the passenger door, which she reluctantly did as Dog's head pushed between the seat and the door sill—he was growling. "No."

The dog retreated, watching as Henry deposited Artie into the front seat. "So, you have made the acquaintance of the young man who owns the hotel?"

"I have."

"What is his connection to all this?"

Artie remained silent.

Vic pointed a finger at him as she pulled the keys from her pocket. "You get blood in my truck, and you ride in the bed or tied to the hood, got me?"

He nodded. "I have something, that I suppose I should go ahead and give you now."

She stared at him. "What?"

"After the crash, I found something he would want me to give to you, specifically." He glanced at Henry. "The assurance you both want, it's on a chain, around my neck."

Henry watched Vic, who felt around under Artie's shirt. "I'm liable to catch something . . ." She fished out the chain and swung it so that Henry could see the large silver ring in the available light, reflecting a pale glaze of blood, the embedded turquoise and coral wolves chasing each other in the silver loop.

"Wherever he is, Walt has a powerful ally." The Bear raised his head to look at her and smiled. "Virgil White Buffalo."

I lowered Madie's head back onto the wooden floor planks, still looking into her toothless mouth, remnants of a thought echoing in the back of my head. The empty safe made some kind of sense, but what about the teeth? It seemed familiar in some strange and removed way, but why in the world would anyone do this?

I blew the lamp out and sat it back on the windowsill, feeling the cold air creeping from a crack there, then I looked up through the black bars that framed the moon, which was almost being crowded out of the sky by fast-moving clouds. What was it she'd said there at the kitchen door about the ghosts being restless on tonight of all nights?

Wallydraigles, indeed.

Crawley, had to be.

I'd just started to turn when I heard the last thing I expected—the giant bell in the tower began ringing, vibrating the entire building.

I moved to the door, looked to the right and into the main hallway where I could see Simon Toga Kte heaving greatly on the ropes that lifted him from the ground in the entryway to the circular staircase that led to the tower. No one else was there, so I stepped out and moved in that direction, staying next to the wall in case anybody happened to turn the corner.

He finished ringing, and I watched as he picked up his lamp from a tread on the stairs and looked worriedly up and down the hallway.

I was relatively sure he hadn't seen Madie's body unless he'd seen it before I arrived, but then why ring the bell?

He hurried off toward the dormitory, and it dawned on me that it was likely that the two boys had been discovered missing.

The far door to my left slammed open and Superintendent Spellman strode down the hall in his dressing gown, heading in the direction Simon had disappeared, only to have the young man reappear at the end of the hall. "Mister Toga Kte, what is the meaning of this?"

"Two of our young men are missing, Mr. Spellman."

"Which two?"

"The small one, Thirty, and the new one, Marcus."

The tall man sighed. "Have all the regular precautions been taken with the other boys?"

"Yes, sir."

"Do you need assistance? I'm sure Mr. Crawley . . ."

"If I need help, I can always take Ty with me, sir."

He scooped a watch from the pocket of his robe. "Very well, do we have any idea how long they've been gone?"

"No, sir."

"Well, it's 8:17 so they haven't gotten the lead they had the last time Thirty escaped." He paused to think. "How many times is this?"

"Four, I believe, sir."

"Hmm . . ."

"I'll take care of it, sir." He started to go but then turned back to the man. "Have you seen Madie, sir?"

Staring at his watch with a perplexed look, he finally replied. "What, she's missing too?"

"It's all right, sir, she may be in bed. She's usually the first to respond to the bell, but she was up late baking bread."

The older man nodded. "Well, be sure to take some with you, you'll need that and water if you have to go far."

"Yes, sir." He tipped his cap and ducked through the door toward the kitchen. The superintendent turned and strode back toward me.

Watching him pass, I saw him glance toward his office but then he continued, so I crossed the now empty hall and pushed open the door to the short entryway that led to the stables only to find the place empty. Going straight to the unoccupied stall, I looked around but could find no sign of Virgil, the boys, or the horse.

I could see the stable door hanging ajar and skiffs of snow blowing horizontally across the ground outside. The heavy door thrummed against the other as I placed a hand on it to steady it and to steady me, finally pushing it aside to reveal a trail of prints leading toward the outcropping at the end of the knoll, where they disappeared.

The wind pushed at the sides of the boarding school as if in an attempt to blow it away, but it stood, the tall tower reaching up to scar the speeding storm clouds. I trudged out into the wind and wondered what could've come over this Virgil that he would take two children out into something like this?

I started to set off when I felt something to my right and behind me.

I turned to find Simon Toga Kte kneeling in the snow. He was examining a print as he rested the butt of an 1873 Winchester— the rifle you could "load on Sunday, shoot all week long." His head slowly rose as he settled a hand on his belt, where I noticed a Colt 1892 revolver and an impressive skinning knife. He stood, looking very concerned, buttoned up his great coat, and with good reason pulled his hat down tight. Then he walked past me.

I took one step and then stopped to look down at where Toga Kte's prints joined with those of the big bay gelding's. I could now see that there was another set of tracks, into which I placed my hand, the print engulfing it.

The largest grizzly bear tracks I'd ever seen.

He was hurrying, but I had little trouble keeping up, finding that I couldn't seem to get tired or cold.

At the edge of the knoll, I got a look at the rest of the country to the east, an unending fold of falling shelves that I assumed led down to a river, likely the Milk or Missouri. There was a strong ridge to the right toward the Canadian border, which, if I was escorting two fugitives to freedom, was a direction I might try.

The wind keened and there was little doubt that the weather was arriving in force. What was this Virgil thinking? He was likely as impervious as I was, but what about the children and the only horse? The snow was already about mid-shin, and likely to get a lot deeper.

Toga Kte had stooped and studied the tracks that curved down the slope toward the ridge. Shaking his head, he stood and started off again.

I felt for the poor guy—I had little doubt there was some kind of relationship between him and the dead girl. Who knew if I'd ever see the boarding school again? The gateway to the school was my only way back to Fort Pratt, but did I really want to go back there? Was there anything there for me, other than attempting to find out who I was—and did I really want to know?

I was overwhelmed by a wave of panic as a voice rang like a bell in the back of my head, the strongest message I'd heard there yet—yes.

Which meant it was my responsibility to retrieve the children and make sure they were safe, no matter what the cost, before I headed back to another unknown.

Keeping the young man in sight, I kept to the left to follow him but watching the tracks and keeping an eye on the weather as the wind picked up as well. Soon we'd be at the top of the landscape and, as they say, there would be nothing between us and the north pole except a little barbed wire.

Angling up the ridge, I caught up with him, watching him struggle with his leg and decided to try an experiment. "Were you born with a clubfoot?"

He stopped and looked around, glancing past me and then starting off again.

I repeated the question. "Were you born with a clubfoot?"

He kept hobbling this time but began mumbling. "Yes, it was always like this, which may be the reason they left me at the gate of the boarding school."

"No parents, nothing?"

He trudged on. "No."

"I'm kind of in the same position myself." He stopped again, but this time he didn't look around, instead he shook his head as if to clear it. He stood there for a moment more and then started off again. "I'm still here."

He stopped and looked around. "Who the hell are you?"

"Just a voice."

He slung the rifle up on his shoulder. "How come I've never heard you before?"

"Maybe you weren't listening."

Barking a laugh, he struggled up the slope. "Are you here to help me?"

"Maybe."

"Why maybe?"

"You're awfully well armed for a rescue."

He kept moving and said nothing.

"It was interesting what Crawley had to say about never retrieving any escapees alive."

He continued fighting his way up the shelf of snow that had drifted over the ridge, batting at what hung over his head. The snow fell and was carried away in the wind. "It's not my fault, those boys . . . I tracked them as best I could, but they just disappeared."

I shouted to be heard over the oppressive wind. "Was the weather like it is now?"

He stopped again, sheltering his face. "No, sometimes it was in the middle of the summer, and it was beautiful." He said nothing for a moment and then sadness crept into his voice. "I'd be tracking them, and it was as if they simply vanished." His voice cracked. "I'm very good at what I do—I was taught by an old guy who used to be in charge of the stables. He was part Indian but from a tribe down south, a long way from here. If there was any way to find those children, I would've done it."

"So, what are all the weapons for?"

"Did you see the size of those bear tracks? Besides, I don't want to end up like you."

"Like me?"

"A ghost, or whatever you are." He broke over the top of the ridge and the blast of wind felt like a slap in the face, or at least it looked that way from my perspective. "Am I going to die? I mean, is that why you're here?"

"Why would that be the case?"

"Are you here to take me to the other side?"

"No." I scrambled over the shelf and looked down into another valley floor that must've been a frozen lake and saw a curious sight. I was a mile away and could see where they had gone farther down the ridge than we had, but with the sharper angle we had a better chance of catching up with them. There were two figures, one on four legs and another on two, neither of which appeared human.

"You swear?" Toga Kte slipped, and it looked as if he might tumble back down the area we'd just climbed.

It was an involuntary response, but I reached out and grabbed the lapel of his great coat in order to pull him back up and settle him on the knife-edge of the ridge as the wind blasted at us.

"You . . ." He sat there with an utterly astonished expression on his face, looking just to my left. "You're really here."

I stood there on the ridge, feeling as if the snow were blowing through me, and maybe it was. "Yep."

He looked more than a little panicked and if conditions were a little more conducive, I think he might've even run for it. "What are you?"

"Well, that's a little tough—I thought I might be a ghost, but I don't think I'm dead."

"Why are you here with me?"

"To help you save those two boys, if that's your honest intention."

"It is."

I glanced ahead at the disappearing figures. "Then let's go."

He stood and we began tromping down the slope. He didn't speak for a while, but then his imagination got the better of him. "If you don't know what you are, then how do you know you're not a ghost?"

"It's a long story."

He tromped along, all the while gesturing at the endless nightscape. "We've got plenty of time."

I thought about what Virgil had said, that time was limited. "I think I'm from another period."

"And place?"

"No, actually from this place but a long time into the future."

"Do you have some kind of connection to the school in the future?"

I thought about what it was I should tell him, and more important, what I shouldn't, but finally settled on the best tact— the truth. "There isn't any school in the future."

"I was afraid of that." He continued walking as the snow began racing around us and the small amount of light from the full moon began to be encapsulated by the long clouds reaching it like taloned fingers. "Are my people, the Assiniboine, still around in the future?"

"Yep, they are."

"That's good."

"Yep, it is."

The slope had started to flatten—we must've reached the surface of the lake—and we were gaining on the figures, no more than what seemed a half mile ahead in the limited vision. He started to raise his hand to the side of his mouth, but I reached out and pulled his hand down. "Not yet and let me do the talking."

"I know those boys, well, at least one of them."

"I know them both, and more important, I know who's with them."

It was about then that one of the figures turned and stood fully erect, sniffing the air and looking directly at us through the gusting snow.

He swallowed and then whispered. "Oh, God . . ."

This grizzly bear stood every bit of twelve feet tall, and I watched as it stretched its nose into the breeze in which our scent was being carried.

Toga Kte raised the Winchester and started to take aim.

I pushed the barrel down. "Don't, you'll just piss him off."

"What?"

"Make him angry." I took a step forward as the visibility dropped even more. "Besides, I think I know him."

He looked after me. "You know a bear?"

"Maybe." I took another step forward as the grizzly dropped onto all fours and began swinging his head back and forth before stepping toward us and huffing. "I hope I do . . ."

"Hey, can that bear see you?"

"I think so or maybe he can smell me; I don't know."

"Well, I can't see you and if he can't see you, then he's going to be coming after me."

He had a point. "You stay here, and I'll go talk to him."

"Talk?" He leaned forward, again trying to see me. "To a bear?"

"It's the end of December, if that was a real bear, then it'd be hibernating—well, usually. Males tend to den up in mid-December."

"It's only late December . . . Besides, if it's not a real bear, then what is it?"

I took a few more steps toward the beast, who huffed and then pushed off with his forelegs, pounding the ground and giving every impression that he was going to charge. "Just stay here, but if he comes at you, feel free to shoot."

"Believe me, I will."

Just as a test, I angled to the left to see if the bear would track me rather than him, but he was still so far away I couldn't tell. I kept trying to look past the monster, attempting to spot the horse with the two boys but couldn't see anything. I'd been working on the assumption that this bear was Virgil in his bear-skin, but this seemed to be a real grizzly, and the closer I got, the more I thought that it had decided to have a snack before set-tling himself in for a long winter's rest. If he was actually track-ing Virgil and the boys on the bay, he must've become aware of us and decided that two men afoot or, better yet, one man afoot might provide an easier challenge.

The grizzly was only about a hundred yards away now, the gusts of snow swirling and making it hard to see.

It seemed as though he bluffed a charge in our direction, and then what looked to be him rose up again on two feet and sniffed the air. Was that bear smelling me? The beasts aren't known to have the best eyesight, but their sense of smell is very keen.

The horse in the barn had recognized me.

What was I going to do if the bear decided to charge?

It dropped back down onto all fours and then began ambling in a direction positioned between Toga Kte and me.

I kept moving forward and to the left, still trying to attract the bear, hoping that because I was closer, he'd focus on me.

A voice called out from behind me. "Are you still out there?"

I turned, forgetting that he couldn't see me, but then made a shushing sound, which I was pretty sure the grizzly had heard too. Wiggling his hindquarters, he leapt forward and then shook his head back and forth as he advanced, possibly confused by and annoyed at seeing the shadow of something in one direction yet hearing it in another.

Unsure of the young man's marksmanship, I wasn't willing to bet Toga Kte's life on my gambling with a real grizzly. "Virgil?"

He definitely heard me that time and stopped, looking directly my way.

"Virgil, it's me, Walt."

It didn't move at first, but then the great head thrust forward, and the mouth widened into an ear-shattering roar.

Definitely a bear.

A real bear.

I began arcing left in a circle. "Hey bear, hey bear . . ." Giving one last glance in the direction of Toga Kte, he started straight toward me. "C'mon, bear, c'mon . . ."

I wasn't sure what the results would be, but it seemed that if I could touch other things, they should also be able to touch me, and just because the bear couldn't see me didn't mean he couldn't cause me damage.

Maybe I was on my way to being a ghost after all.

The grizzly was about fifty feet away, a dark shadow in the terrible whiteness. Then he stopped, sniffing the air again, and then turned its great snout back toward the young man.

"Bear!"

He looked straight at me.

"C'mon, bear!"

He started off at a lope in a beeline toward me. Whatever he could or couldn't see, smell or couldn't smell—he'd made up his mind. Roaring out of the pixelated whiteness came into full view in a matter of seconds and even if I'd had something to fight with, there was little I could've done.

He pounded into me, sending me sideways as I slid along in the snow. When I attempted to rise, I saw him there, only twelve feet away and in perfect profile, the saliva dripping from his mouth in strings. He gulped once and then began sniffing again, great lungfuls of the frigid air that were telling him a million things I would never know.

He looked in my direction, exhaling strongly enough to scatter the crusted snow that covered his clawed feet.

I didn't move at first, but then drew a leg in to allow me to try a crouch in case I needed to move again.

He turned toward me this time, sniffing and then pawing the snow.

The big head moved closer, and I wondered if he'd let me get by him again. His snout widened, and I watched as his nostrils flared.

A small blip of snow fountained up between us and I heard the report of a .44-40 scattering through the snow like shrapnel.

That damn kid.

The next shot slapped the snow just short of the grizzly's

right paw, which caused him to swing his head in that direction and roar again.

Toga Kte held the Winchester to his shoulder and fired again. This round skittered underneath the colossal bear as he turned and crouched, ready to propel his great weight at the young man who drew nearer.

I'm not sure what I was thinking, or if there was any thought involved, but I threw myself onto the bear's back, clutching at his wet fur. He'd already lurched forward when he must've felt me on him and then it spun, the third round from Toga Kte whizzing by both our ears.

The grizzly slid to a stop and heaved sideways, sending me flying through the air and then skidding in the snow. I looked up and saw Toga Kte leaning over me. He was fighting with the lever action of the Winchester. "It's jammed!"

I stood and turned to see the bear homing in on us, his ears forward and his eyes glistening.

He'd just started to launch himself toward us when I felt that something was looming above. I looked up and could see horse tails in the swirling snow, brass beads and deer hooves, red stripes painted on bone, and the empty eye sockets of a coyote skull looking back at me.

The wind pitched the tails, swishing them as the hooves clicked and the fangs of the skull bit down into the red felt on the shaft of the war lance, white ermines circling like chain lightning. "Kammatbaluússaala!"

Virgil's massive hand stuck straight out, the barrel stave blade pivoting toward the bear.

The grizzly froze, uncertain as to how to respond, but then lowered its head and bellowed at us once more.

I looked back and could see that Virgil was standing over us with the bear hood pulled up over his head, looking every bit like the grizzly's brother. "Kalakoowáxia itbuushpíte!"

The bear began raising his front legs as he lifted himself up, towering above the three of us—and then something strange began happening: the snowflakes that had been darting past suddenly stuck in midair like dust motes and those that had been flung off the bear's enormous paws also began sliding backward and away from us.

The snow moved slowly at first, but then barreled backward to form a tunnel that surrounded the huge animal, tugging at his great weight. He turned and snapped at the vortex as if it were a living thing.

The snow howled around us, cartwheeling in circles as we felt ourselves being pulled forward in the same direction.

Pivoting, the war lance turned sideways and pulled back against Toga Kte's chest and mine as we grabbed hold. I could feel Virgil's strength as he held us all, fighting against the flow of the darkening hole that seemed to be opening behind the bear.

Something was reaching out and taking hold of the grizzly as its movements became more frantic, teeth gnashing. There were thousands of hands clutching at the animal as it thrashed for its life, digging its six-inch claws into the ice, digging against the inevitable.

The rush of the wind was deafening and through half-closed lids I watched as the grizzly was swallowed whole. The three of us lurched forward as the intensity of the void increased, but Virgil held us back, though I didn't know if he could for much longer.

We slid another foot in that direction as the hands reached out to us.

I felt Virgil push us down into the snow as he turned the war lance and held the point out toward the phenomenon, trembling in his hands until he let go.

The lance shot forward into the vacuum, metal tip striking its center; an implosion swallowing everything in an instant, with a noise that threatened to crush your skull.

Stretching my jaw in an attempt to clear my ears, I struggled to my hands and knees, Toga Kte lying there with his face buried in the snow. The wind had stopped, and now the flakes fell vertically to the ground, and the full moon shone on the flat surface of the frozen lake.

Virgil walked to the spot where the bear had disappeared.

He looked in all directions and then tucked two fingers into his mouth and whistled with the tone and volume of a steam train. Behind us, we heard the unmistakable clop of horse hooves. I turned to see the big bay moving toward us with the two boys safely on its back.

Virgil kneeled to retrieve the war lance from the snow, holding it aloft and examining the smoldering end of the barrel stave blade; it sizzled with the touch of a snowflake.

I reached down to shake Toga Kte by the shoulder. He raised his head, shaking it clear. I turned to Virgil. "You did that?"

"No, but I stopped it." He stood, looking over his shoulder and then back at me. "This time."

10

Vic used the hem of her Carhartt to rub the blood off the ring, held it up to the light, and studied it quietly, while Henry attempted to stanch the bleeding in Artie's chest.

"His breathing is becoming more labored, and to treat it I will need to remove the bandage." The wounded man lay on the bed in room 31 of the Baker Hotel, breathing heavily as the Bear examined the bandages, on which was a continual froth of pink bubbles. "He is going to need proper medical attention—more than I can do here."

Vic continued to study the ring.

The Bear turned to look at her. "He is possibly the only one who knows where Walt might be."

"When he tells us, I'll start giving a shit about what happens to him."

The Cheyenne Nation sat back in the chair by the bed and wiped his hands on a bath towel. "If he dies, we may never find Walt."

She lowered the ring but still wouldn't look at him. "So, what are you saying?"

"Either someone goes and brings back a doctor, or we have to take him somewhere where he can be attended to."

"He's not leaving here until he tells us where Walt is."

Folding the towel, he placed it on the arm of the chair. "He cannot."

"Why?"

"He is unconscious and in shock." Vic approached the bed as Henry reached over and felt the wounded man's pulse at his throat and then pried open one of his eyelids. "If dead, he is really of no use to us."

She stared at him.

"Our choice is simple: either we take him to where medical attention can be had or bring it here to him, and considering his condition . . ." He watched as the man's chest rose and fell. "It would be better not to move him, but the nearest cell phone service is almost an hour away, which means two hours at best, and he will undoubtedly be dead by then."

"You want to take this fucker in my truck?"

"I want you to so that I can stay here and continue looking for Walt."

"Why don't you take him?"

"I cannot drive your truck as fast as you and you cannot search as well as me."

"Fuck you."

"So, you know I am right."

"Fuck you some more."

"If we do not find Walt in the next six hours . . ." He considered the watch at his wrist. "He is likely dead; you know that."

She sat at the end of the bed and stared at the ring in her hands again.

"Artie either could not or would not tell us where Walt is." He glanced at the man. "Now, he cannot." He stood and walked to the window, looking down on Main Street. "Our best chance is to try to keep him alive and you are our best chance of doing that." He turned to look at her. "When you get back in range, use your radio or cell phone and contact the authorities and keep Artie alive, no matter what the cost."

She looked up, eyes glistening. "Promise me you'll find him, Henry."

"I will do my best."

She punched him in the chest. "Promise me."

He sighed deeply. "I will find him."

She stood and snorted, wiping her eyes, and then clutching the bridge of her nose between thumb and forefinger. "Help me get him loaded in my truck."

They used the bedspread as a gurney, carrying the wounded man down the stairs and into the lobby, with Dog following.

Outside, they lay him on the sidewalk and opened both back doors of the cab; then they gently arranged Artie across the back seat. Folding him up in the blankets from the room, Henry fastened him in with the safety belts before closing the door and turning to face her. "That will hold him relatively well, but if you have to make any kind of evasive maneuvering, I doubt he will stay in the seat."

"Do you want to put him on the floor?"

"No, I am hopeful that he will be more comfortable in the seat."

She pushed the Bear out of the way and pulled on her gloves. "You want me to get him there, or not?"

"I would like you to get him there, alive."

She nodded without looking at him. "I'll see what I can do." She stood there a moment more with her hand on the door handle. "I really didn't have any choice but to shoot him, you know that, right?"

"I never doubted it."

She stared at her reflection in the driver's side window. "I just didn't want you thinking I'd pulled some dumbass rookie move."

"I would never think that."

She turned her head to look at him. "Find him, Henry. Find him, or I don't know what I'll do."

He grinned a grim smile. "Me either."

He took Dog by the collar and stepped back as the hopped-up half-ton sprang to life, rumbling at the curb. Vic lowered her window. "I'm betting I can get there in forty minutes and I'll try the radio until I get someone. I'll deliver Artie to them and head back, but probably not alone."

"Perhaps you should stay with him, so that if he talks . . ."

Her eyes flashed at him. "I'm coming back."

"As you wish." He stepped away, drawing Dog with him as she slipped the truck into reverse and backed up, drawing it into gear and lowering the passenger's side window.

"I'll be back in an hour, with the troops."

Henry watched as the Banshee throttled away. He looked down at Dog. "Personally, I am glad I am not in that truck, how about you?"

Dog wagged.

He went back to the darkened hotel, slipping around the bar and pushing open the kitchen door as Dog followed.

The moonlight shone through the aged windows, reflecting off the stainless steel in the empty kitchen. He walked to the back door, which led to an outdoor cooler and a foreshortened walkway that ended with some truck skids and a tiny trailer with a light on.

Pushing open the trailer door quietly, he stepped inside, looking around and then studying the Coleman lantern, knowing full well that the things couldn't run any more than fifteen or twenty minutes without being pumped.

He closed the door behind Dog without a sound. Ducking his head, he scanned his surroundings—an empty, unmade bed; an old computer; books tucked away in a shelf above the bed. He read the titles, shaking his head, and then took notice of a small metal box that sat, slightly ajar. Taking it from the shelf he opened it and stared at the contents, scooping the two items out and stuffing them in his pockets. He returned the box to the shelf and noticed the book next to it and pulled it out.

The Judeo-Masonic Conspiracy—he allowed it to fall open to where a windowed envelope had been used as a bookmark. He plucked it out, thumbed the ragged edge where it had been opened, and pulled out an electricity bill for the Baker Hotel.

Peter Schiller in care of Riley Schiller, he read the name on the paper—over and over. The dead man, Schiller, the neo-Nazi, Brotherhood of the North, Schiller.

Carefully, he returned the envelope back inside the book, closed it, and then replaced it on the shelf in the exact same spot so that no one could ever tell it had been moved.

He looked at Dog, who sat near the door. "We are also in danger, my friend."

Dog stared at him in return.

Henry stepped toward a small propane refrigerator, opened it, reached in, and gathered two uneaten hamburgers from a plate. Shutting the door, he turned to look at Dog, held the plate up high and then moved back to the bed, where he placed the plate before turning back. "Treat."

The monster leapt onto the bed and began devouring the burgers. Henry picked up the hissing lantern in one hand and opened the camper door, closing it behind him and making sure it was secure. He stood there for a moment, listening, as Dog leapt off the bed and now stood on the other side.

"Forgive me, my friend, but I cannot allow anything to happen to you—and I am afraid that from this point on things may become more calamitous."

Dog barked, frustrated by the door being shut, going so far as to scratch at the linoleum tile on the floor of the camper. He jumped up, pounding his paws on the door as Henry stood there behind it.

"I am sorry." Turning, Standing Bear held out the lantern, studied the snow beside the camper, then followed a set of prints that led away from the hotel. Dog continued to bark as the Cheyenne Nation kneeled to examine the tracks and then stood. Pulling the stag-handled bowie knife from the sheath at his back, he scanned the hill in the distance and the remains of the boarding school; he then set off at a limp.

The horse was happy to see the school in the distance and so was I, but hardly anybody else was.

As the bay tromped along with the two boys on its back and Simon Toga Kte leading with the reins, I hung back with Virgil. "Now that we're returning to this place, I have something to tell you."

He inclined his head; the wind continued to rise, and the snowfall increased.

"There's been a murder." He stopped and looked at me. "The young woman who works here at the school, Madie? She's dead."

His eyes dropped, and he studied the snow on the ground between us, and it was almost as if the wind was silencing itself to hear his next words. "So, it has already begun."

"What's begun?"

Ignoring me, he continued to study the ground. "How did she die?"

I stared at him for a moment. "You don't seem surprised."

"I am not." He sighed. "You have not said how she was killed."

Virgil had continued walking and I caught up with him. "I found her on the floor of the superintendent's office, with the safe open; someone had cut her throat."

"Who do you think did it?"

"I'm not sure, but there was an argument between Spellman and the man, Crawley. It would appear that Spellman has been embezzling from the school for years and Crawley discovered it and said that if Spellman didn't split the money with him that he'd report the theft to the state."

"What did the girl have to do with this?"

"I don't know, but she was lying on the floor of Spellman's office and the safe door was hanging open—and strangely someone had pulled out all of her teeth."

He regarded me. "Do you know if she had fillings in her teeth?"

"I don't know."

He grunted. "Knowing you as I do, I assume you have a suspect."

"Crawley confronted Madie in the kitchen earlier this evening and threatened her in more ways than one; evidently there was a history between them." He nodded his head but said nothing. "Is that the reason I'm here?"

He shrugged as he walked.

"You know, as a shaman you're not being very insightful."

He laughed. "You must remember that we are also valuable

not only in action but because we are more than the sum of our memories."

I looked up at him. "What the hell is that supposed to mean?"

His head turned, and it was as if the spirit of a grizzly bear was there with him, mimicked in his every move. "Sometimes we are simply here to bear witness."

"Bear witness, I like that." The wind kicked up, scouring our unprotected faces with the hard snow. "So, then why did you save the boys?"

"They both have a future purpose, and also because it was something of a challenge."

"You mean that thing, the Éveohtsé-heómėse."

"Exactly."

I thought about it, shaking my head. "Whatever it is, why did it come for the bear?"

"It did not come for the bear, the bear simply got in its way."

"Then what did it come for?"

"Me." He stopped and turned. "Or possibly you."

"Why would it be after me?"

"You must have thwarted it, and it does not like that."

"You know what it is?"

"I have encountered it before. I know, because of its presence here, that someone is dying."

I turned and studied the side of his face. "What?"

"It is a postulation, but probably a good one."

"Well, the young woman . . ."

"No." He chuckled. "One of us."

"What do you mean 'us'?"

He pursed his lips and blew out some air, cloaking his face with his frozen breath as he nodded toward the three ahead of us. "One, if not all of them. We were the only ones in its presence."

"Except for the bear." I took a deep breath and blew out a cloud of my own. "Well, I don't know about you, but I feel fine."

"Here, in this place you feel fine, but this is not your place or, more important, your time." He stopped, glancing at the retreating riders. "You would not be here unless it was the direst of circumstances, which leads me to believe that your life is in danger, grave danger." He rested the staff on his foot and scanned the barely visible, snow-covered and desolate landscape. "You are dying, Lawman."

I stared at him. "What?"

"I am now sure of it." He looked around again. "Somewhere, on some other plane, your life is about to be forfeit. This is the only thing that could summon the Éveohtsé-heómése—a temptation it could not resist." His dark eyes came back to me. "Where were you last?"

"I don't understand. You mean before here and now?"

"Yes."

"Fort Pratt, this general area but in the future, or something like the future."

He studied me. "What do you mean?"

"When I was there, I was pretty sure it was contemporary, my contemporary time period, but I kept noticing things that weren't quite right."

"Such as?"

I thought about it, finding it hard to explain. "It just wasn't exactly the way it should be."

He took a deep breath and then slowly let it out. "As if these things had been assembled for you—almost as if the whole thing had been staged."

"Yep."

"And the people?"

"I didn't know any of them. But then I did . . . in some strange way."

"As if you had met them before."

"Yes."

"Did they all have anything in common?"

"I can't say I'd know . . ."

"I will ask the next question plainly: Were they all dead?"

I stared at him. "What?"

"The people in the place before this one, were they dead?"

Confused by the question, I laughed again but then noticed that he wasn't. "No, they were walking around and talking . . ."

"Yes, but in your experience, were they people who you know to have died?"

"What are you talking about? It was a town with people in it going about their lives."

"Perfect in almost every way, almost . . ." He began walking again. "Which leads me to believe that whoever constructed that place for you knows you very well but is impaired in reaching you in some way."

I followed. "Someone who knows me?"

"Yes, but it would take a great deal of energy to create such a thing, don't you think?"

"I guess."

"There are only certain feelings that can bridge the gaps of existence—emotions like regret, longing . . ."

"For what?"

"For things to be different, to change or to take things back that we have done."

"Such as?"

He made the next statement as if it should have been obvious. "Killing, for one."

"I haven't killed anybody."

"How do you know?"

I stopped and watched him walk ahead.

After a moment, he turned and looked back at me, raising his voice above the wind. "Do not be surprised, Lawman, I have killed many myself—those who are not meant for this world and must be sped upon their way. It should not come as too much of a surprise that you yourself have killed."

I thought about it. "What? I'm being punished for my sins?"

He opened his arms like great wings, spreading them out and taking a deep breath. "Does this feel like punishment?"

"Not exactly, no. Maybe the not knowing does . . ." I quickened my pace, catching up with him as he turned and started off. "Am I dead?"

"Do you feel like you are dead?"

"Not exactly, but if I've never been dead, it might be hard for me to tell. I feel . . . disassociated, like I'm being prevented from remembering things—things that are important to me."

"People."

"Excuse me?"

"Forget things and concentrate on people. They are what will lead you home."

I reached out and gripped his arm. "Why can't you help me?"

"I have."

"No, I mean tell me what the hell is going on."

"Because I do not know or, more important, I cannot be sure. If I were to give you answers and they were the wrong ones, I would only make your situation even more confusing."

"I'm not sure that's possible."

"Oh, trust me, it can be. You can be confused like this for the rest of your existence, but I have faith in the strength of your mind. You will come to conclusions and those conclusions will lead to others that will finally produce a universal truth. It is what you have done your entire life."

He began moving again, and I spoke after him under my breath in a voice he couldn't have possibly heard. "I wish I had as much faith in me as you do in me."

But nonetheless, did.

"So do I."

When we got to the stables the horse was happily munching away, but the boys and Toga Kte were nowhere to be found.

As Virgil stood by petting the horse that had had the bridle and saddle removed, I continued down the aisle, checking the empty stalls and general area but finding nothing. "Where could they have gone?"

"We should not have let them go on their own."

"It couldn't have been any more than five minutes." Circling back, I saw something on the floor on top of the dirt and straw. Kneeling, I picked up a strand of hair, holding it for the giant to see.

"Horse?"

"Human, I think." I stood, still holding the strand. "When Marcus first got here earlier this evening, they cut his hair but allowed him to keep it in a small bag." Continuing toward the inner doors, I stooped again, picking up more. "Another one."

Virgil approached. "You miss nothing, Lawman."

"Part of the job."

He stared at me.

"What?"

The giant smiled. "So, you know what your job is?"

I pushed the door open and stepped into the entryway across from the offices where I'd found Madie. "C'mon, I'll show you the body."

We crossed into the hallway, where I could see a large puddle and wet boot prints, a lot of them having come from the stables and turning left toward the dormitory.

"You think they were discovered?"

"That, or Toga Kte had to take them back to the dormitory because with all the hell that's about to take place around here, that might be the safest place for them."

Virgil followed as I entered the office and looked down on the floor in front of the safe, to find nothing. "What the hell?"

First studying the floor and then me, he stepped to my side. "You're sure of what you saw?"

I stooped down and stared at the unstained wood. "She was here, right here." I glanced over at the safe, which was now shut. "And somebody closed the safe."

Virgil kneeled beside me, the bones, hooves, and beads rattling. Placing my hand against the floorboard, I pressed the tips under the wood edge. When I lifted them, there was a thin line of blood there. "She was here, someone took her body away and cleaned up." I held my fingertips out to him, confused at how the residue of anything could be attached to me. "How can there be traces of blood on my fingers?"

"Because she is dead."

"Of course." I sighed. "Something bad is going on here."

"Yes."

I stood, wiping my fingers on my jeans. "And I'm going to stop it."

———

The hallways were empty, but as I followed the wet boot prints toward the dormitory, I could hear loud voices in conflict. "You will do as I say, or I will take action myself."

Turning the corner, I looked through the open gates that led to where the boys slept. All three men stood in the center of the room. They were arguing while the trustee, Ty, strung a length of chain through the footboard and across each bed; the boys, tucked under the covers, were watching him.

"You almost lost two more this evening and I won't have it." Spellman stood over Toga Kte, pointing toward the pile of manacles that lay beside the remaining chain at their feet. "The boys will have to be constrained so that we have no more of this foolishness. Do you understand?"

Toga Kte nodded but continued to speak. "What if there's some kind of emergency, or they need to relieve themselves?"

"They will learn restraint."

The younger man glanced at Crawley and then back to the superintendent. "I don't understand why we . . ."

"You don't have to understand, you must simply do as you are told." Spellman turned with Crawley and they both walked out the doors between Virgil and me.

Ty looked at Toga Kte and began attaching a clasp around the ankle of the first boy, who started to cry.

"This is not right."

We all turned to see Ma'heo standing on his bed so that he could address the others.

"This is not a prison—I will not be chained like an animal."

Toga Kte's head dropped as he faced them. "There is nothing I can do."

Ma'heo stepped to the foot of his bed. "Stand up to them, tell them that you will not do this thing for it is bad."

"Shut up." Ty still held the manacles in his hands but stepped away from the chained boy who was crying. "You are the reason we are having to do this." He raised his hands, gesturing with the metal clasps. "You have done this to all of us."

The small boy pointed toward Marcus. "We are the only ones who will stand against this?"

Ty took a few steps toward him, and then suddenly threw the manacle that had been in his right hand, hitting Ma'heo in the face.

The boy fell with the impact, tumbling off the bed, but then he jumped to his feet and ran around the bed toward the trustee before being grabbed by Marcus, who stood and held the struggling boy.

Bleeding from his mouth where the manacle had struck him, he jerked in Marcus's arms. "Let me go! Let me go!" The larger boy held fast and after a while Ma'heo slumped against him. "It's not right . . . It's not right."

I started to take a step forward when Virgil reached out an arm and blocked me. "No."

Turning to him. "No?"

He said nothing more as Ty smirked at the two and began attaching the manacles to the next boy, the next, and then the next.

Ty attached a manacle to Ma'heo's leg as the boy lay on the bed. With his face buried in his pillow, he made no sound. After it was padlocked, Ty turned and walked around the bed where he came to Marcus, who launched himself, swinging the manacle that Ty had thrown.

The sound was tremendous as the larger boy's head snapped

to the side and he fell, summersaulting over the footboard and then crumpling on the floor.

Marcus stood there with the manacle in his hand. He turned to look at Toga Kte, then crossing back and sitting on the bed, he attached the clasp and locked it on himself.

Toga Kte stood there for a moment and then, fetching the remaining manacles on the floor, he began the process again on the other side, patiently making his way down the row of beds, each boy dutifully extending a leg from under the covers.

"Isn't there anything we can do?"

He shook his head. "Again, no. Anything we do, the results will remain the same."

Having finished the second side, Toga Kte walked over and helped Ty to his unsteady feet.

I shook my head. "We can't leave them like this. If this is the night I think it is, then there is going to be a fire and all these children die, all thirty-one of them."

"We have no choice."

Ty gripped the footboard, stepped toward Marcus, and stuck a finger in the boy's face. "You'll pay for that."

Marcus said nothing.

The smaller boy cried out. "Leave him alone, Ty."

The older boy turned to look at Ma'heo in the next bed. "Shut up pip-squeak. If I want anything from you, I'll call your number."

The Cheyenne boy sat up straighter in his bed. "You gonna lock yourself up too?"

"What I'm going to do is none of your business, now go to sleep." Shaking Toga Kte's hand from his shoulder, he walked back, picked up the oil lamp from the floor, and went to the nearest stove to open it and add more wood. He turned and smiled at the two boys, and it wasn't a pleasant smile. "I've got something in mind for the two of you."

Then he took the lamp and carried it toward his bed, setting it on the nightstand and turning it down very low before climbing into the bed with his clothes and shoes on.

Toga Kte said nothing but turned and followed in the direction of the other men.

I glanced at Virgil, and then followed in the direction that Spellman and Crawley had gone.

By the time I got to the office, Toga Kte had disappeared, but I could hear the two other men arguing, so I turned the corner and stood in the doorway to listen to them.

"I won't do that, it's simply inhuman."

"How else will you explain what has happened?"

I moved to a better spot where I could see Spellman standing behind his desk. He was now wearing a great overcoat and remained silent.

Crawley circled to the window and looked down at the floor. "It is a harsh world, Superintendent, and it is the small and weak who pay the price—you must've learned that lesson when the Seventh took their revenge on Big Foot and the rest of the Miniconjou and the Hunkpapa at Wounded Knee . . ." He turned and looked at the older man. "You have the money we discussed?"

"I do not."

"What do you mean, you don't?"

Spellman gestured toward the open safe and then tucked his hands into his pockets. "I came in here only a few moments ago and discovered the safe open and the money gone."

Crawley pulled the cigar from his pocket, striking a match and carefully relighting it. "And you expect me to believe that?"

"Believe it or not, it is a fact."

Crawley turned back to the dark windows where sheets of snow blew against the glass, as if trying to get at him. "Who else has the combination to the safe?"

"Madie."

"The Scottish girl?"

"Yes."

He looked around as if Madie might appear. "Where is she?"

"I don't know, either in the kitchen or in bed I would suppose."

Crawley puffed his cigar and then placed it between his teeth, fanning his fingers under the lapel of his suit coat and withdrawing the revolver from his shoulder holster. "Then it must've been you."

It was silent in the room and the superintendent spoke in a low voice. "I beg your pardon?"

Crawley raised the pistol, pointing it at Spellman's face. "It would behoove you, sir, to be completely honest with me at this most critical juncture."

Spellman didn't move.

"I have come here at a grave inconvenience, and you will give me what I am due."

The older man did something I wasn't expecting: he smiled. "What you are due."

Crawley transferred the cigar to the other corner of his mouth before speaking. "Yes."

"Stealing half of my money, money I have slaved to accumulate over the years."

"Don't you mean money you stole over the years?"

Spellman was silent again.

"And another thing." Rolling his thumb back, he cocked the pistol. "There's been a change in plans, and I think I'll be taking all the money."

"You know, that is something that has always dumbfounded me about people such as yourself, Mr. Crawley." The superintendent leaned back against the wall with his hands still in his pockets. "As an amateur, you consistently think you have the upper hand in any given situation."

Crawley breathed a chuckle, turning the gun to the side and considering it. "Well, this amateur certainly seems to have the advantage in this instance."

There was a loud report as a shot was fired.

I fully expected Spellman to fall to the floor, but I could see only one point of interest—a smoking hole in his great coat just about where his right pocket would've been. Calmly, he lifted the Colt New Army, double-action revolver from the pocket and retrained it on Crawley, who stood there looking as if he were attempting to catch his breath.

The barrel-chested man swallowed and then slumped back against the window and I heard it crack, then he cast about the room as if unsure about what was going on before firing his own pistol into the floor. He slowly slid down into a sitting position, his legs stretched out in front of him like a discarded doll.

He raised his confused face to Spellman, who took three steps toward him and then kneeled.

The cigar fell from the wounded man's lips and into his lap, smoldering.

Spellman watched as Crawley's features stilled, his eyes relaxing and growing dull. "You see, that's the difference between an amateur and a professional, Mr. Crawley—a professional always has his weapon at the ready and knows precisely when to use it."

11

He was always running off and doing this shit. What was he thinking, and more important, what had happened?

Vic thought she heard a noise behind her and glanced back for just an instant. The whack-job was still trussed up in the back like a Christmas turkey, leaking blood on the brand-new seats. "Damn it to hell . . ."

The truck topped off at 140 in the long straight and the only thing that crossed her mind was that the fucking deer better stay off the road. Why? Why did he run off and do this shit on his own? She shook her head. "If you're dead, I'm really going to be pissed."

Launching into the next turn, she tightened her grip and touched the brakes, expertly slowing before the curve and not in it. It was a bad bank, leaning toward the outside, but she negotiated it and accelerated.

That's when a hand came up and touched her throat.

She lurched in an attempt to get away but instead sent the truck flying over the berm and down a hillside, where it crashed into the ground before bouncing once and then rolling into the creek upside down.

The airbags expanded and the horn blew as she slumped against the wheel, both arms draping to the headliner as the cab slowly filled with creek water. She hung there trying to clear her head, the horn blowing loud enough to drown out the sound of the motor as the half-ton's wheels spun in the air.

She pulled back from the bent wheel and felt a wetness on her nose where it had struck something. After smearing the blood away with the back of her hand, she reached up and disconnected the seatbelt, allowing herself to fall onto the liner where the water was now about an inch deep. Splashing around in it, she pulled a mini flashlight from her breast pocket and shone it onto the back seat where Artie hung from the belts like a marionette.

Crawling into the back, she pulled at the belts, but couldn't get him free. Slipping a hand down into her side pocket, she pulled out the stag-handled RussLock knife that Walt had given her and began cutting the belts away to free him.

He coughed and then reached a feeble hand out to her.

"Stop moving, you moron." Finally cutting the one belt free, she dragged him forward, slipping him out of the nylon grasp of the rapidly filling cab. Pulling him on the soaked headliner, she tried to gauge the angle of the truck to see which way was up and out. The water couldn't be that deep, but it could be deep enough to easily drown in.

Shining her flashlight to the right, she could see that the cab was crushed at the top, and to her left there might've been the slightest glimmer of light as if reflecting from the surface of the water.

She struck at the glass with her tactical boot, but it bounced off with no effect.

Dragging Artie into her lap, she pulled the Glock from its holster and took aim at the window, screaming as she fired. She continued to fire until suddenly the window shattered and imploded toward her, carrying thousands of gallons of water with it. Quickly shoving the gun back into her holster, she gripped the wounded man with both fists and, struggling against the flowing water that rapidly filled the cab, kicked out the remaining glass before finally pulling him through the window. She dragged him up with her as she broke the surface and pulled him behind her. She stood but felt her boots slip in the mud as the truck shifted toward her. "Motherfucker!"

She flipped him over and placed her arm around his neck in a lifesaver lock. The truck still spun its wheels as it slipped sideways and the high-powered motor gurgled, gasped, and then stilled, the only sound her heavy breathing as she attempted to pull Artie from the water. Slipping and falling she finally reached up and grabbed a naked willow branch, which she used to get the two of them out of the stream.

She lay in the hardening mud, trying to catch her breath, staring up at the starless dead sky, aware of something lying across her face. Reaching up, she felt a thin rope or chain, finally getting one of her fingers underneath it and threading it out to where she could see the silver ring hanging in front of her face, the turquoise and coral wolves chasing each other in an endless dream.

Feeling the frigid air freezing her saturated clothes, she shivered.

"Fuck!"

The Cheyenne Nation kneeled in order to examine the blood on the ground and then looked up at the piles of snow as big as houses, where he noticed a metal fence post sticking out from a hole in the miniature mountain range.

He stood and began climbing steadily. When he got to the area, he held the lantern up and stepped to one side in order to see, looking down into the open area of the crushed three-quarter ton and the gold and black lettering on the door.

The Bear slid down the incline to where the plows had hard-packed the snow and then stood, looking to the distance.

The doctors had told him to stay off it and rest.

Looking up, he sighed and started off, limping a little more heavily now but setting his jaw with a bit more determination. There are those who don't feel pain and they have an advantage, and then there are those who do, and they have an even greater one—they use it as fuel.

Every muscle, every sinew fought to counterbalance the weakness, a weakness that could not be tolerated. Finding a rhythm, he started off at a lope, the leg crying out as he ignored it.

The wind had picked up in the night and sheared at the unprotected skin at his wrists and the side of his face. The only sound was the wind, except that he thought he might've heard something else.

He waited; it was one of the things he did best. Closing his eyes, he emptied his mind, allowing the feelers of his senses to reach beyond his focus on the listening: a faint sound, not steady as was the wind, everything departing with it.

Opening his eyes, he looked up at the ridge and saw movement near the rubble of the ruined school.

The hole in Crawley's jacket was still smoking. Spellman walked over and closed the door, effectively trapping me in the room with him and the dead body. He then reached into the left-hand pocket of his coat and pulled out a pair of short-handled fencing pliers.

Crossing back to the body, he kneeled, picking up the cigar and snuffing it out on the floor. He spread Crawley's shirt and dug the slug from the man's body. Then he tilted back Crawley's head and began methodically pulling out the dead man's teeth.

I watched for a few moments and then decided I couldn't see any reason to witness much more. I turned the knob, enabling the door to ease open. When I looked back, Spellman had stood and turned with the bloody pliers and a couple of teeth in one hand.

He was looking around the room.

"Are you there?" I stood still taking in the frenzied zeal of his expression, almost rapturous, as his eyes darted about. "Another one for you—two in all, and there will be many more."

I watched to make sure he couldn't really see me and then slid out the door, leaving it ajar.

Virgil was waiting for me in the hallway but said nothing as Spellman stuck his head out of his office and then retreated, closing the door behind him.

I turned to the giant and whispered, "What the hell is going on here?"

"More than you wish to know."

"He killed the girl too?"

"It is likely."

"We have to get the children out of here."

He turned toward the dormitory wing. "To where?"

"Anywhere, anywhere but here." I glanced back toward the superintendent's office. "That man is insane—he's a monster."

"Or at least in the service of one."

"Are you saying he's connected to whatever that was out there that took the grizzly?"

"It would make sense, would it not? An endless source of young souls to sacrifice to the Éveohtsé-heómėse, which is always hungry?"

I stared at him.

"You do not believe me."

"It's a little hard to swallow, but then everything that's happened to me in this endless night has been."

He nodded. "Endless night, yes . . . Sleepwalking in circles."

"That's exactly what it feels like."

"You do remember this is not your place or time?"

I walked down the hall a few steps and then turned to look at him in frustration. "Explain that question please, in simple terms?"

"You were some other place and time before this, and from your description another time and place before that, even though you do not remember?"

"I think so."

"This is how it will defeat you, by distracting you—it is like life, you can live it or be continually distracted until you are surprised to discover that like smoke from a dead fire, it is gone."

I took a step toward the entryway that led to the stables, looking out the window at the storm, the hard flakes peppering the glass. "So, this thing that's out there, this Éveohtsé-heómėse, it's responsible for all this?"

He walked in my direction but then stopped. "I cannot say."

I thought I smelled something . . . "Can't or won't?"

"There is no difference."

"So, what you're saying or not saying is I need to concentrate and get back to where I was and deal with what is happening to me in my life, that is, if I still have one?"

"I am saying nothing."

"Well, whatever you're saying or not saying, I can't do it." I shook my head and sighed, turned, and looked up at him as a smell began to permeate the room. "I can't leave these children here, not knowing what's happening to them—it's not right."

"And you must do what is right?"

I barked a laugh. "What else is there in all this unholy mess?"

He said nothing but smiled.

I turned my head, sniffing the air. "Do you smell smoke?"

When I looked back down the hall, I could see a thin bluish haze suspended near the pressed-tin tiles of the twelve-foot ceiling. "Something's burning."

As we got to the end of the hallway the light from the fire could be seen flickering against the walls, and as we turned the corner we found Ty, the trustee, battling a blaze in the center of the room.

Looking past him, I could see where the nearest stove was hanging open and a stream of flames led across the middle of the floor, where someone had strung what I assumed was lamp or coal oil. He was slapping bedclothes on the flames, but every time he struck, he strung the remnants of oil through the air and onto the beds and the gauzy cloth curtains between the beds. Small flames were catching everywhere.

The boys were all screaming and struggling at the chains that held them in the beds as Ty continued to wrestle with the fire.

Rushing into the room, I turned back to see Virgil stop at the iron gates that filled the sides of the hallway and look at the floor as if he'd never seen such a thing. "C'mon!"

He stood there, his eyes rising to look at mine.

"What is it?"

"I cannot enter this room."

I yelled at him, thinking I had to in order to be heard above the din. "What are you talking about?!"

"If I enter this room, the results will be worse, and I will be compromised."

"What do you mean 'compromised'?"

His face was emotionless. "Destroyed."

I froze for a second. "Destroyed?"

"Yes."

"By this Éveohtsé-heómèse?"

"Yes."

I peered around, half expecting the vortex of hands to begin gobbling up the room. "It's here, now?"

He took a step back. "Very near, yes."

I hurriedly stumbled toward him and waved for him to enter. "Well, come on then and bring that damn spear. You stopped it before."

"I would not delay it this time."

"What are you talking about?"

"Sometimes—and in some places—when its power is greatest, it is almost impossible to defeat." He looked around at the flames and general chaos. "To attempt to change this moment would put both of us at grave risk."

I glanced behind me where the boys struggled, yanking at the chains that attached them to the beds, and screaming for help. "You're going to let them die?"

He took another step back. "There is nothing I can do for them."

I stared at him, completely uncomprehending. "Well, then go . . . If you can't help them, then you can't help me, and I'm not leaving them."

I snagged part of Ty's sheet in my hand and yanked it from him. I'm sure seeing the cloth hanging in the air must've scared him more than the fire itself.

Looking past him, I yelled to Marcus. "Tell him who I am, and why I'm here!"

Marcus stood on his bed and yelled at the older boy as I threw the sheets onto the floor and began yanking the separation cloths from their braces and the drapes from the walls, throwing them toward the middle of the room where the plaster had burned away, revealing the exposed lath that had now caught fire.

Moving my way down the nearest side, I continued throwing the burning cloth toward the center as Ty watched, unable to move as I yelled at Marcus, who still stood on his bed. "Ask him where the keys are, we need to get all of you out of here!"

Marcus held on to the metal bars at the foot of his bed and screamed at the older boy. "Where are the keys?! He wants the keys so he can unchain us!"

Ty turned to look at him, suddenly shaking his head as if coming to from a trance. "The keys . . ."

Marcus continued to yell as all the other boys joined in. "Where are the keys?!"

Ty began patting his pockets, first in his pants and then in his jacket as the others continued screaming at him. "They were here, I saw them here, they were just here."

I moved forward, stood over him and watched as the panic grew in his eyes, and he raced back to his bed where he scrambled around, feeling under the covers and yanking back the sheets.

I looked up at the walls and could see they were filling with flames, black smoke pouring from the cracks, attempting to fill the room from the top. You could barely see the ceiling now, and before too long the boys would all be dead from asphyxiation.

I was about to grab one of the stove tools to see if I could use it to break the chains when Ty cried out, grabbing the key from the floor, beside the bed.

I'd just started to move in his direction when I heard a strange sound behind me and turned to see Spellman closing the iron gates at the end of the dormitory.

He slipped a key into the lock and turned it, trapping all of us in the burning room.

I threw myself against the bars, pushing as hard as I could. No use. I turned and reached a hand through, attempting to grab his throat. He must've felt me as he stepped back, his glowing eyes taking in the entire room as it rapidly became an inferno.

"Mr. Spellman?" Ty was beside me now, holding the bars next to me and pleading with the man. "Take me with you!"

Spellman started, as if awaking from a dream and then looked down at the boy. "I'm very sorry, Ty. You've been useful to me, but there's nothing I can do." He took another step back. "I must leave here now, and I cannot take you with me."

Ty turned back to look at the flaming room and the encroaching black smoke. "You can't leave me here to burn to death with them!"

Spellman seemed startled by the idea. "Oh, you won't burn,

Ty. None of you will . . . Can't you feel it coming?" He walked away, making the turn at the end of the hall and disappearing.

The boy began sobbing and slid to the floor, his hands still clutching the bars as the key fell onto the other side of the gate, where it bounced once and then landed an arm's reach away.

Scrambling and pressing himself against the bars, he reached out desperately for the thing but fell short.

Calmly, I kneeled and placed my arm over his in order to extend my reach. Then picked the key up, closed my fist, and carefully pulled it through the bars. Turning, I stood and peered through the enveloping smoke, then moved down to the far end and unlocked Marcus. Then I handed him the key. "Unlock them all as quickly as you can."

He moved toward Ma'heo's bed but then yelled over his shoulder. "What are you going to do?!"

Glancing around at the heavy bars that sealed the windows, I sighed. "Find us a way out of this place."

I could just make out through the smoke that the iron gates at the opposite end of the room were not only closed but also wrapped with a chain around them and padlocked.

Moving to the nearest window, I dodged some of the falling and burning wall coverings, finally getting my hands around the heavy bars and tugging, all to no avail. They were probably threaded into the steel.

Brushing past Marcus, I looked at the gate that Spellman had locked and figured that was the weakest link.

Taking off at a full run, I crashed into the thing shoulder first and felt it give just a bit before rebounding back, sending me sprawling across the floor in the opposite direction. I started to roll over, grab my hat, and stand when I heard a tremendous thump, somewhere in the walls or floor.

My first thought was that the structure itself was preparing to give way, but then I heard it again. It sounded like something striking the building. Maybe whatever the thing was that Virgil had held at bay was attempting to get inside.

The boys, who had been released from their chains, followed Ma'heo's lead and scrambled to my side, holding on to me and one another because there was simply nowhere else to be safe.

The hammering against the building continued. Sitting up, I pushed my hat back, but could see nothing but the black smoke, the air above us looking like an impenetrable storm cloud.

The sound struck again, vibrating the entire building as pieces of plaster and dust fell. It struck again and this time larger amounts of debris crumbled down.

Many of the boys were crying now.

If it was the thing we'd seen, I'd have to get free and find some kind of weapon.

The thundering crash sounded from above again, and the smoke on the ceiling began swirling toward the center like a drain; the monster must have been preparing to enter.

And that's when something even stranger happened.

"Lawman?" As the vapors dissipated, Virgil's great bear head appeared, the magnificent war lance poking down through the ceiling. "We haven't much time . . ."

"Virgil?"

I couldn't see through the dark, but his voice held a smile. "You didn't think I would actually leave you, did you?"

I laughed.

"Stand back, I need to make this hole larger."

"You better hurry, or this place is going to go up."

In answer, the war lance struck between the rafters above, sending down more detritus that caused us to cover our faces.

He reappeared, lowering the lance down to where the end of it hung about eight feet off the ground, the horse tail end swishing in the air currents. "I cannot lower it any farther."

Glancing around, I grabbed the footboard of the nearest bed and dragged it toward the middle of the room, kicking the accumulation of debris to the side. Placing a step on the bed, I felt that it would collapse if I put my entire weight on it, let alone my weight and the weight of the boys.

Stepping back down, I saw the metal plate underneath the nearest stove that guarded against the heat igniting the floor. It meant toppling the stove with the coals in it, but at this point that wouldn't amount to much in adding more flames to the environs.

I slipped off my coat to provide a little more padding and then put my shoulder into the thing, watching it fall over in three parts, scattering the glowing coals and ash onto the tiled floor.

The only thing left standing on the plate was the legs and platform, which I flipped off and then grabbed the metal, still warm from the proximity of the stove. I carried it back and placed it on the foot of the bed at an angle, allowing two corners to hang over the sides in order to gain support from the rails.

The walls were now crumbling away as had the ceiling, and I only hoped that the structure would hold long enough for me to get the boys out.

I put my coat back on and stepped onto the makeshift platform and could easily lift the boys up. I turned around to see that Marcus was now standing with the entire group, clustered around the bed. "Since you're the only one who can see or hear me, you're going to have to get them up here where I can lift them to Virgil's war lance . . ."

He yelled up at me. "They can!"

Cupping a hand to my ear, I leaned down. "They can what?"

"They can see the war lance, and they can see you too."

"How is that?"

Yelling over the roar of the fire, he shrugged. "I don't know, I'm just a kid!"

I glanced up at Virgil, who yelled down. "It is as I feared, the longer we are here, the more likely we are becoming of this place!"

Pointing at Ma'heo, who stood beside Marcus, I gestured for him to help. "C'mon, you're first."

Ma'heo stepped up onto the plate, and I grabbed him by the waist, lifting him to the point where Virgil had lowered the lance. The boy stared at me as he wrapped his arms around it and the giant lifted. "You are real . . ."

The other boys exclaimed in wonder, crowding in closer for their turn, the heat in the room intensifying. The building creaked and moaned as the flames consumed it, and if not for the hole in the ceiling where the smoke continued to funnel out, I was sure the boys would all be dead by now.

I lifted the next boy and watched him disappear as if I were hoisting him up through a tornado. I grabbed the next child and the next until we'd established a pretty good rhythm, all the time trying to do my best to forget the danger of our situation before looking down to see that Marcus was the only one left. "You're it?"

He stepped up on the platform but then pointed toward the other end of the dormitory. "There's one more, but he won't come."

I nodded. "Okay, we'll get you out of here first and then I'll go get him." I watched as Virgil pulled up the lance, elevating Marcus from the room. "Are you okay up there?"

Virgil's great head appeared again, along with a ring of the boys' sooty faces. "That is thirty, there is one more?"

I held up a finger. "I'll be right back."

The walls were still crumbling and some of the timbers and studs were falling inward with all the beds on fire, making it difficult to navigate in the direction Marcus had indicated.

Moving forward, I called out. "There's nothing to be afraid of, I'm going to get you out!"

There was no response as I made my way around the other potbelly stove and could see someone curled up on the floor against the chained gate.

It was at that moment that the windows burst out of their casings, the heat from the fire expanding them into the frigid air outside with shards of glass and flame rushing back in, reinvigorated by the cool oxygen.

Ducking my head, I ran forward, gripping the shoulder of the huddled boy and turning him toward me.

It was the trustee, Ty.

"C'mon, we've got to get going."

Without a word, he snarled and from nowhere produced a large kitchen knife, jabbing it toward me as I fell backward.

"What are you doing?"

He slowly stood, holding the knife at the ready. "It is coming for me."

"Who?"

His jaw clenched as he held the knife out. "I have served it well, and it won't leave me here to die."

The room was rapidly collapsing, the flames becoming more and more unbearable. "You mean Spellman—he's long gone."

Ty sliced at the air between us, his eyes glowing the same as the superintendent's had, rapturous, erratic, and insane. "I thought you were a part of it, that you were here to save me, but you're not. You're just another lost soul waiting to be fed upon."

More incendiary debris fell from the ceiling and walls. "Ty, we've got to get out of here . . ."

"It's too late." He pointed the knife past my shoulder, to the room behind me. "It's already here."

I slowly turned and could now see the smoke pulling away from the hole in the ceiling where Virgil's lance hung, waiting for us.

The smoke and fire began circling at the far end of the room in the same vortex I'd seen out on the frozen lake with the bear, the petals blooming at the center, the same petals that would soon rotate out like shark's teeth, changing into the thousands if not millions of grasping hands.

I watched as the flaming debris and cloth flew toward it, disappearing in its maw as it grew to fill the entire hallway. The rushing sound of the fire faded away and the only thing I could hear was my own breathing.

I turned back to Ty. "You fed the missing boys to that thing with Spellman?"

He took a step toward me, knife leading the way. "You don't understand."

"It was you, you're the one that killed Madie."

"I was young when I got here, and Mr. Spellman took me under his wing—he allowed me to see the world for what it truly is, that sacrifices have to be made." He smiled. "We're all going to its domain."

Over my shoulder I could now see that the thing was beginning to take full shape. I turned back as he advanced with the knife. "I don't want to hurt you, Ty . . ."

He drew the knife back. "Alive or dead, it takes us all."

I could feel my legs bracing to move forward even though I had no idea what it was I was preparing to do. Instead I just went into the autopilot that had saved me a couple of times before and watched as things unfolded.

He swung, and I stepped forward, bringing my arm up to stop him, and then grabbing the back of his neck and bending him forward as I drew my knee into his body. The blow lifted him off the ground, and he collapsed.

I held him, keeping him from falling to the floor as he caught his breath, but then felt his arm drop. Throwing myself back from him, I tripped and fell into the second stove behind me, scattering its parts and coal across the floor as the blade lashed out and continued in an upward swipe, missing my chin by inches.

I grabbed his knife arm and held, finally bending his wrist back until he dropped it. With little choice, I folded up the fingers of my hand and pounded a fist into the side of his head.

He fell limp, and I picked up the knife and hoisted him onto my shoulder before turning and confronting the creature that was devouring the room.

The lance hung there through the hole in the ceiling, and through the deafening silence I could hear Virgil yelling down at me, almost as if I was underwater. I stood there for a moment, gauging the distance and figuring I'd get two strides before hitting the bed and leaping up. If I missed, however, I'd be flying right into the mouth of the Éveohtsé-heómése.

I looked around another time and wondered if Virgil would be able to withstand the impact of the two of us grabbing hold of the lance at speed.

God hates a coward.

It felt like slow motion as I pushed off, realizing I was only going to get one chance to escape. Thundering forward, I could feel the momentum of the thing pulling us as Ty began moving on my shoulder. Ignoring him, I felt my boot strike the edge of the bedframe as I pushed us up and stretched both hands out to capture the lance.

The momentum of our flight pushed us even closer to the thing, hanging at a thirty-degree angle, and I expected Virgil to let us go at any second. Our legs dangled toward the hands as they reached for us, but there was a jolt as the lance jerked again. We were stopped and then pulled away and drawn farther up as the lance bent, becoming more perpendicular to the hole in the ceiling as the giant began pulling us upward.

It was then that Ty drew his head back and began scrambling to get loose.

I could feel the lance as it stopped moving, the weight of us becoming more active as Virgil attempted to drag us to safety.

Ty screamed. "Let me go, let me go!"

He landed a particularly vicious knee to my chest, and as I gasped, he slipped from my arm, my hand ahold of his as he swayed and spun, the mouth of the Éveohtsé-heómése directly below him, thousands of hands reaching up.

He looked at me, a beatific smile on his face.

"Don't let go," I said.

And he did.

I watched him fall into the many hands, and they pulled him in, smothering him at the same time as the unsated hands, all of them, reached out for the tips of my boots.

The jolt of the lance came again, and I felt myself being pulled upward toward the hole in the ceiling as the many hands still attempted to grab at me. The lance continued to ascend, and I was just getting to the edge as I reached out with my free hand in an attempt to get my shoulders through.

The hole was barely large enough, but I got past the edge and flattened my arms onto the floor, trying to climb the rest of the way out.

There was a crowd around the hole, but with the flames backlit behind them, I couldn't make out who they were. I assumed it was the boys and Virgil, which was confirmed when a powerful set of hands grabbed the shoulders of my coat and began lifting me.

I'd just started to come free, when there was a tremendous tug, but this time in the other direction.

Feeling my arms jammed upward as I was dragged back into the burning room below, I looked up into the face of the giant as he strained to hold me. "Virgil?"

—And I was gone.

12

Having dragged Artie's body from the water, Vic could feel her core temperature dropping. There was an emergency kit in the bed of the crashed truck that she might still be able to get to, but that meant climbing back into the water.

Propping him up against the trunk of a twisted silver willow, she peeled back an eyelid and listened to his short, labored breaths and was glad he was unconscious. Glancing down at his still duct-taped abdomen, she shook her head, thinking about how much of the unsanitized creek water must've gotten into his ruptured lung. "You can't catch a break, can you?" Then she looked up at the blackened hillsides, only slightly darker than the endless sky, getting an idea of her situation. "And fuck, neither can I."

She pulled her cell phone from her jacket pocket and placed it on the ground beside him. Then she stood and braced herself, quickly wading back into the freezing water, the ice around the truck now floating downstream. She felt her way to the tailgate, unfortunately unable to reach it without ducking her head under water.

With a growl, she dunked her head and reached up into the overturned truck bed to pull open the plastic box and take out the sealed liner. Then she lifted her face from the water, shook her head, and struggled through the soft bottom to get to the safety of the bank, where the thick mud surprisingly provided an amount of insulation that at least kept her legs from freezing.

She unzipped the liner, pulling out an emergency blanket and tucking it in all around Artie.

His lips moved, and he mumbled, "Where are we?"

"Truly and deeply fucked, that's where we are, Artie."

His eyes flickered and, seeing the truck overturned in the stream, he chuckled. "It certainly appears that way." His eyes shifted to her as she picked up the cell phone, shaking it and then hitting the button to fire it up. "Think it survived the swim?"

"Waterproof case, asshole." She held it up for him to see and then stared at the screen. "You mind telling me why it is you touched my neck while I was driving?"

"I was trying to tell you that I wasn't going to make it to a hospital." He watched her, waiting for the screen to appear. "You don't like me very much, do you?"

She glared at him. "The guy that just tried to kill my boss—yeah, I don't like you so much."

"More than just a boss, I think."

"Shut up, I'm trying to save your life." The screen illuminated her face.

"Do you ever think about the things you'll miss, those brief moments before you die?"

"You're not going to die."

He studied the flowing water. "I suppose we all think it will be these dramatic, bigger-than-life moments . . ." He chuckled. "Bigger-than-life, that's good."

"You're using up valuable breath, and you don't have any to spare."

"But it's not, at least not for me."

She held the cell phone up at arm's length to get a signal but then lowered it in disgust and looked at him. "You know, I like you a lot better when you're unconscious."

"I have made some very large mistakes with my life."

Replacing the phone in her pocket, she began rifling through the emergency supplies. "No shit."

"But I think I may have struck upon something that might make up for it."

She stood. "Artie, I'm going to have to hike up one of these hills and see if I can either see a house or get a signal."

He raised a hand to her. "Please? Sit with me a moment more?"

"Artie, every second I spend monkeying around with you is another second I'm not saving Walt."

"You love him."

She took a breath. "Yeah, okay? I do."

"Why?"

Her hip kicked sideways. "I don't have time for this."

"Love is a strange thing to me; I don't think I've ever known it. My mother loves me, but that is a mother's love, which is very different from any other; she is similar to you: ferocious." He coughed drool with a little creek water stringing from his lips. "It is the one thing I'd like to understand before I go."

"He completes me, he makes me whole, and I've never been that my entire life. You want to talk about the wind and shit? If I'm a body of water, he's my calm, the thing that gets me thinking about other things than myself and believe me that's a relief." She kneeled, reached out, and, cupping his chin in her hand, looked into his face. "You're not going to die you buttersnap fucktard, because if you do, I don't find him, and that is a no-go. Capisce?"

"You truly are beautiful."

"There is something seriously wrong with you." She stood. "Look, you stay here and talk to yourself, and I'll be back—got it?"

She shook her head and walked away. Artie called after her at the top of his diminished voice. "I know where he is."

The wind was stronger on the ridge where he stopped to take a breath and give his leg a few seconds of relief. He was sure he had heard the noise from up here, but why would Riley have come back to the place where they had apprehended Artie?

Was it possible they were working together?

With the newest revelation, it was unlikely.

Henry stood there listening, the wind scouring the ridge as he took another step, waiting for the cloud cover to move on as he lowered the flame on the Coleman and held the hissing lamp at his side.

What would it be? Likely a gun, but you could never be sure.

It would not be a bad place to die, but not at the hands of such as this, and not before finding his friend.

He was out there somewhere, he could feel him standing there upright with his eyes gleaming, unnaturally alert, the sentry against whatever it was.

His voice was deep, stirring, and dangerous—but it was reluctant too. He allowed it as if he were compelled to communicate with whatever it was, even though he would be robbed of the power he stored for a higher use. "I am here."

"Yes, you are."

Turning, the Bear could see an outline amid the stone rubble, standing inside what would have been the school. Riley stood differently, almost transformed, straighter and more confident, and he was not alone.

———

I woke up on a hard, cold surface with the knife still in my hand.

I blinked twice and then pushed myself up on my elbows, all I could see was white in all directions. "This is getting monotonous."

Slowly, my eyes started to focus, and I could see a horizon forming, a familiar dark strip miles away that separated the absolute flat from a high ridge. Even with the wind, I could still make out the tracks and scuff marks on the frozen lake in the valley where the Éveohtsé-heómése had swallowed the bear. I sat up and my hat skittered across the ice to the east, flipping over and cartwheeling away.

But what had happened to me? Is this all that happens when you fall into the Wandering Without alive? You just hop, skip, or jump to another location at the same time?

I stared at the knife in my hands. Something about metal . . . Something that Virgil had said about metal when he had replaced the spearhead on the war lance with the one he'd fashioned from the barrel stave.

It doesn't like metal.

Metal.

The thought shot through my head like a streak of chain lightning—Madie, the young woman from back at the school. Her teeth had been pulled, likely after her death, and even though I'd returned to Spellman's office only a short time later, there had been no sign of her body.

For that thing to take its victims there mustn't be any metal on them, but will a knife be enough to do the trick? I lifted the weapon in my hand and studied it—had that thing released me because of the knife?

Reaching into my pockets, I took out the silver dollars that I'd collected back in Fort Pratt at a time that hadn't even happened yet. Counting them, I dropped each heavy coin from one hand into the next and then sat there looking at them.

Maybe with the knife and the coins it had been too much metal.

I wondered if I had metal fillings—I'd have to look.

I slowly stood, dropping the coins back into my pocket and tucking the knife in my belt as I started off for my hat.

The brim of my hat had lodged itself in a drift, and I didn't have to chase it all the way to North Dakota. Kneeling, I swiped it from the snow and then cranked it down on my head, flipped up the collar of my sheepskin coat, and retrieved my gloves from the pockets. I tugged them on, buttoned my coat, took a deep breath through my mouth, and started to head back to the boarding school.

That's when I noticed there was something out there, a dark shape in the landscape.

I'd just taken the first step when I saw a figure in the distance, picking its way down from the ridge and following the flat on the same trail that Toga Kte and I had taken when we'd pursued Virgil and the children. If it continued its current path, it would be to me in a matter of minutes.

Even with the limited visibility, I could see it was a person on horseback, and I was willing to bet I knew the horse since the poor bay appeared to be the only one in the county.

I might not know the bundled figure in the saddle, but I could make a guess.

As they continued toward me, I started off in that direction, figuring I'd meet them halfway.

They were about a hundred yards away when the horse saw

me and balked. I opened my arm as a show of meaning no harm, so that when the rider gigged him again, the bay continued forward.

The individual had his head down, tucked in a great coat with a scarf covering up his face and a hat was pulled down low. Evidently, he trusted the horse to know where they were going or didn't care where he was heading.

The horse stumped up to me, cautious on the ice, and then pulled to a stop, allowing a few strides to keep between us as he recognized me.

The man gigged the horse again, and it started forward, but I reached out a hand and gently touched the velvety nose. "I'd appreciate it if you didn't run me over."

He started and then pulled the scarf down to see me if he could. "Goodness, stranger. What are you doing out here on a night such as this?"

I placed a hand on the reins and moved in closer. "Aren't you headed in the wrong direction?"

I nodded west. "Helena is that way."

There was a long pause as he dropped the reins and reared back a bit, adjusting his glasses with the fingers that protruded through his fingerless gloves. "Do I know you?"

"No, but I know you."

"Do you, now? Then perhaps you could tell me why I'd be going to Helena?"

"To report the burning of the Fort Pratt Industrial Indian Boarding School."

From under the wide brim, he stared at me. "And what, sir, do you know about that?"

"Everything, I know everything."

His hands now free, I figured he would go for the big revolver from his pocket, and I was right. Lurching sideways, he attempted to wrestle the thing clear. I was at a disadvantage attempting to reach over the pommel, but I was able to grab his forearm before he could draw the big weapon.

Struggling with firearms can be a tricky thing because usually during the process the thing will go off—and it did.

Fortunately, the way Spellman was seated, the revolver was resting on his leg and pointing out and to the side to keep him from shooting the horse, which as I understand had been a common occurrence.

At the thunderous report, the horse leapt forward, knocking me to the side as it galloped off with Spellman lying fully back.

Rolling, I watched as the bay tried to turn but slipped on the glass-like ice underneath the snow, causing him to slide to one side, his legs kicking as he tried to gain some amount of traction.

Spellman came unseated and rolled across the animal's rump, and the horse crashed onto the frozen surface of the lake.

There was a tremendous thump as the ice began cracking in all directions, but the horse was able to scramble and began running again, loping off another hundred yards toward the shore before stopping and turning to look back at us from a safe distance, the reins draped on the ground.

Standing, I massaged my shoulder where I'd hit the hard surface and then looked to my right where Spellman's Colt lay in the snow.

Walking over, I picked up the double-action and started toward the superintendent but paused when I saw his saddlebags lying a little farther off. I veered over and picked them up, throwing them over my shoulder.

As I got closer, I could see blood on the snow, but I wasn't sure if it was from the man or if the horse had been injured. "Friend, I say . . ." I got my answer as Spellman's hand came up feebly, pulling his coat away. "I appear to have shot myself in the leg."

"I'd say you are correct." Staying out about twenty feet, I surveyed the damage. "Worse than that, I'd say you shot yourself in the knee."

Spellman lay there unmoving on the cracks that seeped water, sprawled on the flat surface on his back, one knee raised, looking all the world like a fly caught in a spider's web.

"I bet it hurts."

"You would be correct." He attempted to straighten it and grimaced. "For what little good it will do me . . ." He paused to absorb the pain. "Who, may I ask . . ." He paused again. "Are you?"

I looked off in the distance where the horse was now pawing at the ground, looking for grass. "I'm not so sure these days."

"Excuse me?" He jerked and then grimaced again, breathing through his mouth, the clouds of condensation fogging his face and subsequently the glasses that sat crooked. "I'm assuming that's an attempt at levity. You'll have to excuse me for not laughing."

"I wouldn't be either, if I were you."

"Is that my gun you're holding?"

I held the Colt up for examination. "It is."

"And my saddlebags."

I slipped them off my shoulder and placed them over my knee. "Yes."

"I don't suppose you'd like to give them back to me."

I sighed, wondering what I was going to do with him. "I am not in the giving vein today."

"Richard III, act IV, scene 2 . . . A man of letters." He attempted to sit up, but the exertion was too much, and he slumped back on the ice. "And what vein would you be in to assist me?"

I thought about it and then just gave him my most honest reply. "None."

He lay there for a moment. "What if I were to tell you . . ."

"I already know what's in these saddlebags."

He lay there for a long while and then finally spoke in a soft voice. "So, this is a robbery."

"I prefer to think of it as just deserts."

"Just deserts, here in the wilderness? Surely, you're joking, there's no justice here."

I examined the Colt. "Was this the sidearm you used with the Seventh at Wounded Knee Massacre?"

"Apropos, eh?" He clutched the leg, rolling over to one side to face me. "In the first instance, it was not a massacre, it was a battle."

"Two hundred women and children killed?"

He studied me through the fogged glasses. "To rid yourself of fleas, you must first destroy the lice."

"You really are a charmer, you know that?" I studied him back. "Is that where you first saw that thing, the Éveohtsé-heómése, whatever it is?"

For the first time, he smiled. "You've witnessed its glory?"

"I don't know if I'd call it that."

"Then what would you call it?"

Ignoring his question, I posed one of my own. "Why don't you tell me about it?"

He choked a laugh. "Why should I, if you're just going to leave me here to die?"

"Maybe you can convince me."

His head fell back as he lay there, looking up at the ghostly gray clouds in the torpid darkness and saying nothing.

I stood. "All right then, you have a nice trip."

His voice was so faint I barely heard it. "Wait."

Adjusting the saddlebags on my shoulder, I turned back to look down at him again.

"On one condition."

"Which is?"

"You kill me." He took a breath and then let it out slowly with the words—"I've seen what happens when it takes you alive, and I don't particularly cherish the thought of that."

"Like I said, maybe you can convince me."

He stared at the sky. I was preparing to turn and walk away for the last time just as he spoke. "I have no one else to tell my stories, so I am thinking that you will have to do."

The wind was still blowing, and his voice was thin, carried away with the wind, but there was enough of it there that I could hear him, although the words sounded as though they came from another room and certainly from another time.

"Back in '90, it was just after Christmas, the twenty-eighth I believe, when we came upon the Miniconjou camp twenty miles northeast of the Pine Ridge Agency near Wounded Knee Creek." His head rolled to one side, his dead eyes staring at me. "Big Foot, the chief, informed our scouts that his people would come quietly."

I said nothing.

"The next day Colonel Forsyth met with them to confiscate their weapons, but I cautioned him that we should herd them into a clearing and surround them with our cavalry, along with the Hotchkiss guns." He stopped for a moment to try to breathe and then continued. "Once we'd grouped them together and started taking the weapons, there was a shot and we opened fire . . ." His eyes came back to mine. "Have you ever seen what a Hotchkiss gun can do to a human being?"

I still just watched him.

"Fifty two-pound shells a minute, and we had four of them, mind you. Men with no weapons, women and children attempting to escape by running into a ravine . . . All of them, lying there in the snow. There was a trench dug, but we left them, using the survivors as bait. Even days later, others would sneak back in to carry away family or friends—we shot them too." He laughed. "I was part of the burial detail and spoke a bit of their devil language, so at night I would walk out there and converse with the dying, sometimes shooting a few for the pleasure of it."

He took a deep breath, sighing. "There was one, Sits Straight, one of the original Ghost Dancers—he denied it, but I had seen him before and knew who he was. I asked him about the dancing and all-powerful medicine that they had hoped to conjure in their sacred shirts. I asked him what he thought as he looked upon his dead people."

He smiled at that thought. "He said that he and his people would be joining the Great Spirit, but in a moment of weakness he told me that as long as he remained with the others that he would be safe. He admitted that he had done questionable things in this life, but as long as he did not die alone, he would be safe from the Éveohtsé-heómèse." His head turned, and he looked at me, enraptured. "That was the first time I had ever heard the name."

He struggled to sit upright and rested on his elbows. "I thought it a lie, but his statement was so fervent that I decided to test it and dragged him by his broken arm away from the others, over a ridge and off by himself. He struggled, but he was mortally wounded, shot through the guts, and it was only a question of time." He looked at me. "I wanted to see it."

"And did you?"

His eyes fell to the snow between us. "It was very late, and I sat there listening to him moaning, when suddenly something miraculous began happening, he commenced singing a death song. I suppose he thought it would protect him, or maybe he had accepted his fate and decided to meet it."

He shook his head. "The first thing I noticed was the absolute lack of sound, no wind, no moaning or crying of the other miscreants or the soldiers playing cards and talking among themselves—the only sound was the song of the old man. At first, I thought he was playing some kind of trick on me, and I thought I'd end it." He gestured toward the revolver in my hand. "I raised that very pistol and pressed it to his head, having grown weary of the small, sad, and miserable spectacle. And that's when I first saw it . . ."

His eyes came back to mine. "A swirling, florid spinning that opened up into a great maw. I remember slipping and falling as I scrambled away from it, sliding down the embankment as the world began spinning and consuming everything, including Sits Straight. I watched as he was swallowed up by the thing, something more powerful than anything I had ever known—and I knew I had found God."

"You're insane, you know that?"

"Oh, no, quite the contrary." He cocked his head. "So, you're not a believer then?"

I stood. "I don't know what it is, but I know it's not what you think it is."

"You have a great deal to learn."

"Maybe, but at least I'll have the time to educate myself." I shifted the saddlebags on my shoulder, feeling the guilty weight in them.

The expression on his face changed as he breathed a laugh and then adjusted his glasses. "You intend to leave me here?"

"Yep."

"Alone?"

"Oh, you're not alone." Feeling incredibly tired, I scanned the horizon. "It's out there, I can feel it." I scrubbed my eyes with a thumb and forefinger. "I guess after you've been around it for a while you get a feeling for it, or maybe now that it's taken a bite out of me, I've gotten to know it better." I lodged the revolver in my belt with the knife. "All I can tell you is that it's not divine, I know that—it's just an empty nothingness that feeds itself in an attempt to sate its hunger, a craving that's been eating it from the inside for as long as it has existed, a ravenous appetite that leaves nothing." Turning back to him, I gave a half-hearted wave and began walking away. "All I know is that it's something I want no part of, in this world or the next."

He called after me. "We had an agreement."

"You didn't convince me, so I'm leaving."

"I'll wager you bourbon to sump water that you won't, as a God-fearing man . . ."

"God-fearing, that's rich coming from you." I started to turn.

He swallowed. "I . . . I don't fear it, you know."

"Really?" I stared at him for a moment and then turned and walked away. "Got any metal on you?"

He still cried out. I didn't want to turn, but I knew I was going to have to, not because I wanted to see it, but because I didn't.

I planted my boots in the snow and just stood there as the sound drained from the world, and I knew it was here, that it had arrived.

My hands grew still, and a coolness came over my face like a caul.

Turning only my head, I could see Spellman attempting to drag himself from the depression in the ice, but try as he might, he couldn't. I watched as the ice began to undulate, small tufts of powder springing up in tiny explosions as the plates of ice crashed against each other.

I could feel the wind changing direction around me, rushing into my back, and pulling me toward Spellman, but I braced my feet and just stood there, this time watching the swirling force throw both the man and the shards of ice upward like a waterspout that had expanded, twirling the great chunks of ice.

I took a step forward.

The hands began forming below him, reaching up through the water and catching on his body and clothes as they slowly began dragging him down into the icy water.

The churning formed a funnel at the center, and I watched as he turned his face to me one last time before being dragged below when another explosion of water and ice shot into the air like a geyser.

The great slabs of water fell back to earth and splattered on the ice. Whitecaps frothed against one another as the water began settling and then, finally, a trail of bubbles drifted to the now still surface.

I turned to go, but then gave the hole one last look before turning for the last time and walking away.

By the time I got to the shore the horse had joined me, like any herd animal, figuring the chances of the two of us making it were far greater than one—or knowing he was a lot faster than I was and that I might distract anything that would eat us long enough for him to get away.

Figuring I'd save the old fellow, I'd slung the saddlebags over the saddle and trudged along, leading him by the reins. I'd made it to the knife-edge of the ridge and had just started over the top when I saw something glowing in the distance. It was the school, still burning.

Trailing back in the path the horse had cut with Spellman, we took the direct route and had just started to climb the rise to the bluff where the conflagration lit up the surrounding area, casting an orange light on everything. There was something between me and the fire, a large personage with a group of smaller figures following it.

I stopped at the outcropping where I'd seen what I first thought was a bear and waited as that same bear lumbered up, resting a large sack on the ground between us. "Hello, Lawman."

"Howdy, Virgil." I gestured where thirty children trailed along behind him. "Looks like you've got a following."

He smiled, resting the end of his war lance beside his foot. "All of them."

"You don't look surprised to see me."

"The knife."

"Is that what did it?"

"I can only guess."

"Toga Kte?"

"I could not find him."

I nodded. "Where are you headed?"

"South, to Crow Country—the children will be safe there."

Reaching over, I handed him the bay's reins. "Here, you might need her for some of the little ones."

He stroked the horse's nose and then noticed the saddlebags. "What are these?"

I patted the bay's flanks. "A donation."

"I will not ask how you got it." He glanced behind himself, at the orange flames consuming the boarding school, the upper floors collapsing with a crashing noise as sparks licked and rose into the darkened sky. "Where will you go?"

"Back, where I have unfinished business."

He studied me. "Business with what?"

"I'm not sure."

He reached out the same finger, tapping my chest where the leather-bound booklet rested in my inside pocket. "Perhaps you should now read the words I have left for you." He studied me and then finally smiled as he reached behind him and scooped up one of his young charges, seating him on the saddle.

"Hello, Ma'heo."

The boy smiled at me. "Thank you for saving us."

"My pleasure."

Virgil deposited Marcus behind Ma'heo, and the young man stared at me from over the younger boy's shoulder. "Maybe you should come with us."

"Oh, I think I have some work to do."

He looked behind him at the crumbling building. "That place is gone."

"No, somewhere else."

Marcus allowed a tear to streak from his eye. "This is not a bad world."

"No, but it's not mine." I reached up and took the hands of

both boys as words bubbled up from my throat, words I didn't think I knew but evidently did. "Stay calm, have courage, and wait for signs." Stepping aside, I looked up at the giant. "See you on the other side?"

He said nothing.

I waved at them and continued toward the burning building.

The heat was tremendous, and the snow was melting quickly. I avoided the stable side of the building, which appeared to be burning brighter, and approached the corner of the structure where I could see the front lawn and the opening that led to the interior square in which I'd first arrived.

I continued in that direction, giving the burning building room as I came to a bench beside the archway at the fence that surrounded the place.

There was someone seated on the bench with a rifle, leaning there as he fussed with a rucksack.

"Toga Kte."

Starting, he pushed his hat up and looked at me, his hand resting on the rifle. "Hello?"

Backlit by the fire, I was pretty sure he couldn't make me out, not that it would've done any good. "Going somewhere?"

He stood. "Do I know you?"

"No, I'm just . . . passing through." I looked back at the fire. "What about you, where are you headed?"

"Helena. As you can see, there's been a fire that needs to be reported to the state, but first I need to find someone."

"Madie?"

He stared at me. "Yes."

"She's dead." His face moved as if I'd struck him, but he didn't say anything. "Ty killed her, and Spellman killed Crawley."

"I thought something had happened to her." His face dropped as he looked at the ground between us. "You're sure she's dead?"

"Yes, I think she stumbled in on Spellman as he was emptying the safe in his office and then Ty killed her."

"And Crawley?"

"He was trying to blackmail Spellman, but the superintendent shot him."

He suddenly looked resolute, reaching for the rifle leaning against the bench. "Then I need to go find Spellman."

"I already have."

He moved to the side in an attempt to get a better look at my face. "What does that mean?"

Pulling open my coat, I handed him the Colt revolver and the knife. "Here, take these. Where I'm going, I don't think I'll be needing them."

He stared at the revolver. "This belonged to the superintendent."

"He's dead as well, and no one will ever find the body. He was carrying the money, but I took it and gave it to my friend who is taking care of the children."

He stuffed the armament into his belt and lifted the rifle up, holding it between us. "Who are you, and how do you know all of this?"

"That's not important—what is important is that you get to Helena and tell them what happened here. Somebody has to tell the story."

"They won't believe me."

"They'll have to, you're the only one left."

There was a noise, and we both turned to watch the bell tower collapse into the square, flames flying out the windows and doors. We ducked and covered our faces with our arms and listened to the bell, which tumbled and echoed off the stone walls as it crashed to the ground.

I glanced to the west. "You better get going, you've got a long way to go before sunup."

"You're sure she's dead?"

"I'm sorry." I sighed and then placed a hand on his shoulder. "Get going and tell her story, all their stories."

He nodded, lacing the rucksack onto his back. He started to go but then stopped and turned to look back at me. "You . . . You're the voice, the voice I heard out there on the ridge."

I stared at him awhile and then laughed. "Yep."

He studied the side of my face. "Are you a ghost?"

I thought about it and figured I wasn't, as tired as I was. "I don't think so, I haven't died, yet . . . I don't think."

He stood there for a moment more and then turned, hobbling away before stopping and turning back to me again. "I need to know your name."

"I wish I knew for sure what it was."

He nodded and then turned, limping down the road at a surprising clip.

I turned back to the building, watched it burn for a while, and then took a few steps, positioning myself at the center and then pulled the leather booklet from my pocket and opened it, taking the candy card from the pages, and turning it over, reading the two names Virgil had printed there.

A flood of images, words, and memories swarmed into my mind in an instant as I stood there unmoving and attempting to catch my breath.

I stared down the road at the young man limping away and called after him. "Walt!"

He turned to look at me.

"My name is Walt Longmire."

He nodded and then turned, continuing.

There was no owl as I let my eyes play over the sculpted snow on the landscape that somehow looked less desolate and more natural. Then I stepped through the archway—and disappeared.

13

"Where is he?"

Artie's voice rose, but his body, seeming to have accepted his fate, was conserving the energy that would allow him to speak. "I'm not the one you need to be worried about."

Vic kneeled beside him. "What's that supposed to mean?"

"The young man, Riley—he's not what you think."

She leaned in closer and then raised an eyebrow. "I think he's a moron."

"Possibly, but he's more than that." His pupils wandered a bit, finally finding her face. "I know you think I'm the reason he came here, but I'm not." He wheezed the next words. "At least not the final reason."

"Where is he?"

"It was the only way to save him . . ."

"Where?"

"Even now, he is fighting a battle for not only his soul but the souls of others, and if he dies while trying to accomplish this, then he is lost."

She sighed in exasperation. "I swear, if you don't start making sense, I'm going to kill you myself."

He gasped, capturing a few more words to blurt out. "The

difficulty is that he will likely be unaware that he's fighting this battle."

"What are you talking about?"

"He won't know who to trust, and those he does are likely to betray him."

Pulling her weapon, she held it up for him to see. "Artie, I swear to God . . ."

"He knew things, things I didn't think he could possibly have known."

"Artie."

"Even me. He was trying to protect me, there at the end." He breathed for a moment, attempting to recoup his energies. "I led him here, I wasn't sure why but then it came to me that the only way to stop the Éveohtsé-heómése was through him, and I thought for him to do that I would have to kill him but that turned out to not be true." He shook his head, slightly disbelieving. "For some reason, it fears him and knows he can do it harm."

She grabbed him by the chin and locked her eyes on his. "Artie, I need you to focus. If you know where he is, I need that information."

"Maybe it sensed something in him, something that would warrant its own destruction."

"Artie, please."

He glanced at the Glock in her hand. "Manufactured from the ore of the earth, the machines, they turn off and the spark dies, leaving nothing alive . . . But what if they don't die, what if they are simply waiting to live again?"

"Please."

"Metal, even the bullet you put in me holds me fast to this world, keeping the Wandering Without from taking me." His eyes widened with the pain. "I thought that there was redemption in it, but there isn't, only a chaotic hunger. It is a devourer of worlds . . ." His eyes found hers again. "I'm going to need you to do something for me."

"What?"

"Look at my left wrist under the sleeve."

Lifting the torn thermal she revealed one half of a set of handcuffs, the chain dangling from his wrist. "Peerless 700." Her eyes returned to his. "These are Walt's."

"Yes. You have a key that will fit them?"

"Everyone in the department uses the same cuffs." She fished in her pocket, pulling out the keys. "Uncuff you?"

"Yes, quickly."

Doing as he asked, she rapidly took the cuff off the one wrist and then reached for his other. "Artie, why are we doing this?"

"He is endangered and needs help."

"I know that, so why are we fucking around with this shit?" Holstering the 9mm, she undid the other cuff, tossing them both to the side. "Now what?"

"Throw them in the water."

She stared at him. "What?"

"Throw them in the water."

Shaking her head, she took the cuffs and tossed them into the stream. "Now what?"

He smiled a sly smile as he hunched against the roots of the tree and fumbled with something. "The hard part."

"What's that?"

Pulling the Sig Sauer .380 from the inside of his boot, he aimed it at her face. "You will need to pull the bullet from my body."

———

"How you doin'?"

He said nothing—there being nothing to be gained by talk just yet.

"You lookin' for me?" He stepped forward where the ambient light from the moon shown on the side of his young, smirking face. "You know, I can't get over how stupid you were. I mean, didn't we even look alike?"

The Cheyenne Nation leaned against the rubble, his hand wrapped around one of the broken bricks—now the time to talk. "I had suspicions."

The two other men stepped forward, fanning out so as to not provide too easy a target. "Where's the woman?"

"Taking Artie to the Regional Hospital."

"He's not dead yet?"

"It would appear not."

He stepped over the rubble, coming closer. "I knew he was out here running around, but I figured he would've frozen to death by now. He got here before your friend, and we had a good time with him before your friend showed up. The big guy rescued him, you know; had him arrested and everything after the crazy fucker tried to kill him." He glanced around. "You find him yet?"

"Who?"

"Let's not be cute here. The sheriff."

The Bear smiled. "No, have you?"

Riley nodded, smiling. "I ran into him with the plow after he arrested Artie, but I guess I overdid it because I wasn't wearing a seatbelt and it knocked me out too. When I finally came around, they were both gone. I figured I'd just bury his truck and then go scrape up the bodies, but they didn't show. Artie's accounted for, but where the hell did the sheriff go?" He raised the tactical shotgun, casually aiming it at the Bear's midriff. "You wouldn't lie to me, would you? I mean, it'd be inconvenient if that bitch was running him to the hospital."

"Inconvenient for whom?"

"Well, for us, that's for sure." He laughed and nodded toward the two men who were now standing at the sides, about twenty feet away, their own weapons trained on him. "Not armed, are you?"

"One way to find out." His fingers tightened on the brick. "Riley Schiller."

The young man laughed again, looking down at the snow between them. "You the one that killed my father down in Billings?"

"Peter Schiller, the one who was blackmailing Jaya and Jeanie One Moon?" The Bear shook his head. "No, but I wish I were."

"So, it was that chickenshit Jimmy Lane?"

"Chickenshit enough to kill your father."

"Yeah, well we'll take care of him up in Deer Lodge."

Henry studied the men on either side, placing a boot up on the wall, lodging a heel there. "So, this would be the welcome wagon of the local chapter of the Brotherhood of the North?"

"Why, you lookin' to be an associate member?"

"Not particularly."

"Good, 'cause you're the wrong color."

"Chickenshit yellow?"

This time he didn't laugh, redirecting the shotgun at the Bear. "You know, I don't think you're appreciating the seriousness of your situation."

"Oh, I think I am." The brick came out of Henry's hand with the slightest of movement so that the men on either side didn't have time to respond as the Cheyenne Nation, winging the lantern, launched himself from the rubble toward Riley.

The lantern flew into the air as the brick struck the barrel, forcing it up as it went off, the young man stumbling backward as the Bear drove into him and they tumbled. The two men at the sides fired as the lantern crashed to the ground, one hitting the other one in the shoulder. "Stop shooting, stop shooting, you stupid assholes!"

The one shooter gripped his shoulder. "I'm hit."

The other ran forward and found Riley lying in the snow holding his bleeding face.

Henry Standing Bear and the shotgun, for all intents and purposes—gone.

The Oldsmobile was sitting at the side of the road with its windows partially lowered, idling exhaust into the frigid air. I stood and watched the young couple. They were arguing in the front seat.

I opened their door, sat in the back, and pulled the door closed behind me. "Howdy."

The young man fumbled trying to get his pistol out.

I patted the back of his seat. "Forget the gun, we've been through this before."

He stared at me. "We have?"

"Yep, last night." I blew into my hands, rubbing them together to warm them. "How was your drive?"

He looked at her and then back to me. "What?"

"The drive up from Denver, how was it?"

The tall, mop-headed blonde spoke up. "Do we know you?"

"You knew me last night when you gave me a ride." I looked out of the fogged windows. "At least I assume it was last night, but I've never seen it get truly light here, so who the heck knows?"

"We gave you a ride?"

"Yep. You also tried to borrow some money and when I didn't have any you tried to loan me your pistol. You said that every night you drive off heading north, but then every time you get tired and stop to sleep on the side of the road you end up right back here in Fort Pratt."

She leaned in closer. "And you know us?"

"Yep, your name is Heather, and I know both of you somehow, but I haven't put the pieces completely together." I looked at the young woman. "You play basketball, don't you?"

"Yeah."

"Somewhere, I've seen you play. It was the women's prison in Lusk, now that I can think about it."

"What about me?" He cocked his head. "What do you know about me?"

"Your name is Jamie, and you're a hothead, and . . ."

He studied me. "And what?"

"I think I killed you."

Now they both stared at me.

He cleared his throat. "Well . . . That's fucked up."

"It was something about a liquor store robbery, and I think I shot you after you shot me." I pulled off my sheepskin coat and rolled up a sleeve, showing him the tadpole-like scar on my forearm. "Here."

"You killed me."

"Yep."

Heather leaned in, a concerned look on her face. She put one arm along the back of the seat, and I noticed a scar at her wrist. "Did you kill me too?"

"I don't think so."

He shook his head. "There's only one problem—I'm still here."

"Maybe."

"What's that supposed to mean?"

"Maybe we're here, maybe we're not. You say you're in some kind of time loop where you keep driving off but wake up here every time you go to sleep. I've been here I don't know how long, and I've had even weirder things happen to me. The one thing I can tell you is the time, it's 8:17 p.m."

They both turned to look at the clock on the dash, which indeed read 8:17. "You noticed it too."

"I've been here for at least twenty-four hours and the time never changes, it's always 8:17 p.m.—you were the first one to bring it to my attention the last time we met."

"Maybe it's just the clocks . . ."

"No, not all of them, and there's something about the number thirty-one, but I think I've got that figured out."

"And?"

"I think it stands for the thirty-one children that disappeared at the school, but that doesn't have anything to do with you."

"So, I'm dead and that's the end of the story, huh?" He nodded at Heather. "But she's not dead?"

"I don't think so."

"Are you dead?"

"I'm not sure."

"So, I'm the only one that's dead, and this is hell?"

"Doesn't make much sense, huh?"

"Look, pops," he scratched his chin with the front site of the revolver, "I'm not a good guy, so the only place I'm going after I'm dead isn't gonna be pleasant . . ."

It was my turn to laugh. "You call this pleasant, going through the motions every day and night, nothing changing, waking up exactly where you started?"

He made a scoffing sound like a teakettle percolating. "Sounds like life to me."

"A shitty life."

The young man rested the pistol on the back of the seat, inclining the barrel toward me. "It might be time for you to get out."

He might've had more to say, but the words seemed to slip his mind when the muzzle of a nickel-plated Colt Python was stuck in his ear. "You wanna hand me that gun?"

I slowly turned my head till I could see the flat-brimmed highway patrolman standing outside the driver's door. He was holding his sidearm in his gloved hand. "Officer Womack."

His eyes never left the driver as he spoke to me. "I've met you before?"

I slumped in the back seat. "You know, I'm glad I made such an impression on everybody the last time I was here."

He ignored me and spoke to the driver. "Slowly take your finger off the trigger and wrap the fingers of your other hand around the barrel and hand it to me."

Jamie did as he was told and then started to turn in the seat.

"Did I say to move?"

He froze. "No, sir."

"Turn around and place both hands on the wheel. Now."

Doing as requested, the young man sounded apologetic. "Sorry, sir."

"Don't move." His head dipped, and he looked at the young woman who had her hands in the air. "Are you all right, ma'am?"

"Yes officer, thank you; we were just having a discussion."

"Looks like quite a discussion all right." He looked back at me. "You armed?"

"Nope, you took my .45 the last time we met."

He stared at me. "Excuse me?"

"Never mind."

He returned his attentions to the young man. "Got a driver's license?"

"Um, yeah . . ." He wrested it from his jeans and handed it to Womack, who read the name. "Jamie Fischer . . . You're from Denver?"

"Yeah."

"Where you headed?"

"North."

"Just north?"

"Yeah."

Womack stepped back. "Mr. Fischer, do you mind stepping out of the car please?"

"Officer Womack, do you think we could . . ." I started to open my door when he swiveled the gun toward me. "Easy, easy there." I pushed the door the rest of the way open and climbed out, keeping my hands in plain view. "They're just a couple of kids—why not let them go?"

He gestured with the revolver he'd confiscated. "Have you forgotten this?"

I shrugged. "Keep it. Hell, he won't mind, he gives it to everyone he meets."

He turned to Fischer. "That true?"

"Sure, keep it."

He glanced at me again and then handed Fischer his license. "There you go, Mr. Fischer, let's take it a little easier, huh?"

He tucked the license into his shirt pocket and started the car. "Thanks, officer."

I closed the door and stood there as Womack studied me with a questioning look. "You're not going?"

"Nope, I think I'll stick around." I ducked my head and waved. "Nice seeing you again, Heather." And then added. "Maybe I'll see you again."

We walked back to Bobby Womack's stealthy unit. "How long have you known them?"

I watched the twin taillights of the oversize Oldsmobile as they drifted into the swirling snow, punching dual holes in the non-night. "Forever, it seems."

"Can I give you a ride?"

"Sure." We both turned to look at a flurry of movement at the top of the archway where the great horned owl settled in and blinked down at us. "Howdy, Spedis."

He turned to look at me.

"You told me about him the last time we met—named for a petroglyph from the Columbia River valley in Washington, Spedis is the protector who guards against the water devils or demons that pull people away." I thought about Spellman and the frozen lake. "I'm wanting to stay on his good side."

Womack strolled ahead. "Sometimes you have friends you don't know you have in places you've never been." I stopped, and he turned to look at me again. "What?"

"That's the second time you've said that to me."

I looked down and could see two more large coins lying in

the tire tracks. Kneeling, I picked them both up and stood, examining them, flipping them in the palm of my hand, and listening to the clinking sound as I walked over and looked at Womack across the top of the Crown Vic. "Can I get you to do me a favor?"

"If it's within my power, certainly."

"Take your glove off and let me see you hold that gun with your bare hand."

He looked at me as the silence between us lengthened. "Is this some kind of joke?"

I continued to hold the coins in my hand. "Humor me."

His face grew more somber. "Why?"

"The only times I've seen you take off those gloves was to shake my hand and at the Vietnamese restaurant, and then you used the chopsticks and a wooden spoon." I tossed the coins in the air, catching them. "I've never seen you touch anything that's metal with your bare hands, trooper."

He stared at me. "We've eaten together?"

"Take off the glove and grasp the gun, or I don't get in the car."

He continued to study me but then sat the revolver on the metal surface before raising his hand in a flourish, splaying the fingers. He then tugged at the glove end of each digit before pulling the leather off and slapping it on the roof beside the gun. "Pick it up?"

"Yep."

His hand lowered, hovering over the pistol for a dramatic moment, and then he snatched it and held it pointed at the sky. "Is something supposed to happen? I mean, am I supposed to burst into flames or something?"

"Or something." I had to admit that I was a little disappointed as I opened the passenger door and climbed in. "C'mon, let's go."

He followed suit and hit the plunger, dumping the rounds onto the seat and tossing the revolver onto the dash before cranking the Ford to life. "You're sure you're not armed?"

"No, I told you . . ." Feeling at the small of my back, I paused and then spoke slowly. "As a matter of fact, I am."

His hand slipped to his sidearm as he half turned in the seat and looked at me.

I didn't move. "Easy."

"Two fingers?"

"Two fingers." I slipped the .45 from the pancake holster at my back and held it out to him.

He took the semiautomatic. "There are no firearms allowed in the city limits."

"Yep, I know from when it was a military installation—you told me."

He examined the piece he had handed me back before dropping the magazine, catching it in his other hand, and ejecting the one round from the action. "You don't have any more of these?"

"Nope, as far as I know." He gave me a look and then handed me back the gun. "Just a precaution until I find out who you are." He placed the magazine and loose round in the left pocket of his uniform shirt. "By the way, who are you—and don't tell me you've already told me."

"Walt Longmire."

"And what do you do, Walt Longmire?"

"I'm not absolutely sure, but I think I'm a sheriff."

He pulled the cruiser into gear. "Well, let's go find out."

"Do we really have to go through all that again?" I reached forward and put a hand on his arm, pulling the poster from my inside pocket and holding it up to him. "I'm looking for this girl, and she works at the theater here in town. You picked me up off the street almost in this exact spot just last night, or at least I think it was last night. I'd been wandering around asking questions about her when you brought me in, but there was no way to radio because the storm had knocked everything out including your two-way. You'd just gotten back from a terrible crash involving an oil truck, and I'm betting that's where you were just now."

He stared at me.

"And if you don't mind me asking again, why are you wearing a Wyoming Highway Patrol uniform here in Montana?"

He glanced down, I guess to reassure himself. "Hmm . . . You're the first one to ask me that."

"I asked you last time, but you didn't answer. Got one this time?"

He thought about it. "Not really."

"Something is messed up in this place."

He looked out into the empty road and then pulled away, driving toward the town.

"Bobby, have you ever heard of the Wind River Canyon?"

He blinked, but that was all before glancing over at me. "What?"

"It's a place down in Wyoming, near the middle of the state, an opposed two-lane that follows the Wind River. People say it's haunted."

"Really, by what?"

"You."

He took a moment, pulled the cruiser over, and turned to look at me. "Excuse me?"

"When I was here before, I couldn't seem to concentrate, but a friend of mine wrote some names down for me and I've been having these flashes of clarity."

"Look." He sighed. "How 'bout we get you someplace where you can talk to some people . . ."

"No. Listen to me, I'm not crazy and you know it. I can tell by the way you look at me when I tell you these things. You know something's not right."

He threw the car into park. "So, what are you saying?"

"I know this is going to sound nuts, but Bobby, you're dead."

He didn't move.

"I don't know how I know it, but you died in a fiery crash with an oil truck in one of the tunnels of the Wind River Canyon."

"You wanna run that by me again?"

"You're dead."

"What, you're some kind of seer—this is something that's going to happen in the future?"

"No, it already happened decades ago."

"Are you dead?"

"I don't know, but that kid in the Olds that just drove away, he's dead too."

"He die in a crash?"

"No, I killed him." I thought about it, trying desperately to get my head straight. "I shot him when I pulled him over after he robbed a liquor store and killed a man back in Wyoming. He put a bullet through my arm on the side of the road, and I shot him, and he died."

"The kid that just drove away . . ." He stared at his lap for a moment and then suddenly looked very sympathetic. "Okay. Look, we're gonna get you some help."

I turned, pulled the handle, got out of the car, and walked away.

The emergency lights flickered to life, and red and blue began streaking across the clear canvas of the snow. "Hey, I'm going to need you to get back in the car," Womack said, stepping out of his cruiser.

I turned and looked at him. "Can't you feel it? I don't know where this place is, but we're not supposed to be here." I took a step toward him and watched as his hand went to his sidearm. "I've never even met you, but I heard about what happened— how you sacrificed your life to save others. You're a hero, and I have no idea why you're here in this non-place." I swallowed, "Any more than I know why I'm here."

He pulled the .357 from his holster but held it loosely at his side.

"Honestly, do you remember coming here or how you got here?" I took another step to study him. "You say you came from a crash, but do you really remember driving back to this town?"

He looked off to the distance, but his hand still held the gun. "You say you were off somewhere. Where and when was that?"

I laughed. "You wouldn't believe me if I told you."

His eyes returned to mine. "You mean because all this crap so far has sounded perfectly reasonable?"

"Bobby, have you ever heard of the Éveohtsé-heómése?"

"The what?"

"The Éveohtsé-heómése."

"No. Is that a Native term?"

"Cheyenne—some kind of boogeyman, something to scare kids, but I think it might be more than that . . . Where I just came from, it literally swallowed people alive."

He stared at me. "A monster."

"No, not a monster; it doesn't have a form, per se."

"What does this thing look like then?"

"It's hard to explain, but I know it exists—I know it's out there."

"In this place where you were."

"No." I half turned, looking at the town of Fort Pratt. "It's here too, but it's different . . . Like it's constructed this place and populated it with people I know." I turned back to him. "Dead people."

"But you say we never met."

"No, but I was involved in an investigation that had something to do with you." I began reaching into my pocket when he raised the gun and pointed it at me. "Easy, I just want to show you something."

He lowered the pistol just a bit.

I pulled one of the heavy coins from my pocket and held it out to him. "Take a look at this."

He carefully took the coin and examined it. "Silver dollar, old."

"1888 to be exact, they call them Hot Lips silver dollars because of the double-strike minting error on her mouth."

He started to hand it back to me. "So?"

"Doesn't mean anything to you?"

"No. Should it?"

"It involves a case you were working on before you died." I took the coin and dropped it into my other hand with its brethren. "You leave them, everywhere you go."

"What are you talking about?"

I pointed at his car. "You move that vehicle forward a few feet and we'll find two more of these, one in each of the tire tracks." I pulled the remaining coins from my pocket. "I've already collected more than two dozen of the things."

He pursed his own lips, not looking me in the eye. "Okay, I think the situation here has changed, and I'm going to have to ask you to turn around and place your hands together behind your back."

I moved toward him. "Are you listening to what I'm saying?"

He stepped back, slowly raising the .357 between us. "I need you to turn around and . . ."

"You're arresting me?"

"I don't think I have any choice." He pulled the cuffs from his belt. "Turn around."

"Pull your car forward." I dumped the coins into my pocket and raised my hands. "I'll stand right here."

"You'll turn around and I'll cuff you, and put you in the back of the car, and then I'll pull forward. Deal?"

Not seeing any other option other than being shot, I turned and felt him adjusting the cuffs over my wrists. He then walked me over to the car, where he opened the door and took my hat off, tossing it inside. "Now you have to get in."

I did and then watched as he shut the door, walked around the front, and climbed into the driver's seat.

He pulled out onto the road and started toward town as I turned to look through the back window. "Hey . . ."

His voice called through the metal mesh that separated us. "I said I'd pull forward, not that I'd go back and look around for loose change."

———

I stared at the darkness of the inside of my hat in the hoosegow and listened as Womack continued to try to raise anybody on the two-way. "Are you going to be at that for very long, because I was thinking of getting some sleep."

He continued to dial up and down the scanner's range, but all he was getting was static, including from me.

I lifted my hat and looked at him. "You want to load me up and take me to the next biggest town and see if they've got anything on me?"

"Not in this weather." He tossed the mic onto the desk and leaned back, turning to look at me. "I'll wait until tomorrow; I'm sure they'll have the power back on by then."

"Five poles knocked out between here and Helena, thirty-one hours to get the power back, according to Martha, over at the café."

"How many places did you go before I picked you up?"

"That was on the previous visit."

"So, you keep saying . . . And where did you go in the meantime?"

I thought about it but figured I had nothing to lose in that he already thought I was crazy as a loon. "The boarding school."

He turned the office chair, placing his feet up on the desk. "Where I picked you up."

"In a different time period."

"A different time period."

"Yep."

He rested his face in the palm of one hand. "You know, just when I think you can't get any crazier."

"Well, anything worth doing . . ." I was about to continue when the phone on his desk rang.

"Aha! So much for your thirty-one hours." He picked it up. "Highway patrol substation." He listened for a moment and then stood. "You're sure?" He listened some more. "No, I'll be right there." He hung up the phone and began putting on his overcoat and hat.

I sat on the edge of the fold-down bunk. "Something up?"

"That Oldsmobile you were in just got hit by a snowplow, east of town."

I stood and walked over to the bars. "You're kidding . . ."

"No, I'm not."

"Take me with you."

"No."

"I want to see the bodies."

He stared at me. "I told you, no."

"Make sure there are bodies."

He finished getting ready and then started toward the door before noticing the look on my face. "I know they were friends of yours, but it happens."

He went out the door, closing and locking it, and then I heard the cruiser peel away, the sound of the big-block engine growing faint as it swept through the town.

"No." I stood there with my fingers wrapped around the steel bars. My theories of this place being a continuous loop had just been blown apart. "Not here, it doesn't happen here."

14

Staring at the gun he now held in his wavering hand, she shook her head. "You really have lost your mind, you know that, right?"

"I need you to do this, it's the only way." He stared up at her, having difficulty finding her face but then finally focusing on her eyes and directing the small semiautomatic there. "You must have a knife, a woman like you always has a knife."

Her gaze stayed on him as she glanced toward her right hand where the blade already jutted from her clenched fist, glistening in the partial moonlight like an exposed fang—he hadn't even seen her move.

"I don't want to hurt you, but I need you to do this."

"Then lower the Sig, 'cause there's only one thing I do to people who point guns at me."

"First, you promise to take the bullet out."

She stooped, pulling the medical kit from the bag, and taking out several packaged pads.

"What's that?"

Tearing them open, she stacked them together and looked at him. "Unless it's time for your period, I'm making some absorbent bandages for the incision."

"Good, good . . ." He leaned forward, handing her the gun and then touching a spot on his lower back. "I believe the slug settled here just beneath the skin."

Tucking the .380 in her pocket, she looked at him. "You're serious about this?"

"It's the only way."

"No, the only way is for me to run back toward Fort Pratt to see if I can get help there."

"I will be dead by then, besides, there is no help there for any of us."

She stared at him in the darkness, her voice even darker. "You don't get to die until we find Walt."

He coughed, spitting blood from his lips. "I may have no choice in the matter."

"You don't think me digging this bullet out of you is going to do you any good, do you?"

"It doesn't matter. Either way, it has to come out—trust me." He leaned forward again, pulling Henry's duster away. "No sense in ruining the coat."

Moving to the side, she studied his back. "I'd say that's the least of your worries." Shaking her head, she asked. "Where is it?"

"As . . . as near as I can tell, it's in my back at the point well below the shoulder blade, where it must've struck."

She reached down and ran her hand over his skin, feeling the protrusion. "Jesus, it's right there."

He nodded. "Yes, so it should come out easily enough."

"Not really." She leaned forward, looking him in the eye. "Are you sure you really want to do this? I mean, it's going to hurt like a sonofabitch, and as weak as you are from internal injuries and loss of blood, you're likely to go into shock and fucking die." She glanced at the knife in her hands. "I don't even have any way to sterilize this knife."

"Just so you know, if I die while we're doing this you will need to remove the bullet nonetheless."

Shaking her head, she reached down and placed the edge of the blade against his skin, quickly slicing with impeccable technique. He stiffened but didn't move as she worked the tip of the blade into his wound, attempting to catch the deformed slug and coax it out. "Damn it . . ."

He spoke between clenched teeth. "What?"

"The blood flow blocked my view and it slipped to the side, back under your skin."

"Cut it."

With a face, she did, catching her lip between her teeth. "Fuck!"

"What?"

"It slipped again."

"Cut it!"

She did, this time catching the bleeding metal with the knifepoint and then coaxing it from his flesh with a thumb and forefinger. Holding it up in her bloody fingers, she marveled at the weight of the lead slug. "This is not a 9mm."

He slumped to his side, resting his face on one of the tree roots that protruded from the creek bank, taking his time before answering. "No."

"Where's my bullet?"

"Grazed the lat muscle under my right arm."

"Does it hurt?"

"Yes."

"Good." She held the slug out to where he could see it with one eye. "So, whose is this?"

"Your friend."

"Walt."

"Yes."

"Why?"

He cleared his throat, his voice weak. "Like I said, I thought for my purposes he had to be dead, but as it has turned out he didn't have to be."

She was about to question him more when she noticed the amount of blood he was losing. Quickly, she placed the pads over the wound to stanch the blood. "You're bleeding."

"I . . . I assumed."

"No, I mean you're really bleeding." Bubbles formed and expulsed from the wound. "Artie, this wound opens into your lung too. You're going to need an occlusive bandage back here." Pressing the wound, she watched as the blood continued to saturate the pads and the froth increased. "Fuck!"

Calmly, he placed his hand over hers. "Go . . ."

"What?"

"Back . . . Go back to Fort Pratt." His voice gave out as he gestured for her to come near. She leaned forward as he whispered in her ear. "Go . . . Just go."

Standing, she swallowed and stared down at him, finally turning but then crouching again and handing him the small semiautomatic. "You might need this."

He said nothing but took the pistol and watched as she waded across the creek, climbed the bank to the road, and began running east, swallowed by the impossible landscape.

After a while his breath became even more labored as he tried to straighten, but he couldn't. He breathed a laugh and decided to not do it again because of the agonizing wrack in his chest. He knew there wasn't much left and thought about what he'd told her and hoped she wouldn't be too quick.

Most live in fear of dying alone, but it was something he understood—that there are things that you can only do by yourself, besides, we are never truly alone. There's always something out there waiting, it is the nature of life and the nature of death.

With the last vestiges of his energy, he tossed the useless weapon into the creek and slumped against the willow roots. His eyes stilled and then unfocused as he spoke to himself, but not completely alone.

Never completely alone.

Riley struggled to his feet and looked around. "Where did he go?"

The shooter, who had hit his friend, stared as the wounded man clutched his shoulder and stood. "You shot me, man."

Riley barked at him. "I'm gonna have him shoot you again if we don't find that asshole and quick."

The three of them looked into the darkness as the wounded man joined them. "He couldn't have gone far."

"How many rounds did you have in the shotgun?"

Riley licked his lip. "Two more, I think."

"You think?"

"Two."

The shooter looked around. "Well, there are three of us, even with numb-nuts wounded."

They all looked around again.

"Where do you think he is?"

"It's according . . ." The shooter's voice trailed off as he leaned forward, trying to see around the rubble walls. "According to whether he decided to escape, or whether he's out there aiming that shotgun at us right now."

The wounded man opened his jacket and felt the saturated shirt underneath. "Hey, I'm bleeding pretty bad."

Riley turned to him again. "What do you want us to do, get you to an emergency room or get this fucking Indian and tell everyone that he's the one that shot you?"

"Yeah, well . . . I guess we need to get him."

Riley nodded. "Then we find that sheriff."

They all looked around again.

The wounded man shook his head. "This is where somebody says something stupid, like let's split up."

"All I know is that grouped together like this, we make a great target for an indiscriminate weapon like a semiauto tactical shotgun."

Riley took a few steps away, picking up the wounded man's rifle and calling over his shoulder to the shooter. "You go to the right; the remains of the school are the only place he could be."

The wounded man watched the two of them move off. "Hey, what about me?"

"You take the middle."

"I don't have a gun."

And somewhere, in the darkness, the only sound was the Cheyenne Nation smiling.

As I lay there in the cell, I thought about the individual I'd met in the hotel bar. Thomas Bidarte had warned me that I didn't have much time and that there were people here, including him, who had been waiting for me.

He'd also said there were no police in this town, yet here I was in jail.

I recited the words he'd said to me. "All haunting is regret."

Then he'd run out into the street and been hit by a snowplow that hadn't even slowed.

And then his body disappeared.

I yanked my coat from the bunk and reached into the inside pocket to pull out the homemade poster. I unfolded it and looked at the half of the girl's face that looked back at me. "Find the girl, get out there and find her, and don't let anybody get in your way, okay?"

It was about then that I heard someone fiddling with the lock on the front door. I knew it wasn't Officer Womack because he would've simply unlocked the door and come in—this was somebody attempting to break into the office.

"Hello?"

The noise stopped, but after a moment it recommenced along with a lot of whispering.

"Hey, is there somebody out there?"

Of course there was, but it was the kind of thing you said in these types of circumstance, at least I thought that's what you did. "Hello?"

There were more sounds and then a loud click as the exterior door bumped open and then slowly swung wide.

Now, of all the people I was prepared to see, the entire staff of the Tonkin Yacht Club might've been last. Bao, the head man, moved cautiously into the room and was still holding a couple of lockpicks, then he saw me and smiled broadly. "Beaucoup dinky dau!"

Behind him, what looked to be the entire kitchen staff of the Vietnamese restaurant filed in, all of them smiling and waving.

"Bạn đang làm gì đãy?"

He laughed and ignored me, putting the lockpicks to work on the cell door.

"No, wait . . . I don't want to get you guys in trouble."

After a few seconds, the bolt in the mechanism clicked and slid away and they all cheered as Bao opened the door, motioning for me to follow.

"Guys, I'm in jail, you can't just . . ." Once again, they ignored me, pulling me from the cell and pushing me toward the door as one of them reached over and picked up my sidearm from the desk and handed it to me. "Now, wait a minute . . . Guys, Bobby's going to be back here, and he's not going to be happy if I'm not in that cell and my sidearm is missing."

Opening the door, they pushed me outside where the priest stood in the darkness and the drifting snow. "Father Vanderhoven?"

He moved in closer as I checked the mag and then stuffed the Colt .45 into the holster at my back, all the while smiling at the Vietnamese as they clustered around us. "I'm sorry, have we met?"

"You don't remember me either?"

I watched as he shook hands with all of them, and they started back toward the town. "Sorry for the confusion, but it was the only way I knew to get you out of there."

"But you don't remember me?"

"No, why?"

"Oh, I don't know; no one else seems to." I looked back and watched my rescuers continue up the sidewalk before extending my hand. "Walt Longmire."

"Paul Vanderhoven, but you say we've met before?"

I sighed. "Yes, we had a drink at the Baker Hotel and discussed Richard Henry Pratt and how the town was haunted."

He studied me as we walked. "Are you some kind of investigator?"

"I used to think so, but now I'm not so sure." Turning back to him, I smiled. "Father Vanderhoven . . ."

"Just Paul." He glanced around and then indicated that we should move farther into the town.

"Paul." I walked along with him. "You're kind of an expert in the history of this place, aren't you?"

"Somewhat." Behind him he glimpsed the HP outpost. "Do you mind if we speed things up? I've never assisted in a jailbreak, but I have the feeling that we shouldn't be here when Bobby returns."

Walking a little quicker, we reached the café, and I was disappointed to find it was closed, with Martha nowhere in sight. "So, do you mind telling me why it is you broke me out?"

"This is going to sound crazy . . ."

"Try me, I'm very open to crazy these days."

He looked over my shoulder and into the café. "I really can't say."

I glanced behind me, but the small restaurant remained closed and there was no one inside. I turned back to him. "Martha?"

He nodded. "She came to the church in tears, saying that you'd been arrested and that someone had to get you out of there and she didn't know where to turn." He took a breath. "I tried to reason with her, but she was emphatic that you should be released, almost hysterical." He laughed and then shook his head. "I'm not much use in the face of weeping women, I'm afraid." He looked up the street, smiling as he stamped his feet to keep warm. "Bao has a knack for such things; he's gotten me back in the church after I've accidentally locked myself out." He looked up at me through thick glasses. "I believe this is the first misdemeanor I've ever committed."

I sighed. "Wyoming statutes 7-13-402 clearly states that escape, attempting to escape or assisting others to escape from any confinement institution can include punishment of up to five years of imprisonment and felony charges."

"Good thing we're in Montana." He stared at me. "What did you say you did for a living?"

I looked down at my boots. "I'm a sheriff."

He turned and started up the sidewalk again as the same two drunks stumbled out of Bar 31.

The lean individual in the uniform clutched the lamppost and then puked onto the curb. Wiping his mouth with a sleeve, he turned to face us. "What are you looking at?"

I caught the priest's shoulder. "Let me handle this."

"Gladly."

I turned to look at the security guard. "Look, we've done this before . . . You're going to swing on me, and I'm going to block it and then put your face into that lamppost." I glanced at his buddy, who stood a little way away. "And then Three Fingers here is going to take a shot at me, but I'm going to block him too, and then punch him in the gut and sit the two of you on the stoop there and go on about my business."

The drunk reeled back and looked at his friend in the doorway, who had found his voice. "We know you?"

"Only in the sense of aggravated assault."

He swung anyway, just as I knew he would, and I stepped in, blocking the clumsy attempt with a forearm, and then planting his face in the lamppost just as I'd done before. I turned to look at the other one, who surprised me by raising his hands in supplication. "I'm good."

"So . . ." I stood there staring at him. "Things can be changed here."

He slowly dropped his hands. "What?"

"Nothing." I gestured toward his buddy, now lying on the sidewalk. "You want your friend?"

"No."

"Why don't you gather up your buddy and head back in the bar and tell Big Daddy Delgado I said howdy." Ignoring his puzzled look, I gestured for Vanderhoven to follow me, and we continued toward the theater, where I stopped to look through the doors into the darkened lobby. There was no one inside, and the lights were dimmed as well as in the ticket booth, and there was no signage on the marquee. I glanced over at the case, where I expected to see the poster for Support Your Local Sheriff and found it empty.

"Something wrong?"

"I'm not sure, but I'm thinking I might've screwed things up."

"How?"

"The way you always do, by doing a good deed." I looked around again. "Paul, how come there are no posters for upcoming movies or anything on the marquee?"

"It's been closed for years."

I glanced back into the lobby, and on closer inspection could see that the counters were bare of any concession equipment and the place looked a little shabby and run down. "There was a girl, a girl who worked here . . ." I pulled the plastic-covered poster from the inside of my jacket, holding it out to him. "This girl."

He studied the half face. "She's missing?"

"She is now." I studied the empty street. "Again."

"Is that why you're here?"

"Yep." I studied the poster. "Have you ever seen her?"

"No, I don't think so, but then there's a lot that happens in this town that I'm not privy to." I started to cross the street as he called out to me. "Where are you going?"

I stopped in the middle of the road, stooped to pick up the two Hot Lips silver dollars resting in the fresh tracks, and looked up and down the street. I waved at the priest and threw a thumb over my shoulder at the two-story building behind me. "To the hotel, to see if I can get a room."

He sat back in his chair, his teeth incredibly white embedded in his tanned skin, the mane of dark hair producing a halo effect. He was standing behind the bar in the exact spot where I'd seen him before, pouring himself another shot from the same bottle of mescal. "It is about time."

I sat on the stool across from him. "I knew you'd remember me."

He nodded, picking up the glass and looking at me from over the rim. He still spoke in the same soft Spanish lilt. "But do you remember me, Sheriff?"

"Thomas Bidarte."

"So, you do remember." He smiled and then drank in one swift move. "That scar over your eye, I'm the one who gave it to you." He picked up the bottle, placing another shot glass in front of me.

"This time, I think I'll take you up on it."

He poured and then refreshed himself. "So, you have been sleepwalking in circles?"

"It seems like it, yep." I reached out and touched the glass with thumb and forefinger. "So, why is it you seem to know what's going on around here when nobody else does?"

"Does it seem like that?"

"Yep."

"Because I am livid." He looked out the window at the snow-covered road. "I am infuriated—you would be amazed how that can cauterize your mind."

I lifted my tiny glass. "Here's to cauterized minds."

"The problem is rage is tiring, and you eventually let your guard down, and it uses your own humanity against you." He raised his own glass, and we drank.

"And you can't just tell me what the heck is going on, because there are things you can say and things you can't, but you haven't told me why?"

He said nothing.

I reached over and poured another round. "If you don't mind me asking, are you dead?"

His face broke open into a full grin. "You should know, Sheriff."

"Did I kill you?"

He shrugged. "It was only fair, for me it was simply business, but for you it was very personal—I was threatening something very dear to you."

"And what's that?"

He sat there, staring at me. "What makes you think that you do not belong here?"

I glanced around. "It's not right, this place . . . I can't help but think that it's been constructed for a specific purpose."

"And that purpose would be?"

"To distract me."

"From what?"

"My actual life. It's as if there are blockades set up in my head to keep me from accessing memories or facts concerning my real life, the life I'm living while I'm being distracted by all this."

"So, what do you suppose is happening back in this real life of yours?"

"I don't know, and that's what's so unsettling." I spun the tiny glass and then raised my eyes to his. "Tell me about the Éveohtsé-heómėse, is it death?"

He stared at me, speechless.

"I've seen it; I've seen what it can do."

"You've seen nothing. It can manifest itself in ways you cannot imagine."

"Try me."

"It can take everything you know, everything you love and hold dear, and twist it until it is unrecognizable."

"But to what purpose? The people I've seen it take gave themselves up, almost voluntarily, like some kind of religion."

He reached over, taking the bottle and refilled our glasses. "Do you like eating the same food all the time? Drinking the same drink?"

"No."

He lifted his glass in salute. "Drink as much as you want, there is no drunkenness here, or hangovers . . ."

"There's a guy across the street I just introduced to a lamppost who might disagree with you."

"Oh, you can choose to be drunk—another distraction."

I picked up my own glass. "And why is it I should trust you? I mean, if I'm the one who killed you."

"Because all I want from this place is to be away from it, the same as you."

"But you haven't told me what this place is."

"A way station, someplace in-between, neither here nor there—not a place at all."

"So, this isn't heaven or hell?"

Bidarte waved a hand at me in dismissal. "No, that would require resolution, a luxury this place cannot provide." His shoulders slumped a little. "This is simply an endless cycle of agitation to provide . . . sustenance."

I sat back on my stool. "You talk like you've been here a long time."

"Forever, it seems." He waited a moment before asking. "You mentioned a girl you were looking for; did you find her?"

I pulled the poster from my coat. "I did, but then I lost her."

"How?"

"I was somewhere else and did some things, and when I got back here things had changed." I glanced at the darkened theater across the street. "The last time I was here she worked at the theater, but now it's closed, and I don't know where she is."

He reached across the table, taking the poster and examining it. "What do you mean you were somewhere else and did some things?"

"It's kind of hard to explain, but I believe I went back in time."

His eyes widened.

"I know it sounds crazy, but I just stepped through the gate up at the school, and it was like I stepped back in time."

"How long ago?"

"The turn of the twentieth century."

"And how were things different when you came back here?"

"Well, first off, nobody seemed to remember me."

"That is not unusual, every time you go to sleep or are distracted the cycle starts over again, and it is as if your mind has been wiped clean—that is, if you do not guard against it."

"Other things had changed too."

"So, perhaps the things you did then had an effect on this place now." He thought about it. "That gives us hope."

"Of what?"

"Escape."

"To where?"

He laughed again. "Anywhere, anywhere but here."

"What if they are worse places?"

"At least they *are* places." He stood, looking down at me. "What time is it?"

"Eight-seventeen." I pulled out my watch and looked at it, at the broken glass. "It's always 8:17 p.m."

"Very good." He smiled. "One thing I am sure of is that you are the key to all this, the people who occupy this town are connected to you in some way—it was that way before you arrived here: all these people were here, even me."

I looked up at him.

"Where have you been since you arrived again?" he asked.

"In jail, mostly."

"Excuse me?"

"When I got back, I had an argument with some kids in an Oldsmobile, and the highway patrolman, Bobby Womack, ran them off and put me in jail."

"A highway patrolman."

"Yep."

"How did you get away?"

"The priest, Father Vanderhoven, got the guys at the Vietnamese restaurant to break me out."

"Now, why would they do that?"

"They said that Martha, the woman at the café, had begged them to do it."

The sound of bells began ringing in the distance.

"What?"

His eyes became more panicked. "It doesn't like metal. The jail has metal bars. You were surrounded by metal where it couldn't get at you—why else would they want you out?"

"But if the Éveohtsé-heómėse wanted to get me, it had plenty of opportunities . . ."

"Perhaps it has grown tired of the taste of fear and wants you to give yourself to it, voluntarily."

"You think that's why they got me out?"

He looked onto the street, stood up, and began backing away from the bar as the bells continued to peal. "I must go."

I thought about how the Vietnamese had picked the locks and how Vanderhoven hadn't touched anything metal. I stood and pocketed my watch, retrieved one of the silver dollars, and tossed it onto the surface of the bar, where it circled and then fell over. "Heads."

He stared at it and then at me.

"Pick it up."

He cocked his head and studied me. "And if I don't?"

I pulled the .45 from my back and laid it on the oak surface of the bar next to the silver dollar. "I introduce some more metal into the conversation."

Bidarte breathed a sharp laugh, like a gut-punch. He then burst out laughing until he had no breath but then inhaled, a look of pain on his face. He attempted to speak but then erupted into laughter instead. "I die every night—it is my punishment, like Sisyphus, forever rolling the boulder up the mountain. Every *night*."

He looked out the window at the street where he had most recently met his demise as the bells continued ringing. "It is always a strange kind of night here in case you haven't noticed."

"I'm getting that." I picked up the semiautomatic. "So, like Sisyphus, you cheat death?"

"You cannot cheat death, my friend." The smile fled his lips. "If there is one thing that I have learned in this wretched place, it is that when the bill for our existence comes due, we must all pay the piper."

He turned and walked away into the lobby of the hotel, and after scooping up the big Colt and the coin, I followed. "Wait, I've got a lot more questions."

He pushed open the door of the hotel and walked onto the sidewalk. "That is unfortunate in that I have no more answers."

Reholstering the .45, I caught the heavy glass door before it swung shut. "You've got to help me."

He stepped off the curb and walked into the snow-covered street as the bells rang. "Help yourself."

Calling out to him, I stood on the curb under the balcony of the Baker Hotel, "I don't know how."

In the middle of the street he turned, spreading his arms out and looking up at the yellowish-black sky. "None of us can help you any more than you can help yourself—have you never thought that this place, populated with people you know, is a figment of your imagination? That you are as responsible for keeping us here as the Éveohtsé-heómėse?"

I leaned against a post and then tossed the silver dollar to him.

With one quick snatch, he caught it, looked at his fist, then slowly back up at me, finally opening the hand so that I could see it on his bare skin.

He looked at the sky again as the bells stopped, and even the snowflakes hung there in the air like a myriad of tiny mobiles, dancing and reflecting. There was no sound, but I watched as his lips moved and formed the words. "All haunting is regret."

And that's when he was hit by the five-ton snowplow.

Again.

15

Riley and the shooter were positioned to the sides of the boarding school rubble, weapons at the ready, but the wounded man lagged behind in hopes that they'd find the Indian before the Indian found them.

Quietly stepping over the broken concrete footers, the wounded man moved onto hallowed ground. There were a few old gravestones, most of them unreadable with age. He was standing in fresh snow but began to back up, when he ran into something that felt like cold metal. Glancing behind, he was relieved to see it was the bell, sitting on its stone foundation.

Moving to the side, he tripped over a section of the rocks that had fallen away, barely catching himself as he continued backing up. He discovered a hole and saw that it was large enough for a man to squeeze through. He thought about it, figuring that might be the safest place to be when the shooting started.

Instead, he crept forward and around the bell, keeping an eye on the silhouette of the two armed individuals as they continued their separate ways.

Crouching down he placed his arms on the cool surface of the bell and noticed that a portion of the snow had been brushed away—it was also then that he felt the cold steel of a stag-handled bowie knife press against the skin of his unprotected throat.

"Hello."

He felt the breath on the back of his head and tried to speak, but the words couldn't make it past the blade.

"You are not armed, numb-nuts."

Finally, he found one, and croaked it softly. "No."

"Hmm, you just saved your own life."

He started to move, but the blade pressed harder, pulling at his skin.

"There are only two of them?"

He croaked again. "Yes."

"Do you know where my friend is?"

"No."

"Then you are not of much use to me."

He croaked again. "Please don't kill me."

"I would not think of it."

He felt the blade slip away, but then felt the butt of it strike him in the back of the head, his chin bouncing off the bell as he slid to the ground—and it was the last thing he felt.

"Did you hear something?"

The shooter turned to look at Riley. "You mean you, yelling?"

Riley stepped over some of the rubble, drifting in the direction of the shooter, now not so sure they should be apart. "Something metallic, like a gong or something."

The shooter glanced around. "Sounded like something from far off."

Riley sidled up to him, his shotgun aimed at the shooter's legs. "Maybe back down at the town?"

Pushing the barrel of Riley's gun away, the shooter looked back toward the road where his truck sat parked with the running lights on. "We can check on it later, after we get this guy."

Riley glanced around. "Where's numb-nuts?"

"Probably in my truck, or halfway back to town by now."

"What if the chick comes back with reinforcements?"

"According to how many of them, but if it's too many we say nothing and just play dumb."

Riley turned his head again. "Did you hear something?"

The shooter followed his gaze. "Back toward the graveyard."

"Yep."

He gestured for Riley to move to the right. "You go that way and I'll move around this way on the other side of the wall." He pointed toward the domed shape in the middle of the cemetery. "I think we might've made a mistake, and that bell is the only other thing big enough to hide behind."

Riley kept his eyes on the bell. He stepped over some of the rubble as he raised the barrel of the shotgun, aiming it at the partially covered mound of snow.

Glancing to the left, he couldn't see the shooter and thought he should've caught up by now. He wanted to shout out but fought against it, keeping his concentration ahead.

Movement.

He saw something behind the bell, something edging his way. He waited a moment before realigning his sites and then pulled the trigger, the report of the 12-gauge thunderous.

Lowering the shotgun, he hopped forward and then pointed it again at the body, slumped against the bell, where it had fallen over and backward. "I got him! I got him!"

He looked down at what was left of his friend's face.

Staring at the twitching body, he involuntarily stepped back and watched the booted foot convulse as the bile rose in his throat. "Shit . . . Oh, shit, man." He glanced back at the collapsed walls of the school but could see no one. "Hey!" Riley looked toward the area where his companion had been. "Hey! I shot the wrong guy."

There was no sound in response.

In fact, there was no sound at all.

The crash was monstrous, and I stood there watching his body fly into the air and slam into the wall at the corner of the hotel, his arms and legs splayed at impossible angles.

I watched as the scene played out the exact way it had before. I stood there, frozen, unable to help.

I stared up the road as the plow barreled on, the taillights shuddering, blinking, and then disappearing into the swirling snow and yellowish darkness. I rushed into the street and yelled after the plow, even going so far as to pull out my sidearm and throw a few rounds at the thing.

Giving up, I walked toward the body encapsulated in the plowed snow. I kneeled beside him and reached a hand out to his face as his eyes darted about.

One brown eye sought me from the corner of the bleeding socket.

"Don't try to talk."

The eye widened, as if seeing things I couldn't.

"I'm going to stay here with you."

The eye shifted to his hand, and I reached up and took the collection of broken bones in mine, where he dropped the silver dollar that I'd tossed to him. "How many . . . ?"

"Don't talk."

His jaw was broken, the words hard to make out. "How . . . how many?"

I stared at him. "What?"

"Pieces of silver—how many?"

"I . . . I don't know."

"You'll . . . You'll need thirty-one."

He collapsed, and his one eye grew still, the iris receding into a tunnel of black.

I stared at him, and then at the coin in my hand.

I stood and glanced toward the hotel, where I thought about carrying his broken body. "Thirty-one pieces of silver—a handsome price."

I looked back and the body was gone, just as I knew it would be.

Leaning against the support post of the hotel balcony, feeling overwhelmed by it all, I had the urge to go into the hotel, climb the steps to room 31, and just collapse onto the bed. But would the world be different when I woke up or, even worse, would it be exactly the same?

I swallowed and looked back to where the body had been and thought about what he'd said this time—that this isn't heaven or hell but a way station; a place of continual agitation to provide sustenance. How that everyone and everything in this construct of a place has to do with me, and that I'm as responsible as the Éveohtsé-heómėse for all of the people in this town being trapped here. He had said something about sleepwalking in circles, and the only way to combat the constant malaise of this place is with anger.

Anger.

Was there something I was supposed to be angry about?

I reached into my pocket and pulled out the plastic-covered poster, looking at the visible half of the missing girl's face. "Is it you, are you what it is that's supposed to make me angry?"

Looking down the street, I noticed the lights were on in the Night Owl Café and started walking in that direction.

I stuffed the poster under my arm and stepped up on the sidewalk. Pushing open the glass door to the tinkling of a small bell, I stood in the doorway but didn't see anyone. There was a delicious smell coming from the kitchen, however, so I sat in the same stool as I had before.

I thought about what Bidarte had said about the thirty-one pieces of silver.

Placing the poster on the counter and then probing around in my pockets, I began collecting the coins and stacking them in front of me. Making separate stacks of ten silver dollars apiece, I'd gotten to the last stack when I came up three short. "Twenty-eight."

"Can I help you?"

I looked up to find that the face on the missing-persons poster was standing in front of me. "Howdy."

Still looking a little uncertain, she smiled a wide, nervous grin, pulling her jet-black hair back with one hand. "Talking to yourself?"

I nodded, placing my hand over the poster and folding it so that she couldn't see the half image of herself. "Sometimes I'm looking for intelligent conversation and don't know which way to turn."

"I know that feeling." She laughed, looking down at the coins. "You must be hungry."

"No, just collecting." I gestured toward the stacks. "Almost thirty pieces of silver."

She looked perplexed. "That supposed to mean something?"

"I'm not sure, but generally it refers to the amount of money that had been paid to Judas Iscariot for handing over Jesus."

"Was that a lot, back then?"

"Not really." I thought about the biblical passage equating the value of a slave at thirty pieces of silver if gored by an ox. "It was supposed to be an insult, as if that was all they thought Jesus's life was worth."

She studied the coins. "What'd Judas do with the money?"

"In a fit of remorse, he threw it into the temple to be rid of it."

"And that was the end of the story?"

"No, the religious leaders used the money to buy a potter's field, the place where Judas hung himself."

She leaned her hip against the counter. "You some kind of preacher?"

"No, at least I don't think so." I noted her name tag: JEANIE. "Worked here long?"

"Seems like forever." She pulled an order pad from her apron and then a pen from behind one ear. "What can I get you?"

I plucked a menu from the holder, scanning it. "What's that I'm smelling?"

"Strawberry-rhubarb pie."

"Kind of out of season, isn't it?"

She shrugged. "I don't know, what season is it?"

"Good question. I'll go with the pie and a cup of coffee." I placed the menu back in the holder. "Say, does Martha still work here?"

"Martha?"

"Strawberry blonde, about medium height, eyes that set the stars?"

She continued to stare.

"A woman, she used to work here."

She stuck the pen back behind her ear. "When?"

"I guess before your time."

"Yeah, I guess." She stayed there for a moment but then turned back toward the kitchen. I waited and then took the folded poster, glancing at the image again and then placing it in my inside coat pocket. Gathering up the silver dollars, I began redistributing them into my pockets. When I looked up, I saw a strange-looking individual filling a coffee mug and then walking toward me.

He had long hair pulled back into a ponytail and odd pale-blue eyes, one glass. His name tag read SHADE. He was powerfully built, and after placing the mug in front of me, he rested his arms on the counter, muscles flexing.

"Can I help you?" His voice had a Canadian cadence to it, which wasn't unpleasant, but his quiet, menacing tone was.

"Thanks for the coffee."

"You hassling my waitress?"

I cocked my head, looking at him. "Excuse me?"

He brought his face close to mine. "There's no Martha working here."

"If you say so."

"I do."

I raised my hands. "I'm just here for the pie."

He pulled a washcloth from under the counter and wiped his hands while looking down at me. "You look familiar."

"I was just thinking the same thing about you." I picked up the mug and sipped the coffee."

"I don't usually forget people." He folded his arms. "You staring at something?"

I lowered the mug. "Nope."

"You looking at my eye?"

I sighed, glancing up at him. "No, I wasn't."

"You sure about that?"

"Yep."

"It's not real, you know."

"I never would've known."

He reached out and cupped the top of my mug, sliding it back toward himself. "I think you're lying."

I leaned back on my stool and laughed. "Is this the kind of customer service you usually provide?"

I slowly stood up to my full height. "Look, Mr. Shade, I've had a really long day, night, whatever . . . And I don't feel like playing games."

He stared at me, at first not moving, and then he slid the coffee mug back toward me and took his hand away.

I sat back down and picked up the mug, taking a sip.

The Native girl, Jeanie, approached from the corner near the cash register but then stopped when she saw him.

He reached out and took the pie from her, setting it on the counter and sliding it toward me. "No charge."

I unrolled the flatware from the paper napkin and pulled out the fork. "Thanks."

He chuckled as he turned the corner, coughing into a fist as he pushed his way through the swinging doors of the kitchen.

Jeanie watched him go and then turned to me as I cleaved off a section of the pie. "You live here?"

"No, I don't think so." I shoveled the pie into my mouth and chewed. "You?"

"Well, yeah." She gestured around us. "I've got a little place east of town."

I nodded, swallowing. "What's it like?"

"It's a little place . . ."

I waited for more, but she just stood there looking away. "One bedroom, two? What color is it? Is there a sidewalk?"

She started to speak but couldn't.

"A garage? Can you tell me something about your house, anything at all?"

She stared at me.

"I didn't mean to upset you . . . I've been having the same trouble, remembering things." I forked in another piece of pie and chewed, studying her. "I wouldn't normally push like this, but I've got a feeling I'm working on borrowed time and need to get some answers."

She glanced back toward the kitchen. "About what?"

"About you."

She stepped back. "Do we know each other?"

"No, I don't think so, but I've been looking for you for quite some time, and I think I found you, but now I've found you again—Jeanie One Moon?" Her eyes came up to mine, startled. "You don't live here, you never have." I sat the fork down and pulled the poster from my pocket and held it up for her to see. "This is you, isn't it?" I pointed at the half of a phone number where the sun hadn't faded it away. "Is this your parents' phone number back in Lame Deer? Do they know where you are? Does anybody know where you are?"

Her eyes darted about, filled with terror.

"I'm not trying to scare you, honest."

Her eyes came back to mine.

"I . . . I think I'm a sheriff, and I think I know things about you because you were the last case I was working on. Do you have a sister? Jaya One Moon Long?"

The words stammered from her lips. "Just . . . Just One Moon, not Long."

"She plays basketball, like you did."

"Yes."

"And someone was threatening her, the way they threatened you."

She backed away, knocking over some stainless-steel containers that clattered to the floor.

"Hey!" The guy with the glass eye appeared at the end of the counter near the cash register holding a truncheon, the kind truckers use to check tires. "I need you to get out of here, now."

Stretching my neck and squaring off, I turned to him. "Raynaud Shade."

He didn't point the billy club at me. "I know you?"

"You did."

"What's that supposed to mean?"

"We've met before. You kidnapped a woman, and I pursued you into the Cloud Peak Wilderness area of the Bighorn Mountains."

He made a face. "What?"

"You were a prisoner, on your way to a state-performed execution."

He smiled. "Well, I guess that didn't work out."

"Actually, it did. I killed you."

He shook his head, moving toward me in a menacing fashion. "Look, if you don't get the hell out of here, I'm going to kill you."

"Walt?" Turning, I saw her standing at the door, holding it open. She wore the clothes she'd worn in the library the time before, but now had on a long wool overcoat that looked familiar. She held a hand out to me, stretching her fingers. "You need to come with me."

I stared at her.

"You're confused, and you need to leave these people alone."

I glanced at Jeanie, still backed against the counter. "I've been looking for this girl."

"And now you've found her, but we need to leave them alone."

I slipped my hand behind my back and onto my sidearm. "I think she's in trouble."

She paused at my movement, knowing all too well what it meant. "We all are, but right now, we need to talk."

"I know you most of all, don't I?" I took a step toward her and then stopped. "Are you my wife?"

"Yes."

I took a quick intake of breath. "Are you dead?"

She breathed deeply. "That's what we need to talk about."

"Am I dead?"

She indicated the two behind the counter. "Not in front of them; they won't understand."

"Are they dead too?"

She swallowed, tears forming in her eyes. "Walt, please? Don't make this even more difficult than it already is."

I looked at the two people behind the counter and then lowered my hand. Her eyes widened as I walked toward her, so I stopped and waited until the tension left my body before crossing the rest of the way and reaching out my hand. "All right."

She took it, and I turned back toward the man and Jeanie. "I'm sorry if I caused any trouble." I then turned and pushed open the door, holding it for Martha as we stepped onto the sidewalk and into the cold.

We both automatically turned to our left and began slowly walking through the town, holding hands. "You remember this coat—you bought it for me, and I remember the one you're wearing."

She smiled. "You do?"

"Your mother bought it for you the first year we were married because she thought I couldn't take proper care of you and that you'd freeze to death."

She laughed but then stopped when she saw the look on my face. "What is it?"

"You . . ." I was finding it hard to breathe. "You didn't freeze to death."

"No."

I released her hand and stepped back, still looking at her. "It's all I can do to talk to you, when all I want to do is feast my eyes."

She grinned a stunning smile. "I'm here now."

"Are you?"

Her smile faded as she turned away, walking to the edge of the sidewalk. "Doesn't it seem like I am?"

"Almost too much." I stepped toward her. "What's going on, Martha?"

She wrapped her arms around herself, still turned away. "You talk as if there are absolute answers to all these questions, when that's just not the way it works."

"Then why don't you tell me how it works."

"Because you're not going to like the answers."

I stepped down off the curb and into the street, turning to look her in the eye. "Try me."

Her hair blew across her face, hiding it. "You like rules, Walt. Laws, logic, and things like that don't count for much here."

"Where is here?"

"Wherever, whatever you want it to be." She glanced around, the stars sparkling in the reflection of her eyes. "I didn't create this place, Walt, you did."

"Then why don't I know it?"

"It's a collection of your thoughts, bits and pieces of places you've been, places you've never been, places you've wanted to go, and even some places you dread."

"Which one are you?"

She shuddered with a breath at my unkind words. "I would hope that I'm here to help you."

"To do what?"

"Let go."

The street suddenly felt much colder. "So, I am dead."

"Not the way you think."

"And how do I think?"

"Lying a-moldering in the grave."

"But my soul goes marching on?"

"Something like that."

"Why can't I remember dying?"

She stepped off the curb in order to walk out to meet me. "Sometimes it's a traumatic event and it takes awhile for your mind to work it through."

I sighed and shook my head. "That doesn't sound like me." I looked east, toward the curving road that led to the boarding school and then turned back to her and tried to be gentle. "How was it for you?"

She seemed at a loss for words. "I don't really remember, so I guess it wasn't really that important."

"It was to me."

"I know that." She took my hand again as I remained silent. "I wasn't making slight of it."

"I've missed you."

She looked down. "I know that."

"Is that why you came back for me?"

"Like I said, there aren't many rules . . . But I suppose so." She released my hand, turning and smiling her sad smile. "It's been a long time."

"I didn't used to think so."

She turned and raised her hands like a benediction, clutching the lapels of my coat. "Well, it has been."

"Are you seeing anybody?"

Chuckling, she shook her head. "No, we don't date here in the afterworld."

"Is that what you call it, the afterworld?"

She smiled, and her hands slipped away. "It seems appropriate, don't you think? I've never really referred to it as anything—it just is."

"And you've been waiting for me?"

"I suppose so."

"So, what happens now?"

"We get to be together."

"Forever? Here?"

She looked back up at me with earnest hazel eyes. "If that's what you'd like."

"What I'd like? That's a little noncommittal."

"You have to be sure it's what you want, Walt. That's the only thing that can ruin this, is if you make the wrong decision or commit to something you don't really want to do. As they say, your heart has to be in it."

"The problem is, I'm not so sure I'm dead here in this little town of sinners and saints."

"Then how are you here?"

"I wish I knew—but the one thing I do know is that some-one is looking for me, maybe a couple of very smart and capable someones, and when they find me this'll all be over, one way or another."

There was a blip behind me and suddenly the revolving streaks of red and blue lit up the street. I turned to see the '79 Crown Vic with its emergency lights on and the driver's side door swinging open to reveal Trooper Womack with his sidearm drawn. "Ma'am, I'm going to need you to step away from this man, please."

"Howdy, Bobby." I moved away from her. "Don't shoot."

Stepping to the side, he came around the door and approached. "You wanna keep your hands up where I can see them?"

"Sure."

Martha stepped toward him, holding her hands up too. "Officer, is there a problem?"

Bobby stopped about twelve feet away. "Ma'am, do you mind stepping up there on the sidewalk for a moment?"

She stood her ground. "What is this all about?"

"Probably about me breaking out of jail."

Bobby shifted his gaze between the two of us. "Yeah, it might have something to do with that."

She folded her arms. "I arranged it."

Bobby looked at her. "Excuse me?"

"I'm the one that got him out—are you going to arrest me too?"

"Ma'am, I just need you to get back and up on the sidewalk where you'll be safe." He turned back to me. "You have your gun?"

"I do."

"Two fingers."

"Right."

I began moving for my weapon when Martha stepped toward him between us. "What are you arresting him for?"

He motioned with the big revolver, the nickel-plating glint-ing as it captured the light like oil on the surface of water. "Ma'am, I need you to step aside."

"Why are you interfering with us?"

"Ma'am, step aside."

"No."

He looked past her. "Do you know this woman?"

"She's my wife."

He shook his head. "Ma'am, I might not have to arrest him, but I need him to surrender his weapon. There are no firearms allowed in the city limits of Fort Pratt."

She stood there for a moment longer before stepping aside as I drew the Colt from the small of my back, holding it between thumb and forefinger as I extended it toward him.

Womack started to reach for it when something made me pause, and I drew it back. "What if we do something different."

He held the barrel of the .357 on me, steady. "Such as?"

I nodded toward Martha. "How about I give it to her, to give to you?"

"Look, I'm not playing games here . . ."

"No games, I'll just hand it over to her and then she can walk over and hand it to you, nice and safe."

He shook his head in dismay. "Okay."

"Now I show you what I know." Turning toward my wife, I held the large frame semiautomatic out to her, but she made no move to unfold her arms.

"I'm not taking that."

I glanced at Womack, flipping the Colt and catching it in my hand, aimed at her. "You're not taking it because you can't."

We stood like that for a very long time.

"Oh, Walt." Her head lowered to where she was now looking

at me through her eyebrows and smiled, the sound of her voice echoing in the empty street somewhat familiar, but then again, unfamiliar and flat. "This would've been so much easier if you'd just gone along, but that's just not you, is it? You always have to do things the hard way."

16

Riley was alone, he knew that.

There was no answer, and there wasn't any reason to think there would be. He looked down at the dead man at his feet and then turned back toward the rubble of the boarding school.

Somehow the game had changed and as clever as he'd been, it had come down to this—they'd killed his father, and now they were going to kill him.

He had to come up with a plan, something that would give him an edge.

The only other option was sneaking around out there in the darkness with that fucking killing machine. He needed leverage.

He cleared his throat. "I know where he is, honest I do."

His voice sounded meaningless to him as he took cover behind the bell.

"He's close, and I can show you."

Silence.

"He's close, so close that I can kill him if I have to."

Silence.

"I don't want to kill him, but I will."

More silence.

"I'll make you a deal." Not waiting for the unending silence to continue, he filled it in with more words. "I'll give him to you, and you let me go." He quickly added. "That sounds fair, doesn't it?"

Something flew through the air and clanged against the other side of the bell. He fired into the space where he thought the thing, whatever it was, had come from. The blast broke the glacial air and he crouched against the cold metal, finally sneaking a look over the bell, where the tactical rifle of the shooter lay in the snow, the barrel bent at an angle.

Peering into the dark, he turned and slid his back down the bell, a whimper escaping his throat as his legs collapsed beneath him. The fucker didn't care, he didn't even need weapons.

Trying to still his heart, he called out over his shoulder. "I'm not kidding, I have him and I can give him to you, safe and sound."

Silence.

"Look, if I die, he dies too."

More silence.

"You'll never find him."

Even more silence.

"C'mon . . ." He couldn't keep the pleading from his voice and was about to speak again when he saw something moving in the road out past the gate. In the darkness it was hard to tell, but it looked like somebody running up the road toward him. "What the hell . . . ?"

Raising the shotgun, he took careful aim. He had only one round left.

Whoever it was, they got to the crew-cab and stopped near the quarter panel, partially obstructing his shot. Could it be his buddy the shooter? Did he get away, and was he now trying to get into the truck and leave him?

Riley thought about shouting, but what if it wasn't him, what if it was the Indian?

He'd have to move in that direction if whoever it was didn't come toward him. He waited a moment and then thought about the exact predicament he was in—death behind him and uncertainty in front, and uncertainty was looking better and better.

Struggling up, he tried to remember if the shooter had taken the keys.

The truck door opened, making it impossible to see. The interior lights in the cab had come on, but Riley couldn't make out anyone. Maybe they had just opened and closed the door, hopefully discovering there were no keys.

Had the shooter been driving?

He looked at the body of the man he'd shot, lying at his boots.

Averting his eyes from the disfigured face, he sat the butt of the shotgun on the ground and began rooting through the dead man's pockets. Nothing in the first, he reached over and felt the second and was reassured by a lump there. Leaning forward he worked his fingers into the pocket and pulled out a set of keys on an electronic fob.

Whoever was over near the truck was probably still there, but maybe not. Maybe they'd come this direction; circled around, or maybe they'd headed back for town. There really wasn't anywhere else to go and waiting here to get his head cut off wasn't so appealing.

Clutching the keys in one hand and the shotgun in the other, he looked back toward the school, fully expecting the big Indian to be standing right there, but there was nothing. Turning, he stepped over the dead man and crept toward the truck.

The driver's side window was down, and he couldn't see anybody inside. Numb-nuts had wanted the window open on the drive up, he remembered.

Near the truck, Riley looked around again before yanking the door open and leaping inside. Crouching down in the seat to keep from being a target to the outside world, he fumbled with the keys and watched as they slipped from his fingers and onto the floor mat.

Raking the mat, he grabbed them again and stuck the right one in the ignition, turning it just as the muzzle of a Midnight Bronze Glock 9mm pressed against the back of his head and the blade of an antler-handled bowie knife slipped through the open window, scraping up under his Adam's apple like a primitive and very close shave. "Going somewhere?"

His eyes went to Henry Standing Bear, leaning into the driver's side window as a female hand reached from the back, slipping the shotgun from his hand.

"Where is he?" She nudged the back of his head with the semiautomatic. "Now."

"Okay, okay . . . I don't know, but I'll make you a deal."

She nudged the muzzle into the back of his head again. "Here's the deal, you tell us what we want to know, or I pull the trigger and we watch chunks of your brain slide down the inside of the windshield."

He glanced at the Cheyenne Nation.

"He's not going to help you, Riley. In case you haven't noticed he would just as soon cut your head off and stick it on one of the spikes on that fence around the cemetery." He could feel her breath as she leaned forward, speaking directly behind his ear. "Where. Is. Walt?"

"Like I said, he took Artie, but I ran into him with the

snowplow. Maybe a little too hard, and I thought I'd killed them both once I came to, but when I got out of the plow and got to where the truck had rolled, they were both gone." He turned his head just a bit to look at the Bear. "Didn't Artie know where the sheriff was?"

Vic nudged his head once again. "Artie's dead."

"Honest to God, I have no idea where he is."

The Cheyenne Nation's words rumbled in his chest. "Where did the collision happen?"

"Here, right here."

"Walt was hurt?"

"Yeah, yeah, there was blood and everything." He gestured toward the cemetery. "He couldn't have gone far, but we looked for him everywhere that . . ." His voice caught in his throat as he thought about the stones that were moved near the platform, and the hole big enough for a man to fit through—his eyes rested on the ancient tonnage of the boarding school bell.

Bells rang in the distance as she stared down the barrel of my sidearm and moved to the left, stepping between Womack and me. Martha hadn't changed physically, but there was something about her movements that seemed more lithe, dangerous.

The slightest traces of a smile etched their way onto her lips. "If you don't mind my asking, how did you know?"

I spoke softly. "You never touched metal, even the first time I was at the café, and then just now."

She turned toward the highway patrolman and then back to me. "Bravo, but there was something else?"

I pulled the Mallo Cup Play Money card from my pocket and held it up toward her. "A friend wrote the names down for me to read and I was finally able to remember my daughter and grand-daughter." I centered my aim on her face, as difficult as it was. "You never mentioned Cady or Lola. There's no way my wife would ever ask me to leave our child and grandchild under any circumstance—she would fight as hard as me to get back to them and keep them safe."

She thought about that for a moment and then turned to look at the man behind her. "How about you, Officer Womack. How did you end up here?"

He kept the big revolver trained on her. "I go where the trouble is."

I interrupted. "You didn't summon him?"

"No, I wouldn't be surprised if he was called here by you, but that just makes him available to me." She turned to look back at me again. "You still don't get it, do you?" She took a step forward, closing the distance between us. "You're not quite dead yet."

"If what you're saying is true and I'm hurt and missing, there are very capable people looking for me—and when they find me, this is all over. I've seen what you can do, but for some reason you can't get at me, and time is running out. All this distraction, all this repetition just to keep me here is because you know they'll find me."

She looked sad for a moment. "And what if you're dead when they do?"

"I can be hard to kill." I cocked the .45.

She laughed, shaking her head and studying me. "I have been at this for a very long time—how could you possibly think that you could defeat me."

"I changed things back in Fort Pratt, so I can change things now."

"A minor inconvenience. Besides, once you've been removed, who's to say that the history of this place won't return to its rightful order?" She took another step toward me, the barrel of my gun only inches from her lovely face, a face I'd missed for so long. "You talk as if I'm some enemy, but all I'm trying to do is give you what you want, Walt."

"Don't call me by my name in her voice; you haven't earned that." I looked around the street. "And this is not what I want."

She straightened the collar of her coat, the one that was supposed to keep her from freezing to death in our first year of marriage. "Not even me?"

"You're not her."

"I'm your image of her, and that's all that's left—all that you really want."

I swallowed. "No, you're just a hollowed-out copy of what she was, and if you're relying on me to provide you with everything she was, then you're going to fall dramatically short. That was what made her so magnificent. There was so much of her that I'd barely gotten to know after all those years we were married when she died, and it breaks my heart, every single day."

She stood there, staring at me, her eyes narrowing. "But let's be honest for just a moment—there's someone else, isn't there?"

I thought about it, and once again, the thoughts were becoming more clear. "Yes."

"Is she nice?"

"I don't know if *nice* is the word I'd use to describe her."

She took a few steps to the right and turned her face up to look at me, toeing the snow with the point of her boot. "Does she love you?"

"I think she does."

"And do you love her?"

"That would be none of your business."

"But wouldn't it be Martha's?"

I reaimed the .45. "That's where you miss the point: she would want me to be happy."

"You're sure of that?"

"Yep."

"What about the rest of them?"

"The rest of who?"

She gestured toward the sidewalk behind her, where the denizens of Fort Pratt, at least the inhabitants I'd provided, now stood. There was Tomas Bidarte, Vonnie, the two drunks from the bar, Big Daddy Delgado, the young couple from the Oldsmobile, Bao and the scads of Vietnamese, Vanderhoven the priest, and finally, Jeanie One Moon.

"They're all dead, at least I think they are." I studied the group, looking at all their faces, searching for the young couple in the Oldsmobile. "Except for Heather, the young woman from the car, and she shouldn't be here."

"And what do you think they want?"

"I don't know."

She glanced back at them and then once again at me. "Revenge?"

"I don't think so."

"You killed the majority of them or caused them all to be killed."

I thought about the interactions I'd had with each of them. "Perhaps, but I don't think they hold that against me, at least not to the degree you're indicating. I don't think some of them are particularly happy with me, but the primary purpose in whatever is left of their lives isn't vengeance."

"Then what?"

"Escape. I think what they want is out—to get out of this make-believe world of yours. Whatever fate awaits them, they want to get on with it."

"You're sure of that?"

"They are."

"I don't think you understand the scope of what you're saying—"

There was a sound—a growling sound—a crowd noise, like the murmuring of thousands if not millions of people. Something was moving out there in the darkness at the edge of town.

"Are you sure you don't want to change your mind?" She searched the crowd, at the masses that stood milling in the shadows. There was screaming and even cheering sounding in the distance, which seemed to go on forever, hordes of humanity. "I think I have you outnumbered."

I could see Bobby Womack was now pressed up against his cruiser, aiming his weapon toward the shadowy masses. I glanced at the .45 in my hand and felt the inadequacy of it robbing the muscles from the arm that held it.

Bullets, that's all I had to offer, bullets?

"Perhaps not."

The call had come from down the street behind me, a bass voice so strong the vibrations of it rattled my insides. Off in the darkness there were very heavy footsteps that thudded the ground like falling timber.

He came out of the swirling snow like he owned it, looking every bit like the eight-foot apex predator. A grizzly holding a war lance. He almost sauntered toward us, the teeth of his massive bear head glimmering in the streetlights.

Virgil White Buffalo stopped directly behind me, placing a hand on my shoulder, like an adult reassuring a child, the coral and turquoise wolves in the silver band on a finger of his other hand twirling the lance with the coyote skulls, horse tails, clattering jaw bones and beads, up and across his massive shoulders.

He called to the Éveohtsé-heómése. "Hello, old friend—long time no see."

The smile shifted on her face. "I wondered how long it would take you to arrive."

"I was preoccupied with thirty other souls."

"And how are they—enjoying their freedom?"

"Their ancestral lines are alive, well, and flourishing." His hand slipped from my shoulder as he stepped to the side. "How have you been, all these years?"

"Profitable."

His gaze scanned the crowds that filled the landscape, backlit figures that covered the distance like a moving blanket. "So, the lawman has broken your spell?"

She unfolded her arms, gesturing to the surrounding street as if it were obvious. "Not completely."

"Your spell—his world."

"I suppose we will see which is stronger."

"Yes, we will." Taking a step forward, the giant twirled his lance.

Shaking her head, she continued smiling and not looking particularly threatened. "After all this time, do you honestly think you are a match for me?"

"I think we can weaken you to the point that you can no longer do your evil work."

"Evil?" She laughed. "There is no more honest labor in this existence—to eat or be eaten is the way of things in this world and the next."

"There are better, more noble ways."

"And you represent that?"

"I represent myself." He looked out at the multitudes. "Who do they represent?"

She turned to the unending crowd massed behind her, turned back, and spoke with pride. "I represent them, they are all mine."

"They are not. You have borrowed them and now, the bill has come due, and they must be released."

She studied him, her head cocking to one side, sizing him up. "And you will pay that bill?"

"If need be, but nevertheless, they will free themselves—turning on you when they have the chance."

"Any resolve they had for that kind of action, they gave up in a previous life." She placed her hands in the pockets of her long coat. "I command many."

"While fighting for your life?"

"You honestly think you are a threat to me?"

"Me and those who have been summoned along with me." He gestured toward Womack, then turned to me, resting his heavy hand on my shoulder again. "Allow me to introduce the architect of your demise. We have all been personally selected by the lawman, this place, even the form you use—does it seem so strange that we would now have an advantage?"

He swung around with terrifying speed and, with all his mountainous strength, plunged the war lance into her chest.

I stumbled forward, stunned, an inhuman noise emanating from my throat. I knew it wasn't Martha, but it looked like Martha, and it was excruciating to see. I took another mindless step, but Virgil extended a hand and stopped me. "Stand away."

"Virgil, I . . ."

"It is not your wife, no part of it."

She looked down at the lance in her chest as the spearhead began to glow. Lifting her head, she took the shaft of the thing in her hands as other hands sprouted from her, forming the same vortex of grasping appendages that I'd seen before—and began pulling the spear from her body.

Sound began to drain from the world as the snow began rising from the ground, suspended in midair as if the incredible strike had impacted the earth, causing the flakes to leap upward.

The legion of hands continued to pull the lance free as Virgil leapt forward, driving it even deeper, but still, her body remained motionless.

The snow twirled and danced as I stood there, rooted to the spot. Every time I tried to step forward, my boots stuck.

Virgil had managed to lift her from the ground as the assembly of hands gripped the spear. I watched as he turned and launched her to the center of the street, where she slid on the snow but remained upright. The hands sprouting from her body finally yanked the war lance from her chest, and she began running at Virgil, who also ran at her, intent on meeting the Éveohtsé-heómėse in the middle of the road.

Raising the Colt once again, I took careful aim—but could not fire.

I tried as hard as I could, but my finger wouldn't pull the trigger that I'd squeezed thousands of times before.

It was her, even if it wasn't her. Her face—I'd summoned an image I was incapable of forgetting.

My hand shook as she and Virgil catapulted toward each other, then suddenly hung there midflight, like an unfinished statement frozen in time.

Still training the sights on her face, I too was frozen, although there was something moving behind them.

There was still no sound but I saw something slicing through the snow like an icebreaker. There was a glint of chrome, and the slush and snow sprayed a rooster tail behind it as a 1979 Crown Vic bolted from a parked position in the middle of the street and raced forward with Bobby sawing at the wheel.

The black and white cruiser veered left and clipped Martha. She tumbled across the hood and was thrown into the support poles of the awnings on the sidewalk. The police car knocked her backward, taking out all the poles and burying her under the debris, then continued up the road.

He'd just made the intersection near the movie theater and the church when the same five-ton snowplow blew into the big sedan, the gigantic blade all but cleaving it in two.

I watched in horror as the snowplow climbed the stairs of the church, driving the car ahead of it sideways before grinding to a stop at the heavy wooden doors.

The snowplow lurched as whoever was driving attempted to finish the job.

A pair of headlights swooped down from the road leading to the boarding school. It was a big car, and it slammed its weight with great velocity into the side of the plow, jolting it free from the patrol car and spinning the five-ton truck off the steps and back into the street. The plow's engine quit, but the unidentified driver was still turning the starter anyway.

By this time, the big Olds came out of nowhere and spun around in the street. I could see that the young man who had been driving it was still at the wheel, the girl, Heather, smiling at me as he hit the accelerator and the car leapt forward, slamming again into the snowplow but this time headfirst.

There was an explosion from the impact, and then an eruption of fire that burst from both vehicles. The detonation was strong enough to throw me to the ground as the entire intersection burst into flames.

I watched the backlit street as debris from the blast clattered down on the hard-packed snow all around us.

Suddenly, something grabbed me and lifted me from the ground by my collar and then set me on my feet. "That was a lot of metal." Virgil stood beside me as the burning debris continued to rain down on the buildings. "I think we are destroying your town."

"That's okay, I wasn't so fond of it anyway."

He laughed and then walked up the street to retrieve his lance. He spun it as if to check the balance. "You didn't fire your weapon."

"No." I looked around but couldn't see the crowds any longer. "Do you think it would've done any good?"

"Possibly not, but you never know until you try." He laughed. "You of all people know that."

"I couldn't." I stared at the gun in my hand. "I couldn't shoot her."

"It is to be expected. I am sure she was counting on that." He looked back up the street where the intersection was engulfed in flames. Satisfied, he began walking toward me—it was then that the debris at the collapsed sidewalk rustled and began moving.

We both turned to look as sheets of corrugated tin and broken wood slid aside, and she stood there, backlit by the fire, looking neither bloodied nor bowed. "There is no advantage with me."

Suddenly, a shot was fired from down the street, the echo reverberating from the flaming structures around us as I saw

Trooper Womack approaching, completely aflame with his gun drawn and firing as she turned to face him.

The bullets struck her but didn't seem to have any effect as she slowly walked toward him, directly into the gunfire. The buildings around us were now an inferno, some of them even collapsing as Virgil spun the staff in his hands while walking toward her with resignation.

Still aflame, Womack stopped only a body's length away from her and continued to empty the .357 before raising the big Colt and swinging the cylinder out, hitting the plunger as the empty shells fell to the ground. With a speed-loader, he replenished the nickel-plated revolver in a split-second and shoved it into her face—but never made it.

With one blow, she sent him sprawling across the street into the nearest burning building, where he disappeared with a sudden *whoosh* as the fresh oxygen first blew out and then followed him into the hellhole. However, Virgil had reached her, and the moment she turned, again drove his spear deep into her chest.

She froze, her mouth open.

In agony, she swung at him, but he pivoted around and held her from behind, clamping a hand over her face. Her eyes widened, but even from the distance, I could see that the spear wasn't what was causing all the pain.

Somehow, it was the hand over her mouth.

She struck at him, trying to get his hand away—her eyes continuing to widen.

Couldn't she breathe?

Once again, I found my feet leaden as I stumbled forward, catching sight of something glimmering in the inferno that surrounded us—something small, something circular, with tiny turquoise and coral wolves—the silver ring on Virgil's gigantic hand.

The hands began grouping around the spear again, thousands of them at her abdomen, reaching to grab the war lance. "Virgil!" I cried, hoping he'd hear me through the vacuum of silence.

The hands joined together and gripped the shaft, pushing it through herself and into him.

I watched the giant lose hold of her, the stunned look of surprise on his face as he staggered back.

Collectively the hands continued to drive the spear through her body and into his until he fell. Then she simply slipped through the rest of the shaft, pulling herself loose. She grabbed the lance and hoisted him in the air. Impossibly, she then swung him around and threw him backward into another of the blazing buildings.

She turned as scattered cinders and sparks blew out toward us. We stood there looking at each other, the sound returning to the air—the pop and crackle of the burning town—and great bells ringing in the distance.

Calmly, I shoved my gun into the holster at my back. "This has to stop."

She took a step toward me as I reached into the sheepskin coat Martha had bought me and pulled the poster of the missing girl from my inside pocket, I lifted it, holding it up for her to see. "How much?"

Her eyes sharpened. "A bargain?"

I gestured with the poster. "Me for the girl, Jeanie One Moon."

She stared at me and then strolled toward the middle of the street, a finger over her lips as she pondered. "I already have you."

"No, you don't. I'm still alive out there and every time we hear those bells a little louder, they're getting closer to finding me." I looked at the sky, my eyes following the sparks that rose into the blackness. "If I'm really what you're after, then time is running out."

She smiled. "You would give yourself to me of your own free will?"

"Release the girl."

She continued to study me, the flames flickering on the side of her face. "Very tempting . . . The deliciousness of a melancholy like yours—I've never tasted anything like it before."

"Release the girl."

She studied me for a moment more and then gestured behind me and to my right. "This girl."

I turned, and Jeanie One Moon was there with the same red scarf around her neck, looking exactly as she did in the photo on the poster, only whole. The wind blew the fringe silently as she looked off to the distance, seemingly unaware of us. "Yep, along with all the others you have trapped in this town."

"Why should I?"

"After you have me, you won't need them."

"You are to blame for all of their deaths."

"Even more of a reason to release them." We stared at each other as the bells began ringing again, and I looked up into the sky. "You better make up your mind."

She laughed, gazing at me with a carnivorous look. "Why not? Who else is here?"

"Me."

We froze, then she turned and I leaned to one side to see a thin, shivering man standing in the street behind her. With the flames of the conflagration around him, I couldn't make out who he was, but watched as his long hair swung as he shuffled toward us.

He stopped, having noticed something in the road, then kneeled and picked it up. "Sorry I'm late but . . ." His voice was familiar. He started to rise, but then noticed something else and reached over to pick it up too. "Contrary to popular belief, dying is hard."

Artie Small Song raised his face, grinning.

She glanced back at me and then turned to look at him. "You are already mine."

"You were preoccupied when I passed." He stood, flipping something and then catching it. "And now I am my own." Looking at the object in his hand, he flipped it again and caught it once more. Smiling, he moved toward her. "What are the chances?" He flipped what I could now see was a coin. He held out both fists to her. "Fifty/fifty?" Turning them over and opening his fingers, he revealed a Hot Lips silver dollar in the palm of each hand. "Seventy-five/twenty-five?" Reaching out like a cheap magic trick, he plucked another from behind her ear. "Or a hundred percent?"

He held them up, admiring the three coins as he circled her. "Artie?"

"Hey, thanks for saving my great-great-uncle . . ." He watched me as he joined Jeanie One Moon. "I guess I'm the last one you thought would be riding to your rescue, huh?"

"You died?"

"I have." He shrugged, taking Jeanie's hand and leading her toward me. "Do yourself a favor, if that deputy of yours ever offers you a ride in that hopped-up truck of hers, just say no."

"Vic." I glanced around, half expecting to see her. "Is she okay?"

"Yeah, yeah . . . And don't ever get interrogated by Henry Standing Bear." He gave me Jeanie's hand as the bells rang in the distance again.

I studied the girl. "She hears the bells?"

"Yeah." He gestured behind us where the rest of the citizens of the make-believe town had now grouped. "They all hear the bells . . ." He then turned to the Martha-faced Éveohtsé-heómėse. "How about you, honey? You hear 'em?"

Her eyes narrowed. "You're interfering."

"Yeah, I'm really sorry about that, but you're going to have to let them go." His arm swept toward the assemblage behind us. "All of them."

"I have already struck a deal with him."

"Not till we discuss the price."

"He *is* the price."

"No, I'm actually going to get you something extra."

She studied Artie, a look of distrust on her face. "What?"

"Me, for a start, and then how 'bout I get you some boot?" She stared at him, saying nothing. "Ever heard the term?" She remained silent as he laughed. "Not surprising in that it's an Old World term, maybe even before you started devouring souls on this continent—or did you come over with the véhoe? Seems like everything else that was bad, did . . ." He glanced at me. "Boot, you know what I'm talking about, right, Sheriff?"

The words fell from my mouth. "From the Old English, *bōt*, meaning an advantage or help in making something better— eventually it came to mean something extra or added into a bargain, something you throw in for good measure."

"Exactly." He made direct eye contact with me. "'Throw in,' I like that." He turned back to her, spreading his hands. "Say you trade a car in for a new one and you include some money in the deal, that's called the boot."

She snorted. "I need no money."

"Yeah, well . . . The boot can be a lot of money, am I right, Sheriff? Sometimes it's all the money you've got." With that, he tossed me the three coins, and I released Jeanie's hand to catch them in both of mine.

Artie fell to the ground, barely getting out of the way as I buried my hands in the pockets of my coat to gather the other coins.

Making sure I had all fifteen in my right hand, I yanked them from the sheepskin and reared back, flinging them as hard as I could at Martha.

The coins struck her like shrapnel, boring into her as she fell backward, letting out a scream that pierced my skull and sent reverberations through the air. I scooped the rest from my left pocket and flung them at her, watching them shred their way into her.

The roar of the fire surrounded us, and I could hear the wind as it picked up, along with the sound of Artie's voice.

I could hear him reading aloud from the booklet I recognized in his hands, one his ancestor and I had bound together more than what seemed like a hundred years ago. "Hoéstõtse hoóma tsénémenese . . ." His voice took on a cadence as he read the incantation that was meant to banish the Éveohtsé-heómèse from this world, words that a scared child had assembled before disappearing. "Tsénémenese hoóma hoétõtse énétahe . . ."

His voice droned on as I took a deep breath, moving forward and pulling the last coin from the pocket of my jeans as I kneeled beside her convulsing body.

Her eyes were wild, clicking back and forth as her mouth continued to move, but no sound came out.

I leaned in close. "Let them go."

Her eyes found me.

"You're not my wife, and you never were." I felt as if the valves of my heart were about to burst. "I don't want to destroy you, but I will." I held up the very last Hot Lips silver dollar that I'd had all along, the thirty-first one.

"All of them." Reaching down, I gently took her jaw in my hand and turned her face so she could look me in the eye, the silver dollar suspended above her open mouth. "Let them all go, or I drop this."

Her eyes stayed steady, and then she blinked.

There was a sound in the distance like satin tearing. The noise increased enough to deafen.

I pulled back and sat by her body, covering my ears to retain my sanity as wave after wave struck at me like a surging and crushing surf. Numb and bewildered, I was unable to think.

Suddenly, the noise stopped.

I took my hands away from my ears and opened my eyes.

The town of Fort Pratt was gone. Scanning the snow-covered terrain, I could see no landmarks or anything to give me an indication of where I was.

There was a sound behind me, and I turned to see Jeanie One Moon standing a little way away on the ridge.

I tried to stand, but my legs wouldn't support me. "Hey?"

The fringe of her red scarf licked in the breeze.

"You're the only one left, Jeanie?"

She turned her face to look at me, and I could see only half, just like the poster. "Neaese."

She began walking away.

"Wait, I want to ask you some questions." Struggling to my feet, I noticed the booklet lying in the snow, the Cheyenne emblem symbolizing the end of the world that Virgil had casually traced on the front cover. Picking it up, I dusted the snow off and plunged it into the inside pocket of my coat as I stood.

She continued along the ridge, and it was hard to follow her, even with the wind to my back. My legs felt awkward and stiff, as if asleep. My boots sank in the snow, causing me to weave and stagger toward the small rise over which she'd disappeared.

Above the wind, there was a noise, a familiar noise that held some kind of reassurance, a steady clinking that rattled on and on—a noise I knew.

Down below, on the flat ice of what could only be an enormous frozen lake, like the one where I'd seen the Éveohtséheómése, sat a '79 Crown Vic cruiser with its emergency lights revolving, their beams chasing each other around the landscape like red and blue wolves.

Both doors were open and on each side a man stood, one small, the other very large.

Virgil White Buffalo raised a hand to the side of his mouth and yelled up at me. "It looks like you won!"

I looked at the landscape from my vantage point, but it remained colorless and silent, except for the continuous metallic sound. Feeling something in my pocket, I pulled the last silver dollar out and looked at it. "What does losing look like?"

"Much the same."

The wind pushed at me as I stood there contemplating the coin. "Speaking of . . . ?"

"It is gone."

I looked up at him. "And Artie?"

This time it was Womack who answered, laying an arm over

the open door as he looked up at me, tipping his Smokey Bear hat back. "With the Éveohtsé-heómése."

"You're kidding."

He shrugged. "He figured she needed someone, at least one someone."

"And all the others are free?"

"Yeah." The highway patrolman listened as the bells rang and then glanced over the top of the sedan at the giant. "C'mon, we've got to get going."

Virgil started to climb in as I called after them and took a step forward. "Wait! I'll hitch a ride with you guys . . ."

"You cannot go where we are going, Lawman." He smiled broadly at me from within the grizzly bear headdress and threw the lance in the back seat. "At least, not yet."

I watched as he wedged himself in, and they both closed their respective doors before Bobby started up the cruiser and swung it around in a sliding turn that drifted to the right and then roared for the distance where it faded to a dark speck and then finally disappeared.

It was odd to be thinking so lucidly that my mind was working even though I felt so disassociated. I finally sat there on the ridge, raptly looking to the east, but it was still like looking down from a great height. The smooth snow-covered ground glowed with a brilliance, the veins of creeks and rivers flowing like shining threads that stitched the land together.

Oddly enough, alone there, I wasn't afraid. I felt at peace with whatever fate had in store for me.

What was it Bidarte had said. That all haunting was regret.

Nothing moved now, but the vaporous light was reassuring, along with something else in that far distance—the insistent ringing of bells.

EPILOGUE

The light from the window was white and opaque, just like that lost landscape in my dreams, and I listened to the bells as they pealed, trying desperately to hold on to the reality I'd rediscovered only yesterday.

"Sunday."

I turned and looked at my daughter. "I'm sorry?"

"Sunday night, it's church."

"Chuch!" The two-year-old sat in my lap, playing with her stuffed buffalo, Boomba.

Cady sipped her tea and continued reading the Helena newspaper by the limited light of the lamp on my nightstand. "St. Peter's Hospital, probably connected to the church, I would think."

My mind swung around, recalling I was in Montana as I took the fluffy toy from Lola and galloped it across the blanket that covered my legs as she reached after it. I handed it to her and watched as she stuffed it in her mouth.

"How do you feel?" The Greatest Legal Mind of Our Time was looking at me over the top of her *Independent Record*, paper cup paused at her lips.

"Great."

She continued to study me with her cool, gray eyes, using one of the age-old cop tricks I'd taught her.

"My throat still hurts."

"You were on a ventilator for thirty-one hours, so it's to be expected." Folding the paper in her lap, she sipped her tea. "Anything else?"

"My sides hurt; both of them."

"Four broken ribs, liver and spleen lacerations, and a bruised duodenum—not to mention the broken leg and concussion."

I thought about it. "What's a duodenum?"

"First part of the small intestine."

"Sounds much more prosaic than that." I looked at the heir to the Longmire lineage in my lap. "Duodenum."

"Doo-da-ded-man!" Repeating was one of Lola's favorite forms of communication.

My daughter added, in a somber voice. "It was almost that, Peanut."

After a reputable silence, I asked. "So, I spent almost as much time on the ventilator as I did under the bell in a coma?"

"Pretty much." She continued to study me. "So, let me see if I've got this straight. You'd arrested Artie and put a bullet in him after he'd tried to kill you, and then the son of the neo-Nazi down in Billings ran into you with a snowplow?"

"Yep."

"And you dragged yourself out of the truck and into the graveyard where you hid under the bell?"

I nodded. "It was convenient, at least from my perspective, crawling along on the ground for about a hundred feet."

"Mind telling me why you did it?"

"Hid under the bell? It was the only place I figured they wouldn't find me."

"No. Why you ran up here, chasing after a dead girl?"

I slumped back into my pillows. "When they found the body,

it seemed like the case was over, but not quite . . . With these visions I was having about her, it just felt like there was something that seemed unsettled. I guess I went looking for whatever it was that had caused that unsettling."

"Did you find it?"

I turned and looked at her, eager to change the subject. "You know, you look a lot like your mother."

She studied me, shaking her head. "Where did that come from?"

Lola started fussing, and I handed her over to Cady after she placed her cup on my nightstand. She settled her on her lap. "Schiller's son, Riley, and his friends were there in Fort Pratt?"

I hedged. "Maybe, but maybe something else—something more disturbing."

She eyed me as she nestled her daughter's head at her neck. "Something more disturbing than the three neo-Nazi scumbags?"

"Maybe."

"They said you were talking up a storm when they brought you in."

"About?"

The cool, gray eyes stayed steady. "Mom."

I stared at the sheet covering my legs. "Hmm . . ."

"That's all, just hmm?"

"She was there."

"Mom was in your coma?"

"I'm not so sure it was a coma."

"Then what do you think it was?"

"This is going to sound funny, but there's this boogeyman in the Cheyenne culture, the Éveohtsé-heómėse, and I think I was kind of doing battle with it while I was curled up under that bell."

"Doing battle over what?"

"Who knows, my soul, maybe?" I looked at her and laughed. "Or something like that." She didn't laugh, and I thought about it as we gazed at each other. "Do you ever think we're haunted, Punk?"

She hugged her daughter and looked at me, her eyes growing sad. "I think we're loved, and I think true love is the strongest component in all of us, and maybe the last to fade away. We've had our share of bad luck certainly, but I don't think we're haunted."

"They say all haunting is regret."

"Who says that?"

"They."

She smiled a wan smile. "What've you got to regret, mister?"

I gestured toward the child in her lap. "Your mother not meeting this one."

"And what did you have to do with that?"

"Maybe if we'd gotten the diagnosis earlier? Maybe if we'd tried something different? And what about you? What if I hadn't been at war with Thomas Bidarte, then maybe Michael . . ."

She took a breath. "Dad . . ." She hugged Lola a bit tighter, not looking at me. "I don't think it's healthy to be thinking like that."

"I'm sorry."

She shook her head and then even with her face turned away I could hear the tears welling her eyes. "Do you think it's time you thought about retiring?"

Trying to lighten the subject, I reminded her. "I thought you didn't want me underfoot?"

"Well, I don't want you moving into my spare room in Cheyenne, if that's what you're angling for." She wiped the tears away with an index finger. "But I'm really getting worried about all these concussions and your mental health."

I laughed. "You don't know the half of it."

I was about to say more when the door opened and a nurse was pushed backward into the room by a dark-haired woman with a brown-paper bag and a large, flat box containing what I assumed was a pizza. "You can't, he's only allowed two visitors at a time . . ."

Vic elbowed her way in, closely followed by the Cheyenne Nation, my undersheriff gesturing toward Lola. "That's only a quarter of a person, so we're still under the limit, sort of."

The poor nurse had been overwhelmed from my first series of visitors yesterday, which had included the attorneys general of both Wyoming and Montana, assorted higher-ups of the Montana Division of Criminal Investigation and assorted agents of the FBI.

The handsome strawberry-blond woman in the white outfit and sensible shoes turned to look at me. "Mr. Longmire . . . ?"

I held out a hand to my besieged guardian. "It's fine, really."

She shook her head and started out. "I'll be back in twenty minutes, and then everyone will have to go."

Vic ignored her and unloaded the paper bag on the nightstand, mumbling under her breath. "Fuck you, Florence . . ."

The Bear reached down, taking Lola from Cady as she squealed. "Beeeeeeear!"

Holding her in one arm, Henry swayed back and forth, taking a Rainier from Vic, who then handed one to my daughter and then one to me. Sitting in my guest chair, she smiled. "Here you go; a couple of these and you'll be out of here in no time." She took a sip, glancing at Cady. "How long are they insisting on keeping him?"

Cady held her unopened beer, settling back in her own chair. "Depends."

My undersheriff turned back to me. "Tunnel out at midnight?"

"We're on the fourth floor, besides, I might be asleep."

She dismissed me with a wave of the hand, propped her tactical boots up on the bed beside me, and took a sip. "So, Walt Longmire 1, Éveohtsé-heómése 0?"

"No, she scored, I just built up a lead."

Vic leaned forward, her tarnished-gold eyes alight. "She? The thing from beyond is a she?"

"This time around."

"Oh." She looked at me, then at Cady, finally taking refuge in razzing Henry. "So, why didn't you kill the other peckerhead?"

He grunted. "They had already killed one of their own, and I thought that was sufficient; besides I wanted someone to tell us what actually happened."

I sipped my beer, and it tasted really good. "So, the survivor goes back to finishing school in Deer Lodge?"

"For a very long time."

I looked back out at the dying light of the window. "What about Riley?"

"Three strikes, which means life without parole." In the ensuing silence, Vic reached into the box, taking out a slice of pepperoni and offering it to me.

"I'm not hungry."

She forced the thing into my hand. "It's pizza, what does that have to do with being hungry?" Handing slices out to the others, she then took one for herself. "Just eat the damn thing, will you?"

I took a bite and then sipped my beer. "How's my truck?"

"Totaled, but they knew you'd want it fixed so they took it to Jim at Michelena's and he says he can try to straighten the frame and get the bodywork done and should have it back to you in a month or two."

"What am I supposed to do until then?"

She took a bite of her pizza and chewed. "I have a new truck."

"Oh, no . . ."

She wiped her mouth with the back of her hand. "Yeah, even faster than the old one, which was also totaled."

"This was an expensive venture."

"Yeah, I'm sure the county commissioners are going to have a shit-hemorrhage when they get the bill."

I finally sat the uneaten slice down on the nightstand, noticing and picking up a coin that had been lying there, and continued to sip my beer.

The Bear sidled over toward the window, still swaying back and forth with Lola. "What is that?"

I held it up to him. "Look familiar?"

His dark eyes studied me, along with those of my granddaughter. "It looks like one of the Hot Lips silver dollars from the Wind River Canyon."

"Yep, it does." I turned it over in my hands. "I guess my imagination got the best of me while I was in that coma."

Vic reached under the collar of her shirt, fishing a chain from her neck and holding something out to me. Virgil's ring. "Here. I almost forgot." I took the chain and held it up, the ring suspended in air, reflecting the light of the window as she eased back in her chair, sipping her Rainier. "Before he died, Artie said to give that back to you."

I nodded, taking the thing and draping it around my neck, and then holding the ring up to examine it. "They're taking his body back to Lame Deer and his mother?"

The Bear nodded. "Yes."

Cady moved to the foot of the bed and sat. "Why is it I have the feeling you are not telling us everything that happened to you?"

I rubbed my eyes, the fatigue thrumming through me like a low current. "I've told you everything that really happened, the rest was just my scrambled imagination." I opened my eyes and looked at all of them. "I dreamed a lot of crazy stuff, stuff I now know wasn't real."

Henry moved closer. "In what way?"

I breathed a laugh. "Everybody I met was dead, but they weren't."

Cady looked confused. "Dead?"

"Everybody in this Fort Pratt that I constructed in my head was dead, but not really." I glanced at Vic. "Do you remember Heather, the young woman down in Lusk I keep trying to get out on parole? She was there, and I know she's still alive."

I watched as Vic stared at me, then looked up at Henry.

"What?"

"Nothing." Abruptly, she stood. "We should get out of here."

"Wait, what's the matter?"

"Nothing, you're tired, and we're not helping." She gathered up the beer and pizza. "You've been through a lot and we've got to go talk to the Criminal Division guys across the street." She gestured toward the Cheyenne Nation. "We'll come back in the morning, when you've gotten some sleep."

Cady also stood, reaching for Lola as the Bear handed her over. "You're abandoning me too?"

She smiled, but it was weak. "You heard the nurse."

"But you'll be back?"

"Sure, we'll bring you breakfast in the morning and real coffee."

She carried Lola to the bedside and lowered her for a kiss, and then gave me one on the top of my head before retreating toward the door that Henry had open. Vic glanced back at me before turning and disappearing with my daughter and grand-daughter following.

The Bear avoided my eyes and began closing the door when I called to him. "Henry, what did I say?"

He stopped and stared at the floor, his eyes finally coming up to mine. "Heather, the young woman at the women's prison in Lusk committed suicide two days ago."

He quietly closed the door.

I sat there for a long time.

Placing the coin back on the nightstand, I then opened the drawer there, pulling out the leather-covered booklet with the odd circle with the strike on the cover. I thumbed through the words, reading them, but still unable to speak the language to the extent that it was meant to be read. I started to close it and then looked at the postcard I'd been using as a bookmark, staring at the photo on one side of the students standing in front of the boarding school, underneath the gate—all but one of their faces now in focus. The tall one, Ty, the only one whose face was blurred.

"What's that?"

I looked up to find the strawberry-blond night nurse leaning in the doorway, her hazel eyes watching me.

"Oh, a book I picked up."

Allowing the door to fall closed behind her, she approached the bed. "I guess they took me at my word." Spotting the can of beer on the nightstand, she reached for it, but I snagged it before she could take it. "You're not supposed to have alcohol with your meds."

"Think of it as a med enhancer."

She smiled, still looking at the nightstand. "You have lots of friends."

"Yep, I guess I do." I held the can out to her. "You can have it if you want."

She didn't take it but moved closer so that I could see the lower half of her face in the light from the nightstand. "No, that's okay."

I stayed like that for a moment, the can still extended toward her but then finally returned it to the nightstand. "You know, you look familiar."

"You said that a lot when they brought you in here. You were only partially conscious, but you kept talking to me, insisting that we knew each other." She placed a hand on the visitor chair and stood there looking down at me from the darkness. "You kept calling me Martha." She studied me.

"My deceased wife."

"I'm sorry."

"Even your voice sounds familiar; you're sure we've never met?"

"Yes, I'm sure."

I gestured toward the can on the nightstand. "Really, you can have the beer, if you want."

She made no effort to pick up the can. "That's okay, it might make you sleep better, anyway."

"I'm not sure I'll ever sleep again."

I could hear the smile in her voice. "Oh, you will. Everybody does . . . Eventually."

She turned, and I looked past her to where the shadow of the Cheyenne Nation stood, backlit in the light from the hallway, holding the knob of the door in one hand, the other wrapped around the leather collar of my four-legged backup that he must've retrieved for a visit.

She stepped behind the one chair, placing both hands on it as she positioned it between them. "It's past visiting hours, and I'm afraid you're not supposed to be here."

Henry came forward with Dog. "That is where I have spent the majority of my life, in places I am not supposed to be."

Dog never took his eyes off her.

Attempting to break the tension, I asked, "I thought you were meeting with the Criminal Division investigators?"

"Postponed until tomorrow morning." He came closer and stood at the foot of the bed. He had pulled something from his pockets. "I wanted to return your wallet and badge. I know you always take them out and put them on the center console during long trips."

"Thanks." I tossed them in the drawer of the nightstand. "Where are the girls?"

"In a single hotel room down the block, where we will not be tonight."

"Where are you going to be?"

His eyes returned to the nurse as Dog came around to me. "Here."

The night nurse breathed a laugh, and her voice took on the professional tone. "I'm afraid neither you nor the dog can sleep here."

His eyes stayed steady as he reached across and took the booklet from my lap. "I will not be sleeping, actually I think I will catch up with my reading." He turned the thing in his hands, and his dark eyes scanned the words on the wrinkled pages. "Ancient Cheyenne . . . I have been meaning to brush up my pronunciation." His face rose to her again. "I will be here all night, reading aloud."

"And the dog?"

"He will be here too—just in case I do fall asleep." He turned, looking down at me. "Did you ever consider that being surrounded by all that metal of the bell might have been what kept the Éveohtsé-heómèse from getting at you? You know, when we found you under there, you were not alone. There was a great horned owl that had set up residency around your naked foot, perhaps saving it from frostbite."

"Spedis." They both stared at me. "I think the owl's name is Spedis."

Henry nodded and then continued. "It took four of us to move the bell and when we did, the owl simply flew up to the top of the archway and sat there watching us." He moved to the left and sat, stretching his legs, crossing his chukka boots, and gently placing them on the foot of the bed. "The medical personnel opined that he was waiting for you to die so he could eat you, but I think it was something else." He looked back to the night nurse on the other side of the bed, still standing behind the chair. "What do you think?"

She stood there a moment more and then backed away before turning and going through the door without another sound.

I reached out and petted Dog's great muzzle as he rested his big, bucket head on the bed. "That was odd."

"Yes, it was." I watched as his fingertips traced the lines on the hand-printed paper, his hypnotic voice strong and steady as I felt sleep approaching, as inevitable as the fact that they both would be there when I awoke in the morning. "Hoéstõtse hoóma tsénémenese. Tsénémenése hoóma hoétõtse énétahe . . ."

That, along with the sound of bells.